I will always save you, Firefly.
Always.

understanding fate

Vegas Wolf Pack Series,
Book Three

AMANDA NICHOLE

Understanding Fate

Copyright ©2024 by Amanda Nichole

All rights reserved.

This is a work of fiction. Names, characters, places, and incidents are products of the author's imagination and are used fictitiously. Any resemblance to actual persons, living or dead, businesses, companies, events, or locales is entirely coincidental.

No part of this book may be reproduced in any form or by any electronic or mechanical means including information storage and retrieval systems, without written permission from the author, except for the use of brief quotations in a book review. No AI Training is permitted.

Cover Design by: OkayCreations

Edited by: AKJ Thomas

Understanding Fate
Vegas Wolf Pack Series Book 3
Amanda Nichole

Contents

Dedication	IX
Dedication	
Quote	XI
Prologue	1
Ghost	
1. Chapter 1	4
Bri	
2. Chapter 2	15
Ghost	
3. Chapter 3	23
Bri	
4. Chapter 4	34
Cain	
5. Chapter 5	41
Bri	
6. Chapter 6	50
Cain	
7. Chapter 7	56
Ghost	

8.	Chapter 8 Bri	64
9.	Chapter 9 Cain	72
10.	Chapter 10 Ghost	81
11.	Chapter 11 Bri	87
12.	Chapter 12 Cain	95
13.	Chapter 13 Bri	107
14.	Chapter 14 Dante	112
15.	Chapter 15 Bri	123
16.	Chapter 16 Dante	133
17.	Chapter 17 Cain	138
18.	Chapter 18 Dante	148
19.	Chapter 19 Bri	154
20.	Chapter 20 Cain	163

21.	Chapter 21 Bri	169
22.	Chapter 22 Dante	175
23.	Chapter 23 Bri	182
24.	Chapter 24 Bri	191
25.	Chapter 25 Cain	199
26.	Chapter 26 Bri	206
27.	Chapter 27 Cain	210
28.	Chapter 28 Bri	217
29.	Chapter 29 Dante	223
30.	Chapter 30 Cain	230
31.	Chapter 31 Bri	236
32.	Chapter 32 Dante	241
33.	Chapter 33 Cain	249

34. Chapter 34   254
    Dante

35. Chapter 35   261
    Bri

36. Chapter 36   268
    Cain

Epilogue   277
Dante

Reader's Note   281
Remember I love you

Fate Encoded   282
Presley

Acknowledgements   296

About the author   298
Amanda Nichole

Also by   299
Amanda Nichole

To my husband,
who taught me how to finish.

But things don't just fall apart.

People break them

~Robert Wasserman

Prologue
Ghost

It's interesting how oblivious most people are to the world around them. Wandering in public places, faces locked on their screens. Technology has made them addicts, needing their fix of dopamine to get through the day. They post pictures of the food they eat, places they visit, and events they plan, all while too distracted to actually live in those moments.

It certainly makes my job easier.

In the world we live in, people need to be paranoid and more aware of their surroundings. If they stopped to look around every now and again, they might see something, learn something, or feel something.

These days, blending into any crowd requires simply wearing a hoodie, some headphones, and an illuminated screen in front of my face.

Today, it makes following her child's play. I can tell she's used to being invisible, overlooked, just part of the sidelines. What's more, I can tell she prefers it that way. She keeps her eyes downcast and her free hand firmly on the strap of her carry-on bag as she travels past security to locate her gate.

Her wild brown hair sits tangled on the top of her head, and she, like the rest of the sheep gathered today at the Harry Reid International Airport, has on an oversized hoodie and leggings.

Just like the last time I saw her.

As we find ourselves herded toward the trams, I move casually behind her. Allowing her to gain a bit of distance and not alerting her to my presence here today. Not that she's paying attention. Her phone's out, and she's sliding through screens as she wanders toward Gate D.

For a moment, her attention flies up to scan the overhead signs that guide our travel onto the Red Line Tram. I slow my pace again and feign interest in my phone, taking the time to discreetly scan the other ticket holders. She doesn't appear to have anyone traveling with her, which both irritates and surprises me.

The Vegas Pack Alpha isn't usually so careless with security.

Just as the thought crosses my mind, I spot him. The shifter, I'm betting, is here to protect her. He's doing a proficient job of staying close to her without alerting her to his presence. His problem, he looks like a bodyguard. His eyes scan over the people in the area, track where the cameras are, and constantly search for a threat.

Rule #9: Blend into what's typical for the given environment.

That's the problem with new recruits; they have no finesse. Fortunately for him, she appears too preoccupied with getting to her gate to notice the tail. But I know this: if he's keeping a low profile, she refused to have a security detail, and Dante sent one anyway.

PROLOGUE

This poor guy is in for it when she realizes.

I smile to myself, mentally popping popcorn because I'm hoping I will get a front-row seat to the exchange. I guess we will have some in-flight entertainment on the way to Boston after all.

Chapter 1
Bri

Never in my life have I been more unsure of anything. Okay, maybe that's a lie, but it certainly feels true as I board my flight to Boston. Taking the steps I've been planning for years.

Why doesn't it feel more satisfying?

The last few weeks have been a series of blurred moments. Some have been wonderful, some painful, and some so unexpected that I'm still sorting through the emotions.

I'm a wolf shifter. Or rather, I will be.

Understanding that fact alone has been a whirlwind. The way it has changed every decision I've made since is an understatement. Not one moment has gone by where I haven't questioned how it changes everything.

Worse, I can't talk about why I'm so torn with the two people in the world who know me better than anyone.

CHAPTER 1

Keith and Liv.

They've spent the last three weeks walking on eggshells around me because I've had to close off completely. It's the only way I know I won't slip up and say something that will get them killed.

I hate feeling disconnected from them. I hate lying to them. I hate that all these huge decisions about me are out of my control. I no longer get to have a say in so much of what will happen in my life going forward.

Dante says I have to be Awakened. Cain says it's my choice, but I know deep down how much more difficult that will make my life and his. I don't want to live a life looking over my shoulder, wondering if someone could get to me.

Cain.

Even the thought of him now has my heart clenching and a smile sneaking up on my lips. He's been so patient with me. He's given me space to come to terms with everything but has always been there, reminding me that he's not giving up. He's not going away.

But what if I leave?

Shaking my head to focus on the here and now, I move down the aisle to my window seat, groaning internally at the oversized older man I will have to climb over to get into it.

"Excuse me, that one's me," I say with as much pleasantry as I can muster while gesturing to the seat in his row. The man glances up, eying me appreciatively, before standing up to allow me room to sit. Or at least that's what I think is happening. Instead, he gets so close to me that his protruding stomach slides across my side, and he doesn't make any attempt to move further.

"By all means," he says, a twinkle in his eye that has my spine straightening and me attempting to draw back from him.

Cringing internally, I tiptoe to my seat, disgusted by the amount of my body that ended up pressed against his in the process. I mentally chastise myself for not choosing an aisle seat or splurging on early boarding.

Please let someone be sitting in the middle.

Once I'm adjusted, bag tucked securely under my feet, I throw in my wireless earbuds and plant my face into a book, purposely angling it to create a physical barrier between myself and the pervy forty-something bald man who hasn't taken his eyes off me since I got to the row. My muscles are tense, and my jaw is locked tight as I feign indifference while counting the minutes until I can escape this flying tube.

A flight attendant walks the aisle, closing overhead boxes, which pulls the man's attention, and I relax a bit. After a safety briefing and a roll down the runway, we're up in the air. A few minutes later, despite the music playing in my ears, the sound of deep, rumbled snoring hits me, and I glance over to see my row-sharing compatriot fast asleep.

Five hours and twenty-three minutes to go.

***

Exiting the plane is far less eventful and includes the added benefit of not having to touch the man in my row. I didn't use the bathroom the entire flight, despite needing to, just so I didn't have to repeat my boarding experience. The man had tried to engage me in conversation a handful of

CHAPTER 1

times throughout the flight between his snoozing, and each time, I solidly ignored him, pretending I couldn't hear him over the earbuds.

I wait several minutes, allowing the plane to empty before standing and gathering my bag from beneath my feet and settling my items into their respective pockets and pouches. Head down and hands full, I step out of the row only to have my shoulder crash into a wall of solid muscle. A hand grabs my arm to steady me, keeping me from falling before releasing me almost as quickly. I apologize immediately without looking up and grab the phone that drops out of my hands.

"I'm sorry I wasn't paying attention. I thought everyone had already passed," I fumble through my explanation while fixing my belongings and retreating into the row.

"No problem," the deep masculine voice responds, continuing down the aisle before I can even get a look at him. Exhaling, I scan the back of the plane before stepping out a second time and heading into the Boston airport terminal.

Ethan mentioned in his email that someone would be here to drive me to my hotel, so I grab my bag from the oscillating carousel and make my way to passenger pick-up. A familiar tingling climbs up my spine as I exit the bagging area. Someone is watching me—again.

No. Not here. Damnit.

This feeling has had me on edge since I got to the airport in Vegas. Initially, I shook it off as paranoia, but the longer I stand here, the more I can almost feel the eyes on me. Keeping my gait casual, I intentionally release my breath and casually move my phone to my back pocket to free up one of my hands. I weave myself around slower travelers and try to find a way to figure out who might be following me.

A restroom sign ahead gives me the idea, and I turn into the cut-out for it, deliberately glancing behind me a moment before I disappear into the Women's door.

No one.

Not a single person appears to be watching me.

Fuck. I'm losing it.

I sigh and sink back onto the cold tile wall of the modern restroom, cursing my stupid brain. Ever since the kidnapping, this has been happening everywhere I go—the grocery store, work, and even school. I always feel like I'm moments away from being grabbed by someone from the Reno Pack.

Deacon Marlo appears consistently in my nightmares, his Italian words dancing in my ears, his breath fanning across my neck moments before he succeeds in Awakening me. I've woken up screaming more times than I can count. Each time, Liv appears at my door, worry lining her face, before she silently crawls into my bed for the rest of the night.

I've wanted to ask Dante if he has heard anything since the exchange, but I always talk myself out of it. He has a whole pack to run. He doesn't need to be bothered by the Unawakened girl who just lost him a pack member.

Hudson.

Pain leaks into my overly active heart at the memory of him. His face is permanently etched in my mind from the porch of Ghost's cabin. Pure determination. He just wanted to save them.

He did save them. He saved me, too.

CHAPTER 1

I still don't feel worthy of it, but I'm determined to live a full life. That's why I agreed to come here in the first place: to have no regrets. His sacrifice needs to matter.

Though admittedly, I'm not sure that a 'full life' means hiding in the bathroom on the verge of a panic attack while my mind convinces me that imaginary boogeymen are following me.

Fuck this.

I'm a strong, independent woman who can go on a prospective job trip without having a mental breakdown.

Right?

I exhale, hoping that the tension will leave my body along with the air, before using the facilities and washing my hands in a nearby sink.

Check out the company. Make a decision.

That's why I'm here.

In the three weeks since Hudson's funeral, my life has been a whirlwind. I finished my finals, returned to work, and have tried to keep myself busy working out with Liv. While it feels like falling back into my routine, my anxiety has never been worse.

The only bright spot in these weeks has honestly been Cain. For a few days, he kept his distance, texting me something that made him think of me or dropping off coffee before I left for class. It was always a small gesture before he had to be at work or I had something on my schedule, which ensured he didn't overstay his welcome.

When my birthday came, he bribed Liv, with what I'll never know, but she let him decorate my entire bedroom with small white firefly lights that have me thinking of him every time I walk in. Along with the lights, he left a wrapped box with the lights—a box I haven't had the nerve to open for fear that it's perfect and will make me fall even further in love with him.

My resolve to stay away from him while I sort everything out has been slowly deteriorating. I know that I need this space to figure everything out, but my body and heart aren't on the same page as my brain.

He hasn't pushed for more, but I have found myself looking forward to the moments I get to see him and checking my phone to see if a meme or random text is there.

I want more. I want to rewind time and return to the light banter and sexual tension we had before everything went to hell in a handbasket.

He's my Mate.

That thought unsettles me the most because I wonder if I want him because he's the one The Fates picked or because he's my choice. I've spent my entire life fighting against what the world thought I would be and choosing my own future.

No one expected a foster kid to be a straight-A student, one without a drug problem or teen pregnancy scare. The odds weren't in my favor to be a scholarship recipient for my grades or to become a college graduate. I did those things. I graduated high school with honors, stayed out of jail and shit relationships, and I made a future for myself.

And now, The Fates are trying to dictate who I spend my life with and who I can be entirely myself around. It's driving me crazy.

This trip is about me choosing. Not The Fates, not Cain, not society. Me. I want to be the one who decides where my life is supposed to go. I can't change what's happened, but I damn sure get to decide what I make of this new future I've been handed.

CHAPTER 1

Focusing back on the present, I exit the bathroom, fully aware of those walking around me. The feeling of being watched has dimmed some, and I breathe a little easier, knowing it was all in my head.

As I enter the passenger pick-up area, I scan the signs, searching for my name. Six people appear to be waiting to pick up passengers, but none hold up DelaCourt or Brielle. Last I checked, my name wasn't B. Lopez. I pull out my cell phone to see if I have missed a message or some information from Ethan.

The last text message still shows from this morning.

Excited to have you! Someone will be there to grab you at 730 p.m. in passenger pick up.

Checking the time on my phone, I see it's 7:35 pm.

Maybe they had to use the restroom.

I walk over to the wall, where a few chairs sit empty, and decide to wait. With the extra time, I text Keith and Liv to let them know I landed and everything is good. Then, before I can talk myself out of it, I send a quick message to Cain.

He cares about my well-being. It's only polite to update him.

Hello, denial...

When eight o'clock rolls around, I finally start to think that I've been left and send a message to Ethan asking if I should take an Uber to my hotel.

When my phone buzzes a moment later, I open the text immediately, hoping Ethan has answers for me so my anxiety can relax. Being in a strange city alone is definitely more intimidating than I thought it would be.

> **Glad to hear you are safe. I'm here if you need anything.**

I shake my head, not understanding the context before me. I glance around.

He's here? Where?

I begin typing back into the text message.

> **You're here? Where? I don't see anyone.**

The response is immediate.

> **No one is there to get you? How long have you been waiting?**

I check the clock and see it's 8:06 pm.

> **About half an hour.**

> **Hang on, Firefly, I'm sending a car.**

Firefly? Wtf.

I look again and see it hasn't been Ethan I have been messaging, but Cain.

I mentally smack my forehead.

Shit.

> **Don't worry about it. I'm grabbing an Uber. See you when I get back.**

Damnit.

Switching out of his messages, I pull Ethan's text to find it has been read, but there is no response.

CHAPTER 1

I guess I really am going to call an Uber.

"Ms. DelaCourt?" a deep voice interrupts my inner chastising. I look up to find a man in an impeccably tailored black suit.

"Yes?" I respond hesitantly.

"I'm Sebastian. I'm here to give you a ride to your hotel." He smiles, and the action lights his entire face, giving him a non-threatening, easygoing vibe.

Ethan had someone here, after all.

"Thank you, Sebastian." I stand, gathering my carry-on as he reaches for my suitcase.

"May I take your bags?" he asks as if this is a routine question.

"Oh, um, of course, I'm sorry," I blurt, quickly retracting my arm.

He gathers the items and heads for the exit, and I follow closely behind him.

Cold air assaults my lungs the moment we step outside, and I see a light dusting of snow on everything. My inner child smiles. Las Vegas hardly ever gets snow, so seeing it in real life brings me so much happiness, and I mentally add a point to the "move to Boston" pro/con list I've created in my head. I fight the urge to lie down and make a snow angel.

Get it together, Bri. You're a professional.

We weave through the traffic outside the airport and end up at a black SUV parked in the business section of the lot. While Sebastian loads my bags, I take in the Massachusetts view.

The tall buildings line the horizon, and lights dance off the water. Coupled with the blanket of white, the whole scene looks like a snow globe. There's magic to it that I just can't place.

Wrapping my arms around myself as the chill seeps in, I wonder how much shopping I'll need to accomplish to survive in cold like this. It's early winter for them, only mid-December, and the bite in the air is already more than I have ever had to endure.

Sebastian clears his throat, pulling my attention to the door he holds open for me. Taking a deep breath, I climb in the backseat, settle my backpack on the opposite side, and latch my buckle. I notice how dark the tint is on the windows.

Stuffy business people probably don't look out at the scenery when they drive.

A loud bang into the door on the far side of the car has me immediately defensive before the driver's door opens, and in climbs, someone I never thought I would see again.

"We gotta stop meeting like this, City."

Son of a bitch.

Chapter 2
Ghost

It's a miracle this girl is alive. Her sense of self-preservation must be on vacation because she just got back from being kidnapped over a pack battle, and now here we are, getting into the back of an SUV with a member of the Providence Pack. The pack, I'm assuming, took on the seven hundred fifty thousand dollar kidnapping contract that came out this morning. The one that sent me on this damn trip to begin with.

Reno submitted the contract through a third party I often work with. In the messaging, Reno was vague about the target and the location. Had I not reached out to an old contact, I would never have had any details about it.

So much for not getting involved.

When I see her waiting in the passenger pick-up, I know something has happened to her original ride. She would've had a ride set up otherwise. A quick circle around the area found him with a broken neck next to a dumpster with no identification and stinking of wolf. It still amazes me how they never try to cover their scent. They may not have my abilities, but there are a million ways to cover the tracks of a shifter.

Once I knew her ride was no longer in commission, I hustled back to the loading area to find her engaged in a conversation with Jett Dargis, the head enforcer for the Providence pack and Connor Saint's protégée.

The growl that escaped my throat at the sight of him almost gave my location away. I had to push back my anger and focus on the rules. Keep emotions out of it.

Rule #2: Never let it get personal.

Emotion gets you dead.

While I had never met Jett in person, his reputation preceded him. He was quickly promoted in the Providence pack after a series of accidents took out those with higher ranks. Two deaths may have been a coincidence, but when seven people have that much bad luck in under a year, everyone takes notice. The Providence Pack Alpha, Tobias Ash, rewarded Jett's enthusiasm for the role, and the packs in the surrounding areas have had problems ever since.

I wonder what he's doing on a catch-and-release for less than a million dollars?

Whatever his motives, this isn't good for Bri. Which means this isn't good for me.

Over the last decade, every job I've taken, every contract secured, was in an effort to prevent the one future that still matters to me—My Mate. Every one of my visions leads me to her death. Well, every vision until I met Bri.

CHAPTER 2

One chance encounter in the woods, and the visions have changed. The future has changed. Bri is the key to saving my Mate. All I have to do is keep her alive long enough to find the door.

Shaking my head, I refocus on the interaction to gauge Bri's response. Her smile and the tension that releases from her shoulders instantly tell me she will follow his million-watt smile right into another kidnapping.

Damnit, City!

I look across the area, only to find that her bodyguard is no longer in the room.

What the actual fuck?

My protective instincts flare, and I'm moving before I can second guess it.

Avoiding the open areas of the room, I follow them out, keeping enough distance to stay undetected. The snow-covered ground outside has them moving slowly to the side lot, filled with company vehicles.

He must have checked out the vehicle first to ensure its location and that the chauffeur didn't have another passenger because he guides her right to the SUV and presses the button to unlock it. I remain in the shadows and wait patiently until I have him alone.

Once Bri is loaded into the car, he pauses to do a cursory scan of the lot, his eyes lingering an extra moment on the alley where the body is stashed.

Sloppy work, Jett.
This is why I work alone.

The only person I can count on is me. If my training taught me anything, it's that little mistakes become big mistakes, so if you take care of the small shit, the bigger shit is less likely.

Bri was already waiting for her ride. He had time to properly hide or remove the chauffeur before introducing himself. My guess is he didn't want to mess up his five-thousand-dollar suit.

As he turns behind the vehicle headed to the driver's side, I make my move. I silently close the distance before wrapping one arm around his throat while the other tucks under my forearm, effectively locking in a standing rear naked choke.

At the contact, Jett rears his body backward, slamming me into the door but not rattling my grip. He struggles for nearly a minute, even shifting his hand into a paw to slice the flesh on my arm, giving a commendable effort to escape.

Too bad I feel nothing.

Years of nerve torture left most of my skin numb or scarred. The heinous interrogation treatment actually helps me in my line of work. Though it definitely wasn't his intention to harden my exterior, Saint pushed harder each time I didn't die. Each time he pushed harder, I held onto more and more of the truth.

1,623 days.

Anger builds in me as I squeeze, barely noticing how weak Jett's attempts become. I'd say he has about... three, two, one. At the end of my countdown, his body falls limp, but I hold a few moments longer, ensuring that he is out before laying him down out of the way of the wheels, slightly behind a berm of snow. I retrieve a small vial containing Propofol from the bottom compartment of my boot. I quickly attach the needle and find a vein in his arm before injecting it. Based on his size, his wolf, and the dose, it will only be about five minutes before he's back up.

His hand, now shifted back to human, has my blood coating it. I use the snow to clean it and remove any trace of me being here, scuffing up the boot patterns and scattering the red-dotted snow. I use more snow to slow the bleeding of my arm before surveying the area to be sure I'm in the clear.

The entire takedown took under two minutes, and the only sound was me hitting the door, which didn't attract any unwanted attention. I pull the key fob out of the snow where he dropped it and jump into the driver seat, turning to greet the female who held all of my proverbial cards—the female who, by the luck of The Fates, has a damn death wish.

"We gotta stop meeting like this, City," I offer, purposely taking the bite out of my tone when I hear her sharp inhale.

The fear that flashes on her face a moment before she recognizes me tamps down my anger over her inability to stay out of trouble. Her expression broadcasts her shock, then her confusion, and lastly, her rage. She whips her head around, looking out the window and attempting to escape. My finger slides to the automatic lock before she can open the door, and I add the child lock for good measure.

Never can be too careful with this one.

"What did you do to Sebastian?" she shouts at me accusingly.

"No idea who that is," I deflect before continuing. "You should really put your seatbelt on, seeing as you tend to bring trouble wherever you go."

She huffs. Actually huffs like a pissed-off dragon releasing steam, and I can't help but laugh at how adorable she looks: flushed, jaw set, eyes on fire.

"I am NOT going anywhere with you! The last time I saw you, you assisted my KIDNAPPER with a warm meal and a place to stay. 'Put on your seatbelt,' you've got to be kidding me. Let me out of here. I'm sure there's a poor chauffeur out there with an injury that needs attending to." Her words come out clipped and accusatory, and for a moment, it gives me pause.

She's not wrong about the Hudson thing.

She crosses her arms defiantly, and I assess her momentarily, knowing deep down she's too stubborn to do this without a fight.

Okay. Plan B. It's time to give her the truth.

"Your 'poor chauffeur' is a pack enforcer tasked with kidnapping you on three-quarters of a million dollar bounty from none other than Deacon Marlo, so if you would like to live through this 'fun job-hunting adventure,' I would appreciate less sass, more gratitude, and your buckle clipped." I finish with a smirk before turning around and pulling out of the space, heading toward my hotel.

I have no idea what Jett did with Dante's enforcer, and I make a mental note to reach out to him once Bri's secured. As we exit the airport parking lot, I look into the rearview mirror and see she has, in fact, buckled up, and now that face of hers is just a screen show of emotions. Her eyes catch the gashes still bleeding on my forearm, and I attempt to pull the torn sleeve down, using my gloved hand to wipe away some of my blood in the process.

It's deeper than I realized.

CHAPTER 2

Before checking in, I'll need to replace both the shirt and the gloves. Fingerprints and DNA are too easily traced, and, as far as I know, mine don't exist in any system.

Well, except Saint's.

I'm never without a full change of clothes or extra gloves. Not only do they keep my identity secure, but they keep my visions away. Skin contact shows me everything I need to know about a person's future. The longer the contact, the more I see. So, I ensure everything I wear in public has me covered until or unless I need to use that particular ability.

Her silence as we drive has me flipping my eyes back on the mirror again. I notice the increased tempo of her heart rate fluttering on her neck and her shallow breathing. I worry she's about to experience another panic attack, like the day in the woods, so I try to distract her, speaking casually over my shoulder.

"And to clarify, I recall you also enjoyed a place to stay and a warm meal on the 'kidnapping extravaganza,' several in fact. If I remember correctly, I served your eggs 'just the way you like 'em in the mornin'." I smile my Cheshire grin, enjoying being able to fluster her. I see the flush climb her neck and some of the fire lights back up in her eyes, which shows me she's back in complete control.

Pushing her buttons is so easy, and I haven't been able to push anyone's buttons in a long time—not since Mazie.

The thought of my baby sister is a punch to the gut. Instantly, it's like I'm doused with ice water, and the moment of joy is erased by immeasurable pain as flashes of her frail naked body lay beaten, broken, chained to that breeding table. I fight to hold onto the present, blinking several times and refocusing on the moment I get to light Connor Saint on fire and let him burn over and over for his sins.

That centers me, and when I regain my composure, I realize I have pulled off to the side of the road. Bri is speaking to me, but her words aren't registering. I squeeze my eyes shut for three counts and then open them, allowing myself to process the sound coming in.

"Ghost! Are you ok? What the hell happened? Ghost!"

"I'm fine, City, just made a wrong turn."

I can see she isn't buying it, but she doesn't push, and I proceed back onto the deserted side street. I check for her bodyguard, and find he isn't behind us.

"Am I allowed to ask where you're taking me?" she asks, her voice barely above a whisper.

"Well, seeing as you registered for your hotel under your name, I would bet a handful of assassins, mercenaries, enforcers, and lone wolves are hoping to cash in with you. You'll be safer at my hotel." I meet her eyes again. "No one knows I'm here."

Chapter 3
Bri

Why do I feel like I'm cheating on him?

As I enter the lavish hotel, I try my best not to appreciate how warm it is. The contrast to the air outside is noticeable and almost makes me feel human again. The floor-to-ceiling windows show the blanketed cityscape beautifully.

When Ghost revealed that Sebastian wasn't who I thought he was, it took everything I had to not physically retreat into myself. The cold seeped in and took root.

I can't do anything right.

What the hell was I thinking? 'Sure, person I've never met. I will get into your car without asking for any credentials or checking with anyone to see if you are the right person.'

I'm a fucking idiot.

The sound of the door closing behind me pulls my attention.

"Sorry about the sleeping arrangements. I thought it was just going to be me," he says with a smile that shows how much this amuses him.

Sleeping arrangements?

I turn back toward the room and take in the king bed for the first time.

Mother. Fucker.

"No. Nope. Not doing this. Take me to my hotel. They can kidnap me."

"Awww, you slept with... what was it you called me? Snowball? Just fine." His smile is infuriating, and I have to hold back the urge to hit his perfectly square jaw.

"If I remember correctly, I sent you to the corner. On the floor. By yourself!" I spit back at him.

His laugh is surprising, and it catches me off guard.

"Don't worry, City. I'm perfectly fine on the floor. I'd hate to ruin anything with your 'almost, sort of, kind of, a little bit, not anymore boyfriend,'" he chuckles, coupling the words with air quotes as he walks his bag to the opposite side of the room.

I fight the very tempting and very mature instinct to stick my tongue out at his retreating back. Instead, I huff out a sigh and move my bag, which was left sitting by the door, over to the bed and fling myself onto it. Making a point to moan audibly at how comfortable it is.

Enjoy the floor, Snowball.

"Careful, City. My bite is definitely worse than my bark," he follows the comment with a whispered 'woof' and a lifted eyebrow.

CHAPTER 3

"Yeah, well, I wish we could just get it over with. A bite might actually be the only thing that fixes all of this. Know any Alpha's in the area?" I joke, killing the light mood as I scoot myself back to lean against the headboard. Part of my value to Deacon is his need to take something away from Dante's pack. Awakening me would be a power play, making it hard for Dante to claim me as part of his pack.

Claim... like I'm property.

Ghost freezes, his shoulders tensing before he speaks without turning around, all humor gone from his tone.

"Be careful what you wish for, City. Sometimes those wishes get granted, but not in the way you want."

If I had a dollar for every vague-ass remark this man makes...

I scowl—a memory resurfacing.

"You told me once not to run from my Fate. How did you know what I was, or better yet, how did you know what would happen?" I ask, tilting my head and raising an eyebrow at his back, my tone accusatory.

"You know exactly how I knew what you were—the same way as everyone else in your circle. As for your Fate, this here sure looks a lot like running. How's that going for ya?" he asks.

He's an Alpha and an asshole too.

"Where is your pack? How come you aren't annoyingly in their business instead of here?" I sass.

"Haven't had one of those in a long time," he says, his voice low, almost somber, as he rummages through his bag methodically.

Why doesn't he lead a pack?

Dante told me about the dynamics in the Vegas Pack back when I was in the hospital. He told me about Cain's choice to be Second, about how most packs can't function with more than a few Alphas, but that Alphas are drawn to pack life, drawn to lead. He said their wolves push them into that role. I never thought to ask about Ghost after Dante said he wasn't in his pack.

"I prefer to be alone," he finishes, interrupting my speculation before crossing the room. "I'm going to shower. Try not to die until I get out." His eyes finally meet mine, and his charming Southern mask is back on—a smirk planted on his face.

I mirror his expression, no sweetness behind my snark, before pulling out my charger to revive my lifeless phone. I'd attempted to text Ethan from the car, but my signal wouldn't go through, and then it died from attempting.

This battery is on its last leg. Maybe if I take this job, I will splurge on a new phone.

My eyes glance over to Ghost's bag, nestled neatly in the corner. It's no larger than a carry-on and looks well used. The sound of the shower starting gives me the confidence to scramble quietly off the bed.

Tiptoeing across the floor, I put my ear to the bathroom door, attempting to verify he is actually in the water before I hustle over to the bag. Before I touch anything, I take a minute to ensure I remember its exact position on the chair.

All zippers are in the middle. Every clip fastened, every snap snapped.

With extreme care, I pull on the tab of the main compartment zipper, hoping to minimize the noise. It slides easily to the opposite side, and I let out my breath as I peer inside. It's filled to the top, and I gently remove things to dive in further. I find neatly folded shirts, shorts, boxer briefs, and joggers, a book that looks like it's seen better days, a wallet, a grocery bag containing his shredded shirt and bloody gloves from the car, a small utility bag stuffed full, and several pairs of black utility gloves.

I investigate the wallet and find several driver's licenses, all with Ghost's face and description, but from entirely different states around the country. The names on each are distinct: Todd McNulty, Arkansas; Brian Hasterly, Montana; Dominic Miles, New York; Evan Green, Oregon; William Sharington, Colorado; and Robert Fredrick Rutherford III, Pennsylvania. In addition to his multiple identities, he has a wad of cash, business cards for each, and a single receipt from a gas station for two cokes from over a decade ago.

Weird.

Everything else is meticulously organized, so holding onto an old receipt makes zero sense.

Closing the wallet, I pull the book out to look at the cover— *The Adventures of Sherlock Holmes* by Arthur Conan Doyle. The edges of the detective novel are slightly curled up, and a crease is etched in the spine. I notice a bookmark halfway through, and I open to the page he is reading. Before I can look at the words, I gasp as I recognize Ghost's smiling face looking up at me.

His bookmark is actually a picture, worn out over time, of two smiling teens, a boy and a girl, standing outside a building labeled Bridgestone Arena. A banner behind them boasts 'Nashville Rising Benefit Concert.' The girl looks about sixteen and wears a sky-blue summer dress with embroidered cowboy boots. Her jet-black hair is wavy and falls to her shoulders. Her eyes are exactly the same color as his, and they have an air of mischief.

Next to her is a much younger and more carefree version of Ghost. He stands a whole foot taller than her and has his arm draped over her shoulder. He appears to be almost laughing at something she just said, as his smile lights up his whole face, making him even more handsome than I could have imagined. The sun reflects off his pure white hair, which he has grown long, almost like a surfer, and his skin holds a golden tan. He, too, is wearing cowboy boots but pairs them with stiff-looking blue jeans and a navy button-down short-sleeved shirt.

I never would have pictured him in jeans.

My eyes scan the picture, trying to find the story and the truth behind how the boy in this photo became the man I know today. The Ghost I know is the cranky, lonely, strong-silent type with a strategically flirtatious mask that seems like a form of distraction rather than interest. He's bossy, vague as shit, and incredibly infuriating.

The boy in this picture looks relaxed, happy, fun.

"Find what you were lookin' for?" his voice behind me causes me to yelp, dropping the picture and the book.

Well, shit.

I spin, apologies loaded on my tongue, when I realize he's standing in nothing but a towel, water still beading off his chest and shoulders. He catches my attention, and his damn lopsided grin slides into place as he repeats his words but puts them into a very different context.

"Find what you were lookin' for?" His eyes glance down to his body and the towel wrapped around his waist before slowly returning to me.

"I'm sorry," I finally sputter before doing the only thing I can think of and spin completely around, giving him my back. My skin's hot

CHAPTER 3

from the flush creeping up my neck, and I move as far away from his bag as I can without facing him.

Damn. Damn. Damnit.

I chastise myself for not paying more attention to the shower, for not being faster with the items, and for checking him out.

I'm not interested in Ghost. Not like that, but I'd be lying if I said his body wasn't something to marvel at.

"Feel free to look your fill, City. I know things aren't exactly going well for you in that department," he says before chuckling to himself and waltzing over to his bag to get dressed.

"I don't know what you're referring to, but I was simply looking for your phone since mine wasn't charged," I lie, ensuring my face is solidly pointed at the wall.

"And my wallet and book being out and open..." he says, leaving the question hanging in the air, taunting me because he knows I was snooping.

"Curiosity and all that," I shrug, hearing his zipper close.

"Didn't peg you for a kitty cat, but I guess the adage fits otherwise," he adds, and I roll my eyes before crawling back onto the comforter, attempting to keep space between us as I dare a look in his direction.

He's clothed again, and I breathe a sigh of relief. He grabs a bottle of water from the mini fridge and tosses it at me before grabbing one for himself and sitting at the makeshift office desk on his side of the room.

"I didn't know you had a sister," I say, stating my assumption, hoping I can find out more about him.

"I don't," he says, taking a long pull from his water.

"Her eyes suggest otherwise," I state, watching him flinch ever so slightly at the statement.

For a long moment, he doesn't respond. He just sits sipping occasionally and taking note of the wall decor in the room.

Okay, I guess we're done talking.

I reach for my phone on the nightstand, hoping it has gotten enough charge to restart so I can send some messages and let someone know I'm okay.

"I wouldn't bother with your phone. I'm jamming it. You won't be able to get any messages out," he says with as much importance as if he were discussing the weather or a grocery list.

"You're WHAT?!?" I shout.

"Jamming it. With a transmitter, so you can't make or receive calls. A Faraday cage would be preferable but with limited notice and all." He shrugs, noncommittal. His words are clear, but their meaning is lost as my anger builds.

"I... You.... Argh..." I stumble through, trying to collect my thoughts. I'm in a strange city hundreds of miles from home, and I have no way to contact anyone, including the company I'm here to see.

My fingers fist the comforter, grounding me as I try to communicate my needs, a tactic my old therapist recommended.

"I need a phone. No one knows I'm safe, and I need to contact the company to find out when I need to be there tomorrow morning," I say.

"Need is a strong word. No one needs a phone, and if I remember correctly, a phone is the story you used to lure me in an attempt to get

CHAPTER 3

me to and invite you back to my place last time we were together." His smug expression makes me want to punch him square in the face.

"First, we've never been together, at least not in the way you are implying. A thing you shouldn't continue because if Cain heard you, I don't think I could stop him from killing you, joke or not. Second, I didn't lure you; I begged for help, which you did not give." He cuts me off, laughing out loud before I can give him my third thing.

"Oh boy, City, you have quite the imagination, and your memory must be spotty from the hit to the ground. How do you think Dante knew where you were, huh? Or when you were being handed over to the Reno Pack so he could make an offer? I may not have ridden in on a white horse in a cape to save the day, but make no mistake, you are alive because of me. You aren't headed right back to that pack today because of me. And."

Now, it's my turn to cut him off.

"And what's in it for you, huh? You say you have no pack and like to be alone, yet you keep inserting yourself into this mess. My mess. Why save me at all? What's in it for you?" I shout at him, standing up off the bed in my anger.

His jaw clenches, a challenge looming in his eyes, and for a single moment, I think he's going to snap at me. Yell, shout, answer me.

Instead, his face calms, all emotion leaving it as if it were never there.

What in the psycho shit is this?

"Why is it so hard for you to let people help you? People are actively trying to abduct you in a supernatural political game of chess, and you're here bound and determined to let them succeed. You don't have a signal because your phone can easily be tracked, and I don't feel like adding to my body count attempting to keep you or me alive."

"I never asked you to keep me alive," I mumble, most of my anger gone after his calm and logical statement.

"Well then, I guess it's good that I'm doing it for me and not you. I'm a selfish asshole, not a hero. I don't do anything unless it serves my agenda. Currently, you being alive happens to align with what I need. If that ever changes, trust me, I will let you stumble through your messes all on your own," he finishes his tone cold for the first time, and it's at that moment I see the legend that is Ghost and not the man.

Bullshit.

If there's one thing I'm good at, it's reading people. The foster system teaches you to look for signs, minuscule tells that reveal the people who have bad intentions—the ones who are morally corrupt.

Ghost may be capable of some fucked up things, and I believe the few things I've heard that he's done, but inside, he still has a soul.

The picture of his sister told me all I needed to know.

Releasing my fists, I let out a sigh. I need to compose myself because he isn't going to talk to me right now. He isn't the type to yell, and his control is honed in. I won't get any answers this way.

Turning, I grab my suitcase, place it on the bed, and open it to grab what I need before silently walking into the bathroom to shower.

I need to contact Boston Digital, let Liv and Keith know I'm safe, and let Cain know I'm okay. I can't have him fly across the country to rescue me again. If Ghost wants to play this close to the vest, then he can be my escort this week while I'm here. Maybe I can get him to trust me enough to tell me what the hell is going on and why I seem to be the center of it. Maybe I can get him to tell me the truth.

For now, all I know is that this is starting to feel too much like deja vu, and I'm tired of being a pawn in a game I never asked to play, one that no one gave me the rules for.

He's right about one thing, though: curiosity does kill the cat; I guess I just need to remember that I'm a wolf.

Chapter 4

Cain

*W*hat the fuck did I think about before I met her?

The thought has been bouncing around since she left for Boston last night. Letting her leave for the airport without me felt like a kind of torture worse than I've ever encountered.

She deserves to be happy.

We can make her happy.

Fighting my wolf has been a new challenge placed on my control. Patience has never been a strong virtue of mine, and knowing my Mate is flying across the country nearly unprotected leaves my skin itching.

She asked for space.

She's been reaching out more.

> **Landed safe in Boston**

CHAPTER 4

Thank The Fates for that.

I breathe a sigh of relief, texting her back much faster than is socially acceptable, but my pride went out the window a long time ago when it came to her.

> Glad to hear you are safe. I'm here if you need anything.

I wish I were there, but I think I'm making progress in getting her to trust me again, and I don't want to lose the fragile foundation we've begun building.

I finish the report I'm working on when her text comes through.

> You're here? Where? I don't see anyone.

Anyone? Shouldn't someone be there waiting?

> No one is there to get you? How long have you been waiting?

My wolf reels at the thought of her sitting alone in that airport.

Well, not alone. Dante sent Carter on the flight with her to ensure she made it there without any issues. The LLC investigation has started, and from what we've heard, it's not looking like they are going to let the Tahoe incident go without more information, adjudicators, and documentation.

Part of me is glad they aren't taking this lightly. The kidnapping of female wolves has been too overlooked in our history, and I, for one, like the progressive change this is taking. That being said, Brielle doesn't belong to Deacon Marlo. She's Mine.

> About half an hour.

The buzzing in my hand pulls me back.

Thirty minutes with no ride? Absolutely not. I'll have Jess reach out to her old pack to pick her up and get her safely to her hotel. There is no excuse for that kind of oversight from this company.

I may have disliked that Ethan guy, but he never struck me as incompetent. With as much heat as is on both our pack and Brielle, having her sitting alone in an airport is unacceptable.

Cain: Can you message Carter to find out what's going on? Brielle's ride never showed up at the airport.

My mind link message goes out as I text her back.

> Hang on, Firefly, I'm sending a car.

I've tried not using the nickname with her as often because I know it makes her put her guard up, but I don't want her to forget what she means to me, what she will always mean to me.

Dante: He isn't responding, but I don't feel any stress through the bond.

Cain: Can Jess contact Montgomery to have someone pick Bri up and safely take her to her hotel?

I send before leaving my office, headed for his.

Dante: Jess is on duty; I'll call.

He responds as my phone vibrates again

> Don't worry about it. I'm grabbing an Uber. See you when I get back.

A random Uber isn't safe enough.

"Yes, thank you so much for reaching out, Lily. Tell Doug that Mr. Stone appreciates the opportunity to clear up these allegations."

CHAPTER 4

Quinn's voice is sweet, but her facial expression shows her irritation. "We will get that over to you as soon as we can. Thanks so much. Bye now." She finishes, placing the receiver down before rubbing her temples as I approach.

Her eyes close briefly before she opens them, and she has a new determination on her face. She notices me standing there, grabs a Post-it off her desk, and waves it at me.

"Can you bring this to him? It's the number for the Boston Alpha he asked for. Also, let him know Martin responded." She doesn't need to say more for me to understand that it wasn't good.

"How bad?" I ask, dread filling me.

"He's going to need to call another council meeting later tonight," she answers before returning to her email.

"I'm emailing him the documents with my phone call notes. He should have it... now." Turning her chair, she grabs the Red Bull beside the keyboard and takes a long drink.

Looks like we have a long night ahead of us.

When I walk into the office, Dante's back is to me. Every screen is lit up with legal documents, camera feeds, and web browsers. I glance at the city, remembering how different the view felt two months ago—before everything changed.

Before I found her.

"I don't need any more shit news today, Cain, so tell me she texted back, and her ride was there." He turns in his chair, his face lacking the humor he used to carry.

Looking at him now, I notice the lines that have appeared over the last few months, the dark circles under his eyes. Gone is the kid who took over as our Alpha too young, and before me sits a man who strongly resembles his father instead.

"Wish I could. She says she's getting an Uber. Anything from Carter yet? It's not like him to fail to check in," I say, extending my arm to hand him the yellow Post-it from Quinn. "Montgomery's number," I add before falling into the seat.

He dials, leaving the phone on its cradle and the speaker going. It's just after 8 pm in Boston, so there's a chance he is no longer in his office.

"Montgomery Financing Specialists, how can I assist you today?" A man answers robotically.

The business is a front similar to Marlo's companies. Consulting fees are much more difficult for human governments to trace.

"Yes, I'd like to speak with management about an account issue," Dante responds.

"Of course, can I have the account name?" he replies.

"Dante Stone."

"One moment, Mr. Stone." The line clicks, and hold music plays before another voice comes on the line.

"Stone, I didn't think I'd hear from you this quickly. I guess news travels fast." The voice says, interest lacing his voice as Dante's eyes flash up to mine.

Contacting him for what?

"Thought I'd go right to the source for answers," Dante replies noncommittally.

"Well, I don't know about that. I wouldn't say I'm the source. The contract just happens to fall in my jurisdiction. I don't own it and

CHAPTER 4

have nothing to do with its execution. My Second brought it to my attention today when we started getting access requests to our territory."

Contract? What contract?

I can tell Dante is as in the dark as I am.

"Can you tell me who has accepted?" Dante asks, trying to pull as much information as possible without admitting he doesn't know what's happening.

"Damn near everyone, if I'm being honest. I'm not sure who will actually complete it, though; there is lots of competition. But you've got your own man here, so I guess you have a wolf in this race. I did hear Jett and Dimitri are among them," he adds, listing two of the most prominent contract mercenaries in the US.

"Yes, and I appreciate you allowing him access. We're going to do our best to shut this down. I just wanted to check who the big players were and thought I could see how the Ostler twins are doing for you," Dante says, turning the conversation despite us still not knowing what the contract is for.

It's better to let Pres look into it now that we know it exists.

"Oh, those boys have been great. You certainly trained them well. They keep my young recruits on their toes with the programs they instituted. How's my girl holding up?" he asks, extending the conversation past what I want to hear.

"She's the best. I'll have to give her some time off to go home and visit soon. Thanks for the information. We'll get this cleaned up for you as quickly as we can." Dante finishes and hangs up after a few more pleasantries.

Before I can speak, Pres pops in behind me, headphones blaring and laptop in her hand.

"What do you need?" she asks, her voice all business as her eyes slide between Dante and me.

"Montgomery's got an open contract in his city. Find it," Dante orders.

Pres drops into the chair next to me, fingers flying over the keys as she flips through the TOR network, dark web windows changing faster than I can keep up.

Please don't be her.

Part of me knows it's a long shot. She was just taken. There are a lot of eyes on us about the exchange from before Thanksgiving, but the coincidence of her being there and Alpha Montgomery implying it had something to do with us doesn't sit right with me.

It's then that I realize Presley's typing has stopped, and the room is silent. My eyes flip between her and Dante, and I realize they are talking, just not to me.

"Pres…" I growl out, seeing the expression on her face seconds before the mind-link message hits my ears.

Dante: Conference room ten minutes. Shit just hit the fan.

Fuck!

Chapter 5
Bri

When I creep out of the bathroom, the lights in the room are turned off. It takes a minute for my eyes to adjust to the darkness, so I fumble over to the bed, making an effort not to wake Ghost up. In the process, I stub my toe on the corner of the nightstand.

"Damnit!" I whisper-shout, attempting and subsequently failing to stay quiet.

Movement in the corner pulls my attention, and I see Snowball curled up next to Ghost's bag, head now perked up, a lopsided grin on his face.

"Be up at seven. I'm going to that meeting. Phone or not. Contract or not. I will not spend my life in hiding. You need me alive? You can shadow me to the building and back. That's it," I say, my confidence stronger when talking to him in this form. "Night, Snowball," I finish, a cheesy grin on my face once I get fully tucked in.

If there are people who want to kidnap me, then I will do my best to be safe. I will make sure I'm never alone. I know they can't reveal themselves to humans, so I will stick with ordinary people—safety in numbers and all that.

As I fall asleep, I review my pros/cons list.

Pros: Snow, Dream job, Fresh Start.

Cons: Liv, Keith, Cain

***

Walking into Boston Digital feels surreal. When I imagined coming to work here two months ago, it was the bright spot at the end of a long tunnel. Today, as I stand in the modernly decorated open front lobby, all I feel are nerves.

It could be related to the kidnapping contract, or the man I know is following somewhere in the shadows, ensuring I don't actually get taken.

I wish I knew his role in this.

"Good morning! Thank you for calling Boston Digital. How may I direct your call? Absolutely, one moment, please." Buttons are pushed as the receptionist sends the call through.

I remove the thick jacket I brought to combat the cold and fold it nicely over my arm, which is carrying my leather laptop bag. Both were gifts from Liv's parents for my birthday this year, and, as the chill hits me, I'm grateful they thought of them.

CHAPTER 5

Squaring my shoulders and lifting my chin, I walk up to the desk with a smile. The girl behind it glances up and gives me the gesture for one moment before speaking again.

"Good morning! Thank you for calling Boston Digital. How may I direct your call? Yes, sir, I can get you right over. Just one moment, please."

This time, when she places him on hold, her attention returns to me.

"Hi there! How can I help you?" she asks. Her voice and expression are naturally kind.

"Hi, I'm Brielle DelaCourt. I'm here to see Ethan," I respond, temporarily forgetting his last name and wishing I'd had my phone connection to look it up before coming in.

"Brielle! Yes, he said you would be in today. Have a seat, and I will have someone bring you to his office in just a minute," she says before flipping back to answer the phone call, which has her desk flashing with the red hold light.

Nodding, I turn and walk over to the seating area she indicated. I choose a seat away from the window and place my back to the wall so I can see anyone approaching.

See, look at me being aware of my surroundings. Take that, Casper!

As I wait, I smooth away wrinkles in my navy blue dress and pick imaginary lint from my off-white blazer. My hands cannot stay still without my phone distracting my nerves. Not to mention, I don't typically wear dresses in my current job, so I feel a bit out of sorts.

Liv helped me choose my three work outfits for this trip: two business-professional ensembles for office days and one night-time professional look since I might end up going out with the team. It's a Thursday, and I don't fly out until Sunday night, but I wanted time to explore the city this weekend.

Not sure that will be allowed now.

"Brielle?"

I jump at the sound of the woman's voice.

"Sorry to startle you!" she exclaims, causing me to turn in her direction. "I'm Tristan, Ethan's assistant," she finishes with a polite smile.

"I'm so sorry. I guess I was lost in thought. I'm Bri," I say, extending my hand for her to shake as I stand. She's my height and appears to be about thirty, with her long dark brown hair pulled back from her face. A pop of purple underneath catches my eye and makes me think of Liv, who has wanted to dye her hair purple for years but has never taken the leap.

"No worries at all. Let's get you upstairs, and we can set down your stuff so I can give you a tour."

As we move to the elevator, I scan the lobby again to see if anyone is taking note of us leaving, but everyone seems to be working or engaged in conversations.

I breathe a sigh of relief when the doors close, and we're headed up.

"Nervous?" she asks politely.

"Very. I've wanted this job for a long time," I answer honestly.

"Well, you didn't hear it from me, but I think it's already yours. Ethan has been raving about the ideas you discussed. We've actually already pulled the preliminary numbers on the sustainability initiative," she says, surprising me.

"Really? Huh. I came up with that during the interview based on an article I'd read earlier in the week. It was a big swing proposal at the moment. I can't believe he ran with it," I finish, a little taken aback by the pride I feel.

They're using my ideas.

"Oh yes," she starts as the doors open on the third floor. "One thing you will learn about Ethan is that he loves actionable steps. He jumps into things he believes in with both feet. We're lucky he's right most of the time, or it would cost us a fortune."

She laughs, and I realize my nerves are gone.

"What are you two conspiring about?" a male voice pulls my attention as we head toward Tristan's office.

"Oh, nothing much," she says while winking at me, mischief crossing her expression as Ethan comes into view.

He looks exactly like the photo on the company website. He's in his early forties, clean-shaven, and has salt-and-pepper hair. He's wearing a white button-up shirt with the sleeves rolled to his elbows and grey slacks. Clear-framed glasses hide his almond eyes but do nothing to cover the laugh lines that are etched into his skin.

I can tell he spends a lot of time smiling, which puts me at ease.

"Tristan here was spilling all the company secrets. I think you might need to give her a raise. She's far too valuable to lose, especially with all the information at her disposal," I add, feigning seriousness and causing him to laugh out loud.

"Tris wouldn't leave me. Her kids love me too much," he says, crossing his arms. His confidence oozes from him, immediately making me realize he reminds me of an older Keith.

"He's right about that. Spoils them both rotten."

"Bribery's an excellent negotiation tool; all I need is some sour patch kids or a trip for ice cream, and it's like I hung the moon," he says before turning more serious. "I'm glad you made it in today. I was worried you'd cancel when I didn't hear from you last night. Did you get to your hotel alright?"

His question makes me pause because I messaged him, but he didn't respond. I know my messages were going out because I could text Liv, Keith, and Cain.

I wonder if my phone's been compromised somehow...

"Oh, well, I made the mistake of leaving my phone at the airport in Las Vegas. It must have fallen out of my carry-on when I was loading the plane," I lie, trying for a reasonable excuse for not confirming I made it. "They contacted me this morning at the hotel, and my roommate is picking it up later today, so I get to have this experience without any distractions from social media or the million games I have stored on there," I ramble, realizing it's probably more information then they needed.

"Way to turn a negative into a positive. Well, if you'd like to use a company phone while you're here, just let Tris know, and we will set you up with one. I have a meeting across town, but I should be back for the staff meeting at 1 pm."

"Don't forget the gift bag; it's by Genny's desk," Tristan says, waving me to follow her.

CHAPTER 5

"Got it. It's nice to meet you finally, Brielle. We're excited you're here!" he shouts over his shoulder as he walks onto the elevator.

"It's right in here," Tristan pulls my attention back as we enter her office. "You can put your things over here," she adds, pulling her jacket off to hang it on the back of her chair. She reveals an orange tank top blouse paired with black slacks, but it's her beautifully colored tattoos that pull my attention.

Flowers peak out at her collarbone, and a lion with detailed line work stretches up her arm, with more pink flowers around it, completing her half-sleeve.

Bright hair colors, tattoos... I like the culture here.

Turning away to set my coat and bag down before she catches me staring at her, I tug my sleeve, which covers my watercolor-lightening bug, and feel even more like I would fit in here.

Add to the Pro list.

A beautiful beach picture of her with her family is on her back wall. Her husband and two children stand beside her, all wearing giant smiles as the sun sets behind them.

"Have you had coffee? Breakfast? Where do we need to start?" she asks, pulling my attention from the photo.

"Coffee would be great. Thanks," I return, leaving my stuff and following her out the door. Something about that photo has my heart aching. It's everything I wanted my childhood to look like and everything I want for my kids someday—happy memories, together memories.

My thoughts drift to Cain, and I have to forcibly focus on the now to keep from picturing our future.

Do we have a future?

Forcing a smile, I take in what could be my future office. It has an open concept, with desks and tables set up strategically throughout the space. The main offices and conference rooms line the outer edges of the floor, and the center houses a large kitchen and coffee area complete with snacks and fridges with drinks and water, set out with tables like a cafe.

A few employees sit eating and looking over a tablet in front of them. There's a buzz in the atmosphere that has me smiling as I take it all in. Large screens show current projects and ads that are being perfected for mass media markets across the globe.

"How do you take it?" Tristan asks, making me realize she's already got a cup of coffee in front of her.

"Cream and sugar, please, lots. I like the caffeine but can't stand the coffee taste," I say as she laughs.

"You and me both. We have caramel syrup if that helps," she says.

"Yes, please!" I add.

Once my coffee is made, we tour the floor and talk to several associates. Everyone gushes about their jobs, has nothing but great things to say about the company, and is incredibly welcoming.

Two hours later, I'm pinching myself. This place feels like a dream. I'd gotten to meet everyone I'd be working with and sit in on discussions about current clients for whom the company is creating content. I even met the owner, Vince Gordan, who I have followed on social media since my first year of business school.

It's like this place was made for me.

The imaginary pro list in my mind has gotten incredibly long throughout the day, and I can't imagine any place checking all of the boxes like this one has. The only question still looming in my mind is whether

CHAPTER 5

I can make it work here as an Awakened wolf... that part of my future seems to be the only piece I have no choice in.

Chapter 6
Cain

Sitting in the conference room is giving me deja vu. We were just in here talking about my Mate and kidnappings, and here we are again.

Deacon Marlo's a dead man.

Pres sent everyone the contract while we wait for Jake to join us. Elijah and James are away on business with neighboring packs, trying to realign those who have heard the rumors about the LLC investigation and possible hearing. Why no one thinks taking Reno over now isn't the easiest way to settle this mess is beyond me, but one thing I know for sure is that Bri is mine. No one else will lay claim to her while I'm still breathing.

CHAPTER 6

I try to calm myself by rereading the contract. It uses her UNLV photo and describes her as a Reno pack member. It issues a $750,000 return fee, which is only paid if she's returned alive.

That's probably the only reason I'm not already on one of our jets.

"Have you heard from Carter?" Erik asks Dante, concern evident in his tone.

Carter is Erik's best friend; the two do everything together, and I can see the worry written all over Erik's face as he waits. Jake jogs in, cheeks flushed as Dante answers.

"He checked in a few minutes ago. Someone gave him something. Slipped it into his drink on the plane. The flight crew escorted him off and held him for medical review because he was slurring his words. They thought he was drunk and wouldn't release him until EMTs verified he was coherent. By then, Brielle was gone. She hasn't checked into her hotel, and from what we hear, no one has closed the contract."

Erik's jaw clenches, but I can see tension release from his shoulders at the news. I'm glad for him, but knowing my Mate is still missing relieves none of mine.

"I've been sweeping chat rooms and board posts, and from what I can tell, no one claims to have her yet. A post stated a possible location of her last sighting, but that turned out to be a false trail. So, right now, we have nothing, and until I fix the power issue, I can't bring HUNTER online here. I'd need to be at Berkeley to run it to its full capability," Pres says, eyes flipping to Dante, asking the silent question.

"If it comes to that, we'll send you with a team. We currently have a few leads and friends in the area we can work with. Jess has reached out to her brother, Nyxon, and he's willing to work with us to return her. I've also messaged the twins, and they are waiting for instructions. Carter will meet up with all three of them tomorrow morning to gameplan, and..." Dante's interrupted as his phone vibrates on the table, pulling all of our attention.

His eyes scan the screen before looking up at me.

"She's safe." As soon as the words hit my ears, I let go of the air I'd been holding.

"Where?" I ask, grateful she's okay but not alleviating the worry I'm carrying with the contract still in place.

"She's with Ghost," he says, before continuing. "He will keep an eye on her until she returns."

"Anyone know what his deal is with her?" Jake asks.

All eyes turn to me, and I shake my head. Bri said very little about her interactions with Ghost. I assume he helped because she landed on his doorstep, but having him linked to her a second time does seem curious.

"Is he planning to fulfill the contract?" I ask Dante, knowing Ghost usually steers clear of kidnapping, especially as it ties to women. He mentioned his sister to us exactly once as we prepared for the undercover mission in Detroit. Her death changed him.

He wouldn't do this. He doesn't take women.

"His message doesn't say anything about the contract. It says she's safe and that he will ensure she makes it home," Dante answers, eyeing me before adding on. "However, Brielle spoke to me about Ghost when she returned. She didn't know about his gift; as far as I know, she still doesn't, but he told her she was the key to winning the war. Said that she was the deliverance our world needs."

CHAPTER 6

For a moment, no one speaks as we process this new piece of information, and every part of me wants to yell at him for not revealing that little tidbit earlier.

We don't keep things from each other, especially things about my Mate.

"So he's protecting her?" Jake asks, questions swimming behind his eyes.

"It would appear so," Dante says, his gaze still pinned on me as he gages my reaction.

"Does she know about the contract?" I ask, keeping the anger from entering my voice and trying to be logical.

Dante taps a message into his phone and waits.

Pres interrupts our silence.

"While we wait on that, you should know our girl didn't change any of her login information post kidnapping, well, the last kidnapping. Anyway, even though we no longer have her under surveillance, I still have access to her emails and calendar. She has meetings for the next two days at Boston Digital. Then she booked a day trip to Martha's Vineyard on Saturday and a bus tour for Sunday morning before her flight out that night. If she isn't changing her plans, we know where she will be. We can get that information to Carter so he can reestablish his tail, and it would allow us to send another team in to help protect her," Pres finishes, looking at me with a nod.

Dante's phone vibrates again, and we wait to hear the news.

"She's aware of the contract. He tried to convince her to go home, but she's staying for her meetings," Dante relays. "Jake, take Jess in the Gulfstream. Yelena can be wheels up in an hour," Dante orders.

"I'm going," I interject, knowing he won't be happy but not giving a damn. "Her safety is the only thing that matters to me, and this contract changes things," I state, not leaving room for argument.

Dante purses his lips, bringing his hand to his beard as he considers it, and turns our conversation private by sending me a mind-link message.

Dante: She specifically asked you to give her space.

Cain: That was before she had a kidnapping contract, and Jett and Dimitri after her.

Dante: She's protected by arguably the best bodyguard I could give her outside of you, and we're sending additional resources as backup.

Cain: I need to know she's safe. I need to be there. Please don't fight me on this.

I send the last mind-link, begging him not to force me into a corner. Hoping he understands I don't have a choice.

"Fine. Cain will go with Jess. Carter, Nyxon, and the twins will be rotating shifts with you, so she is always guarded. Pres, I want updates on the contract and anything else you hear. The LLC is pushing for a full investigation. We need her back in our territory as soon as possible so I can brief her on what that may mean. They've already requested to question her. I've been stalling, knowing she's trying to decide what she wants."

My eyebrows fly up at his admission.

They want to speak with her? I mean, of course they do, but why didn't he tell me? Dante answers my question before I can even ask.

CHAPTER 6

"We just received word tonight. Doug Martin isn't backing down. They've requested her for an in-person interview. That's the other reason for the meeting tonight."

"How long do we have?" I ask, knowing the LLC isn't known for its patience.

"He said she needs to be in his office Monday morning," Dante responds.

"And if she isn't?" Erik asks the question flying through all of our minds.

"Then they will side with Deacon's complaint and use any means necessary to return her to his territory and supervision."

The fuck they will.

"We can't let that happen," Jake states, his tone furious, his stare on me. "Bri belongs with Cain."

Yes, she fucking does.

"Then we need her to agree. I told her she had until the new year to decide. Cain, you will need to let her know that's no longer an option. She has 72 hours to make her choice, or there's a chance the LLC will make it for her," Dante finishes, warning in his tone.

No one will take her choice away. I won't allow it, but I can't give her any more time.

I'm sorry, Firefly.

Chapter 7
Ghost

Stakeouts used to be effortless. Observing people as they go through their day was as simple as breathing. If I were to guess, it was easy because I didn't care. It wasn't my job to care. My job was to learn their behavior, mold myself to integrate seamlessly into that environment, and execute the contract, whatever that meant.

Following Brielle to Boston Digital didn't feel anything like those contracts, and it is impossible not to care what happens to her. She is my shot at changing the future.

My only shot.

I had the vision again last night. I arrive at an apartment I've never been to and find the person I'm looking for missing. Instinctively, I know it's my Mate, though I don't know how I know this or whether we've Mated. I just know she's supposed to be there, but she isn't.

CHAPTER 7

Flashes transport me to another scene where I'm walking into a trap. I get no context; I simply know that I've accepted that I will be captured or killed. Brielle's face flashes into my mind, and she speaks so clearly that it's as if she is in front of me.

"This is your chance, Casper. The keycard is attached to his belt loop and secured in his front pocket. We're running out of time."

She disappears, and I find myself alone in an interrogation cell, silver cuffs at my wrists and a solid silver chain connecting me to the wall. Someone enters, and I spot the lanyard immediately. The man doesn't speak, and I don't get to see his face before it flashes again, and I'm running out of a building, blood covering my hands, which clutch the keycard.

Dante drives up, and I pass the card to Cain in the passenger seat before pivoting to jump in the back of a second black SUV. Immediately, relief fills me, and I know he will get her out. As we speed off to the rendezvous point, I wipe the blood onto my black fatigues. Brielle will use her access to release my Mate, and Cain will get them both out. The plan is working. As the thought enters my mind, headlights illuminate the windshield, the tires screech, and the wheel turns too late, causing us to slam into the oncoming vehicle, and I fly head-first, right through the glass.

The doors to Boston Digital open, Brielle walks out with three coworkers, and I shake myself back into the present.

She was supposed to stay in the damn building.

How can I protect her if she can't follow basic fucking instructions?

Her eyes scan the street. Whether she's looking for threats or me, I don't know, but at least she's trying to be aware. She won't spot me, even knowing I'm here, which means she wouldn't spot anyone else either, but she gets a gold star for trying.

My attention shifts to the few people out in this weather. No one appears to be paying them any attention, but I wait until they are several blocks ahead before I move to follow. Giving them space will allow me to see who may be after her, and the tracking device I attached to her boot this morning prevents me from losing her if they make a turn I don't anticipate.

Movement across the street pulls my attention, and I slow, looking into a shop window as if deciding if I'm planning to stop in. Making a fake call, I bring my phone to my ear, click a few pictures, and allow whoever it is a chance to think they are the only ones following her.

Once their movement is out of sight, I look at the photos. Two men leave a coffee shop across from her building. I recognize one of them immediately as the man from the flight, and I make an actual phone call this time. It rings as I follow their path, relaxing some as I wait for an answer.

Come on, Dante. Pick up.

When he doesn't, I dial his office number and insert my earpiece, allowing me to use my phone to follow the tracker.

"VP Securities, this is Evelyn. How may I direct your call?" a courteous voice answers.

"Mr. Stone, please," I respond, trying to keep my voice low.

"Of course, Sir, just one moment."

CHAPTER 7

Light hold music comes on a moment before the call is connected.

"Mr. Stone's office, this is Quinn speaking," a woman says. "How can I…"

"I need to speak with Dante," I state, not allowing her to continue. If there's one thing I hate, it's inefficiency.

Why do I have to go through two people to get to him?

"I understand that. Unfortunately, he's in a meeting currently. May I ask who's calling?" her voice keeps its polite tone as she dismisses me.

"This is more important than whatever he has going on," I say, trying to keep the irritation out of my voice.

"Mr. Stone handles many high-profile clients, so I understand your problem may be more urgent to you. I'd be happy to take a message and have him return your call just as soon as he has an opening in his schedule. Or I can send you to one of the other department leads. Can you tell me the nature of the issue so I can find the right person to help you?" her voice doesn't waver, and I clench my jaw as I turn the corner, bringing the two men back into my line of sight. They lean casually outside an office building across the street from the restaurant Brielle just entered.

"Look, I don't care if he's in that room with the president. I need you to get up, walk in there, and get him on the phone."

"Who is this?" she asks, irritation slipping in.

"Quinn, was it? This is a matter of life or death, so if you could do your job and get your boss on the line," I growl, no longer keeping my voice calm.

"That's what we do here. *Everything* is life or death. My *job* is to prioritize each emergency that comes in. Unless you can give me your name and the reason for your call, there's nothing I can do for you."

"Then you can let your boss know that whoever he has following the asset in Boston is about to die." I hang up the phone, frustration boiling out of me at the woman's inability to follow basic instructions.

I bet she and City get along swell.

Exhaling, I attempt to calm myself down from the interaction as I walk past the restaurant. I can't see Bri, or her associates from the front windows, so I turn down the alley, stopping by the back door to the building.

At least she's not a sitting duck.

Though most of the people after her wouldn't make a scene in such a public place. They would attempt to get her alone, especially since she's worth nothing if she dies.

The vibration in my hand shows me that Dante has responded to my missed call with a text message.

> **Everything ok? I'm in an LLC meeting about Brielle. I can't talk.**

> **Your guy back in communication?**

> **Yes. Carter was delayed at airport security. He should be following her now.**

> **Who's with him?**

> **Nyxon Montgomery. He's assisting until my team lands in an hour. We had FCC issues getting out last night and couldn't clear until this morning.**

CHAPTER 7

> Got it. I'll pull back and let them do their job. Speaking of, you need to fire your secretary. She nearly got them both killed.

Quinn?

> She's incompetent. Wouldn't even put my call through.

That's on me. I told her this meeting was the top priority. I'm trying to stall the Reno investigation. They want Brielle at headquarters.

> She'd be safer there.

That may be true, but I promised her time to figure out where she wanted to be. She only gets this trip.

> Does she know?

Cain's on his way.

> Not sure he's the best messenger, considering.

His Mate. His choice.

> Copy. When she leaves tonight, let your guys know they're off duty. She's staying with me. I'll have her back at 8 a.m. tomorrow.

Cain will want to know where she is.

> **Then he should have told her the truth two months ago, and his Mate bond would have been in place, and none of us would be here.**

> **You aren't wrong. Glad to have you back working with us.**

> **I'm not back.**

> **You sure have a funny way of showing it.**

I bite my cheek at his message.

I shouldn't be here. I shouldn't be getting involved. But ever since I saw Brielle's future, everything changed. The visions changed. Fate changed.

If there's one thing I know about The Fates, second chances don't come around often.

She doesn't know it yet, but Brielle is the only one who can reset the balance.

Walking back to the main street, I step out of the shadows and pull back my hood, allowing Carter and Nyxon to see me. Their eyes snap to mine, and I see their expressions change from feigned disinterest to alert to gawking in a matter of moments.

Typically, I wouldn't have revealed myself before leaving, but they need to know the importance of this mission.

After I allow them the time to process who I am, I raise an eyebrow at Carter and point at the restaurant. He nods, understanding my silent question.

CHAPTER 7

You got her?

I return the gesture and pull my hood back on before disappearing into the alley. I have four hours until I need to be back at Boston Digital to pick her up.

Four hours to find Saint's stronghold in Boston.

It's time to put my focus back on the Fallon Project.

Chapter 8
Bri

Lunch with Tris, Genny, Duncan, and Marie was perfect. I got the inside scoop on their favorite things to do around Boston, and I heard stories about the company's Fourth of July party, which apparently lasted until two in the morning and nearly caught two people on fire.

Duncan, the company's media network liaison, reenacted the event, which had half the restaurant staring at us while we tried to stop laughing. By the time we head back to the office, my worries about kidnapping contracts and life as a wolf are a distant memory.

By one o'clock, I'm energized with newfound motivation. I've got ideas for current and future clients bouncing around, and I've started scribbling down notes to bring up tomorrow with a few of the associates I met with today.

The conference room is large and easily accommodates the twenty-two staff members. Sixteen chairs are poised around the table, and

CHAPTER 8

another ten are along the walls. I sit against the wall nearest the far corner and prepare a new notebook page.

Ethan sits at the head of the table farthest from me, and to my surprise, Vince attends the meeting, sitting at the foot of the table closest to me.

"Good afternoon, everyone!" Ethan begins, cool charisma pouring from him as he quickly gains the room's attention. "Thank you for making time for us to meet today. We have a few items to hit on our agenda today, so please make sure you have the documents either open on your devices or grab a copy from the table by the door so we are all on the same page here."

"Before we start, I'd like to introduce Brielle DelaCourt. She comes to us from Las Vegas, Nevada, through the University of Nevada Las Vegas, and we are desperately trying to convince her to join our citizenship and sustainability team. Please give her a warm welcome today."

Applause fills the room as the smiling faces turn my way.

"Thank you," I say, waving quietly, wishing I could fade into the background.

He quickly shifts the meeting focus back to the agenda items. Watching the staff interact tells me everything I need to know about how this company operates. Everyone has a voice. Everyone is valued.

It's too good to be true.

No. Stop it. That's the trauma response talking.

When the meeting ends, I have an entire sheet of notes with the next steps ready to go, and I laugh at myself because I don't work here—not yet, at least.

I follow Tris back into her office, ready to tackle some of the tasks mentioned in the meeting, when Ethan strolls in behind me.

"So, how is your tour going?" he asks, leaning against the wall and crossing his arms casually.

"Today's been amazing. Honestly, I'm not sure how you have a job opening at all," I say, blurting the question that has been rolling around in my head since lunch.

"Well, that's an easy answer. We're expanding two departments to better handle the volume of new clients we've been receiving and to ensure that as a company, we're staying aligned to our goals for productivity and innovation within the space," he responds.

I nod, feeling better about the lack of turnover, knowing most of the staff has been with the company for years.

"I think you broke her," Tris laughs when I don't respond any further, making me smile.

"No, just processing everything. It's a big move, but I can't imagine finding a more perfect fit," I say.

"Well, that's what we want. This is just as much about you wanting to be here as us wanting you here. In fact, we're heading out for drinks tonight to celebrate a win Genny had with Knight Global. You should join us. See a part of the city. Get to know everyone in a slightly more relaxed environment," he says before returning to his office.

"Tris, can you make sure Brielle has transportation back to her hotel? I don't want her spending money on rideshares," he asks, waiting at the door for her response.

"You got it, Boss," she responds with a mock salute, making him laugh as he heads out. Once he's gone, she turns her attention to me, excitement in her expression. "Guess that means I'm getting a sitter tonight."

She picks up her phone and begins typing out a message. I take a moment to pull out my laptop and send a quick email to Liv and Keith, so they know I'm alive.

At least for now.

The thought reminds me that I currently have a guard dog watching over me, and I'm not entirely sure he's going to love the idea of a downtown bar. Part of me loves that it will annoy him, while the more logical side of my brain knows the risk I will be taking, exposing myself to anyone hoping to get their hands on me.

Well, shit.

I should probably at least let him know the plan.

Once I've sent off the two emails, letting them both know I broke my phone and won't have access until I return, I grab my coat from the back of the chair.

"I'll be right back. I'm going to take a quick walk to work off some of this pent-up energy," I say to Tris before walking to the elevator.

I know Ghost will be outside somewhere. Hopefully, my wandering out will pull his attention so I can talk to him. When we left for lunch, I tried to see if I could see where he was hanging out, but there was no sign of him.

I guess that's why they call him Ghost.

As I exit the building, the crisp cold hits me, and I tighten my jacket, wishing I had a scarf to block some of my face from the chill. The sidewalk is almost entirely deserted at this time of day, but a few people bustle from one building or another. Scanning the area, I know he has to be somewhere that would be able to see the entrance to the building.

Come on. Come on.

I wait there for a few minutes, hoping he will show himself, and I go with plan B when he doesn't.

I spot an alleyway between the two buildings across the street, which appears to lead to the road behind them, so I casually walk toward it.

"Abracadabra!" I whisper.

"Beetlejuice, Beetlejuice, Beetlejuice," I whisper, louder this time, while turning to the other side.

"Bibbity-bobbity-boo?"

"Bodyguardo-appearo?" I try again.

"Damnit, Casper, where are you? I don't have a virgin sacrifice or a Ouija board with me today!" I whisper a shout about halfway through, remembering what Dante told me about their hearing.

"Not sure that's how you summon him, but he's not back yet," a deep voice filled with humor says to my back, and I freeze, instantly recognizing it without turning around.

Cain.

What the hell is he doing here?

I take a moment to prepare myself before I face him.

The moment does nothing to stop my heart from jumping into my throat at the sight of him standing before me. He's got on all black. Long sleeves cover his tattoos, and his cargo pants make him look like he's some kind of SWAT team member. His five o'clock shadow is longer, looking more like a full beard than scruff as if he hadn't shaved it in a few

CHAPTER 8

days. The beanie on his head accentuates his storm-gray eyes. The very same eyes are drinking me in like I'm his first drop of water in a drought.

"What are you doing here?" I ask, my words coming out breathy rather than accusatory.

Get it together, Bri.

He doesn't respond immediately, as if he is weighing his words.

"I would say it's because of the contract, but that wouldn't be the whole truth. I needed to see that you are okay. Needed to be close enough to be sure nothing happened to you," he says, not hiding any of the desperation I see on his face.

"How do you know about the contract?" I ask, surprised.

"Ghost informed us once he had you safe. I never would have let you come had I known." There's pain in his statement, regret.

"Let me? You wouldn't have let me?" I say, trying not to get angry but feeling the same emotions bubbling up inside me from finding out all his lies.

Who does he think he is?

"I didn't mean it like that, Firefly," he says, rubbing a hand down his face.

"No, we talked about this. I needed this trip to make this decision on my own. To see what I wanted without any other variables. I would've come even knowing about the contract, and there isn't a thing you could've done to stop me," I say, trying to keep the anger out of my voice.

"I know. I just... You'll never understand the way it felt to lose you, not knowing if you were alive or dead. To know that it was my fault you were in danger. That you still are. I couldn't live with myself if anything happened to you again, Firefly. I don't want to control you;

I just want you safe." By the time he finishes, he's right in front of me. His eyes plead with me to understand, and I can see him forcing himself to keep his hands at his sides. His warm scent fills my nose, and I have to physically fight the urge to lean into his chest.

I miss his chest.

I'm overreacting.

There's literally a kidnapping contract out for me.

Closing my eyes, I let out a sigh, calming myself before I respond.

"Thank you for wanting to keep me safe. I'm sorry I snapped at you, but I have Ghost looking out for me, or at least I did before you got here," I say, opening my eyes to look at him again. "He can keep an eye on me until I return home," I finish, putting more determination into the statement than I feel.

"You trust him," he says, making it a statement and not a question.

"I do," I respond honestly.

"I trust him too, but he's only one wolf. We know of at least two high-level mercenaries who have taken an interest in the contract and several more trying to make a name for themselves. Let us protect you. I promise to stay in the shadows. I won't interfere with your trip unless you're in danger. I just can't leave knowing what could happen if Ghost ends up outnumbered."

"Us?" I ask, wondering if he is referring to his wolf and him.

"I brought a team with me, and we have a few of the local wolves pulling shifts as well," he replies, making me wonder why I've become so important to warrant such a protective detail.

CHAPTER 8

"Fine. You want to stay. Be my guest, but I'm holding you to your promise. Let Ghost know I'm going to a bar with a group of the staff to celebrate." As soon as the words are out, I see his eyes darken, ready to argue, and I lift my hand in a 'stop' gesture before continuing. "It's called The Tam. I'm riding there with Tristan and her husband. She's making sure I have a ride back to the hotel. Now, before you argue, I'm going. If it's a safety concern, take your team to check it out and post yourselves wherever you want. I will not spend my life hiding," I finish, dropping my hand and sidestepping my way around him back toward the office.

It takes everything in me not to turn around as I cross the street back to the main entrance.

Why does he have to look like that?

As much as I fight him, his protective instincts are really hot, and I love that he has always taken care of me. He walked me to my car after our study sessions, made sure I ate, drove me home when I'd been drinking, flew across the state to rescue me, and flew across the country when my safety was threatened.

He shows up for me.

I file that thought away, heading back to Tris's office to ask for that business cell phone they offered. After all, I will need a way to keep in contact with them, and Ghost can't assume the new phone could be traced to me at all.

Chapter 9
Cain

Not touching her as she stood arguing with me was torture. The flush in her cheeks from her anger and the cold had me wanting to cup them in my hands. The way she tipped her chin defiantly had my wolf itching to dominate her and remind her who she belongs to. I had to forcibly remind him that we're in hot water with her, and until we dig ourselves out, he has to chill.

Fuck, I love her fire.

Even with a contract out on her, she's fearless. Unwilling to back down. Stubborn to the core.

Once she returned to the building, I had Carter and Nyxon move ahead to the bar, I will wait for Bri to leave and follow so nothing happens in transit.

CHAPTER 9

Cain: Text Ghost. Let him know she's headed to The Tam with the staff.

Dante: Quinn's texting you his burner number now so that you can be in contact.

As soon as the mind-link comes through, my phone vibrates with the number from Quinn.

> Thanks Q

I text her back before adding it to my contacts and using the ghost emoji for his name.

> Bri is on the move, headed to The Tam - Cain

> Copy. I'll head there now.

Relief fills me as I post back up on the fire escape to watch the entrance while pulling up the directions to the bar so I know how far we need to go. It's only a mile and a half away, but it crosses over the Fort Point Channel, preventing me from shifting to run over because a wolf on a bridge would be a sight people would notice, especially in after-work traffic.

I'll have to jog it, which makes me glad I didn't wear too many layers despite the temperature. It takes a lot for me to get cold, but I'll be sweating by the time I get there. Google says it will take them about ten minutes by car, which means I should be able to tail them pretty easily with a six-minute mile pace.

A text message from Carter comes in as I close the map.

> We're set. Two points of exit. Both are visible from the bar area. We have a spot at the end of the bar near the back door.

> Copy. She's walking out now. Should be there in 10-15min

I snap a photo and tuck my phone into a pocket as Bri exits the building, all bundled up, following a curvy brunette a few inches shorter than her. They're laughing and head over to a silver minivan that's idling in front of the building next door.

I hadn't seen it drive up, and I'm moving before I can stop myself.

"Brielle, this is my husband..." My heart rate drowns out the rest of her statement, and I change directions as soon as I get to the other side of the street.

This is her ride. The other lady knows him.

I slow my breathing, allowing myself to return to a level of calm as they climb in and pull away. I send the picture to Pres and then call her, throwing in a Bluetooth earpiece, before beginning my jog.

"Who am I looking at?" she answers on the first ring.

"A staff member at Boston Digital. Can you run background on her and her husband for me? I have their plate," I say, finding my stride and turning where I saw the van head right as I rattle off the license plate number.

"On it," she says, and I hear her typing as she gets to work. "Why are you breathing so heavily?"

"I'm jogging behind the car in the snow," I answer.

"Well, you sound like you need to train more," she sasses.

"Thanks for the insight. As soon as my Mate is out of life-threatening situations, I will be happy to kick your ass in a training session," I respond, intentionally trying to keep my breathing controlled.

CHAPTER 9

I haven't been running as much, or sleeping as much, or eating as much.

Hell, I've barely been existing, taking in any moment I could spend with her and then planning the next one like a love-sick puppy.

Which is precisely what I am.

Head over heels, stupid in love with my Mate.

"Alright, we have one Tristan Miller..." Pres interrupts my thoughts with the information as I shake my head to try and focus on the details. As I make it to the other side of the bridge, the van is still in my sights. "Both have clean records, no pack ties that I can see, and a couple of really adorable kids," she finishes.

"Thanks. I'm going to need surveillance tapped for The Tam. We're about four minutes away.

More clicking and the faint rhythm of a bass drop from her office music sound before she speaks again.

"No can do. They're old school, old school. No cameras. No internet. They don't even take virtual payments or cards. Cash only. I can do some digging on ownership, but if I were betting, this place is owned by one of us, so we're probably out of luck there, but fortunately, so is everyone else."

I make a mental note to ask Jess if she knows anything about this place when I get there.

She left from the airport to greet her old Alpha and give our regards. He knew we were coming and requested her specifically. She texted just before Bri wandered out looking for Ghost, letting me know we have two additional rooms at Carter's hotel. I told her to stand by and ensure she didn't recognize anyone in the area.

"Is there anything else I should know?" I ask Pres as I spot the dive bar ahead and see Tristan and Brielle exiting the van out front.

"Report went out today about a fire in a Boston building," she says.

"And this is relevant because..." I ask, slowing my stride as I approach.

"It seems the building belonged to Fallon Industries, a shell company for several other businesses. It hasn't existed on paper ever, and I have only heard of it from finding transcripts from the Fallon investigation run by the LLC."

"Someone torched it? Was anyone inside?" I ask, slowing my stride to finish the conversation before entering the busy bar.

"Three sets of remains were found inside. None of them have been identified yet. They are calling it an accident, faulty wiring," she adds.

"Well, keep me posted. We know at least one person with a reason to burn that organization to the ground. It sounds like he's been busy," I say, finishing the call.

Chatter assaults my ears as I enter the Tam. It's bustling with professionals just off work, and I have to intentionally breathe through my mouth to block out the mix of heavy perfumes and colognes that overpower the musty space.

I spot Bri and her friend waiting in the middle of the bar, and I work to slide behind them without attracting Bri's attention. Carefully, I move to the end of the bar and pat Carter on the back in a friendly hello so I fit in with the crowd.

CHAPTER 9

He introduces me to Nyxon, and I notice how similar Nyxon looks to his sister Jess: almond-shaped eyes, inky black long hair and lashes, and golden-touched skin. He wears a skeptical expression that would instantly tell me they are related. While she leans into her petite stature and uses it to her advantage, Nyxon stands at least six inches taller than she is and leans against the bar in a way that tells me he can fight.

His weight is evenly distributed, his hands are free to move, and his back is against the wall to protect himself.

"She got here just before you did," Carter says, nodding and nursing the beer in front of him. Typically, drinking on the job would mean a lecture, but given the environment, not drinking or appearing to would stand out, so I understand his choice.

It takes us a lot more to be impaired than humans anyway with our tolerance levels.

"Anyone else drop in?" I ask, hinting at Ghost but leaving it open in case other players are in the room.

"Not yet," Carter answers before Nyxon speaks.

"Bartender is Henry. He's pack," he says quietly, nodding toward the bald, bearded man on the far end of the bar. "Charlie owns this place. Lone wolf. He has no pack ties but has been granted permission to operate since his family left him the bar. We make sure to have at least one pack member on staff to stay in the know here. I spoke with Henry, and there was some chatter about the contract last night around closing, but there has been nothing since he got on shift today."

I nod, scanning the room and watching the interactions of the patrons. My focus never strays far from Brielle, and her laugh draws my eyes back to her in time to see a man with his back to me slide a drink in front of her.

Mine.

A growl escapes my throat before I can stop it, and both Nyxon and Carter whip their heads in my direction. I grip the bar, physically holding myself in place.

"Cain?" Carter says my name slowly, trying to gauge whether I'm going to lose it, just as the man turns to speak to Tristan.

Immediately, I relax.

It's Ethan.

Usually, it wouldn't matter to me who it was; she's mine, and no one should buy her drinks, but I looked into Ethan after they spoke on the phone for her interview. Brielle is not only not his type, but he's been married to his partner, Archer, for nearly two decades.

It's part of the reason I didn't have more anxiety about her coming out here. I knew the good-looking Marketing Director wouldn't sweep her off her feet.

The tension in my shoulders releases, and I slow my heart rate just as my eyes catch Bri's.

I want to look away; I'm supposed to be out of sight, but I drink in her expression, catching the desire as it flashes before I see her fight it back.

You're still in there, Firefly.

Her cheeks flush, and her eyes drop, giving me an idea.

I pull out my phone and text her at the number she sent me before she left the office. I know she only gave it to me because she didn't have Ghost's number, but she gave it to me nonetheless.

CHAPTER 9

> You going to be okay to drive?

I send hoping she remembers our last text message conversation in a bar.

She glances over to the phone on the bar when it lights up, and she clicks on the screen. The smile that pulls on her lips sends butterflies dancing in my stomach, and I wonder how she will respond.

The vibration in my hand has hope building within me just as a glass breaks in the middle of the bar, pulling everyone's attention toward the sound. My eyes flash to Bri, not allowing the noise to pull my focus from her. As I scan the crowd to see if it was an intentional distraction or an accidental drop, I notice a man in a black hoodie moving through the crowd away from the commotion and right at Brielle's group. I step around Carter to cut off the man's path just as my eyes meet ice-blue ones. It takes only seconds before Ghost casually wraps an arm around the man, catching his weight as he slumps, and then turns him, quietly escorting him out of the bar. I didn't see the other man's face, but based on Ghost's reaction, he was after the contract money and was tired of waiting for an opening.

The crowd in the bar begins talking again, resetting the noise level now that the dropped drink no longer holds their focus. The large bald man behind the bar throws a dirty look at our group. Nyxon shrugs and continues his conversation with Carter.

"I'm going to check on that," I state, not elaborating further before weaving toward the front doors.

Scanning the crowd as I move, nothing out of the ordinary jumps out at me. I note that Bri's group is talking animatedly, their voices beginning to carry above the crowd as I pass, pulling her attention without even trying.

As much as my feet want to stop and turn toward her, I force my steps to continue, winking at her as I pass.

It's not until I'm out in crisp evening air that I remember the text message she sent me. I pull up my phone and open the messages, a smile splitting my face.

> I may need to be rescued… know anyone who could save me?

> I might know someone, but I can't guarantee you can handle him…

I send back, knowing her stubborn nature just might get me a chance to hold her tonight as I step off the curb, looking for a certain white-haired mercenary who seems to have a habit of saving my girl.

Chapter 10
Ghost

I drop the shifter behind the dumpster a block away from the bar. He should be out for a minute, so I search his pockets, not finding a wallet or ID.

So not a complete idiot...

He looks clean-shaven, in his early twenties, with brown hair cut close to his head. Based on his age and incompetence, he's new to this game.

And here I am, babysitting.

I don't do this. I don't get involved.

On any other job, this guy would stay in this alley with a broken neck, but a part of me knows that Brielle would be pissed to find out I killed someone to save her.

It certainly makes keeping her alive harder when I can't take out the people actively trying to put her life in danger.

I pull off my right glove, placing the palm on his forearm and closing my eyes.

His future plays out in flashes—glimpses of what likely will come to pass.

He doesn't even make it another year.

Removing my hand and safely placing it within my glove, I consider the information I just received.

He's a Beta enforcer for Alpha Simmons from the Hartford Pack in Connecticut. I recognize the Alpha in a few of the flashes. A couple of years back, I took a contract with them. It's kind of ironic he's in the business of kidnapping now, when my job was to return his sister and niece from the same fate.

Footsteps entering the alley pull my attention, and I tuck further into the shadows, removing the blade from my boot while hoping to avoid having to take an innocent down if I can help it.

"Ghost." The name is spoken quietly and wouldn't be heard without enhanced hearing. At the familiarity of it, I step out into the light, seeing Cain standing casually.

"Mingan," I say, stashing the blade back into its holster.

"He still breathing?" His words are clipped, and I can tell his control is wavering as his wolf flashes in his eyes.

"He is," I reply, "And if I'm not mistaken, your Mate would probably want him to stay that way. Compassion is one of those annoying human emotions she has too many of."

A grin pulls on the side of his mouth, and he shakes his head, chuckling as he calms down. "Who is he?" he asks, idly rubbing the knuckles on his right hand.

CHAPTER 10

"One of Simmon's Betas out of Hartford. A recruit on his first assignment," I say, filling in the information I could from what I'd seen. "He should be up in a minute if you wanna question him," I add, stepping away from his crumpled form.

"Probably not a good idea. I'm not sure I will be able to keep my wolf from killing him," he says before adding, "I should be getting back; I just wanted to be sure you were good."

I nod, waiting him out.

He knows me—not just my reputation, but me. He knew one stupid mercenary wouldn't be a threat, which means there's another reason he followed me out here.

"I appreciate you looking out for her, here and before. I owe you one," he says with sincerity.

"Sounds like you owe me two," I state, humor in my voice.

"Yeah, I guess I do. Well, let's see how big the first one is, and we'll talk. But seriously, thank you," he says, turning to head back to the bar.

"You're welcome," I respond, hesitating momentarily as I decide if I should say anything else.

I would want to know.

"And Mingan," I call out to him, halting his progress. "Trust the process. It will work out," I say, trying to give him answers without actually telling him what's coming.

To his credit, he doesn't dig. He simply continues his path out of the alley.

Tahoe was a mistake. Catching her from falling was a reflex I hadn't anticipated having after not being close to anyone in years. When

I know I'm going to be around people, I wear gloves. Always. I hadn't unintentionally seen anyone's future but my own in more than a decade.

Until Brielle.

The second I touched her skin and scented her Unawakened status, everything changed.

I saw Brielle's future; it was all I needed to put the missing piece into the puzzle I'd spent my life trying to solve. Take down Saint. Save my Mate.

Staying away from the exchange took all my willpower because I knew she had a good chance of making it out if I stayed away.

That's the thing about the future: it's constantly changing. Nothing I see is guaranteed, but I've lived long enough to know which visions are more predictable than others. Which come down to chance and which are chosen by The Fates. The more detailed the vision, the more likely it will come true, and the less able to be changed.

When I was younger, I tried to fix it. I would tell people what I saw to save them from it, but in the end, it only changed the details of the events. A death in a car accident driving a white SUV simply morphed into a grey sedan when they avoided getting in that vehicle.

Lung cancer at forty from smoking? Nope, now it's liver cancer or pancreatic cancer.

Nothing I did to save people helped, so I stopped telling them; I stopped touching them.

By the time I was eight, I'd built a shell around myself, closing everyone I cared for outside of it so I wouldn't have to feel their loss long before it happened.

CHAPTER 10

Maybe if I hadn't been selfish, Mazie would still be alive. Maybe if...

Groaning from the lump of a man on the ground has me shaking myself out of my thoughts.

"What the ..." he whispers, confused, before catching me staring at him from the other side of the alley. His eyes flash chocolate brown as his wolf senses danger.

"**Don't**," I say, pushing command into my voice to prevent him from shifting. "We wouldn't want this to get ugly. I just have a few questions," I state, crossing my arms as I see the fear flash at his realization that I'm an Alpha, and if I wanted him dead, he would be.

Predictably, he starts mind-link messaging his Alpha, and I stand patiently waiting for the moment he describes me and his Alpha explains the shit he just got into.

In three, two,... There it is.

His eyes bulge, and his jaw drops open, leaving him looking a bit like a gaping fish.

"You here alone?" I ask.

He nods his response.

"Why no backup?" I continue, knowing how new he is and wondering why they would trust him.

"She's just a human girl," he shrugs. "Waste of resources."

They don't know she's Unawakened.

I realize then that the contract never mentioned her status.

Smart of Deacon.

She's far more valuable if they know that, and they are more likely to keep her.

"You can let your Alpha know his pack is no longer a client," I pause, letting that sink in. "If you come for this girl again, you'll see firsthand why I need no introduction," I finish, turning my back on him in a sign of disrespect and stalking out of the alley back to keep an eye on the woman who is making my life difficult.

Chapter 11
Bri

How much have I had to drink? The thought hits me as I make my way to the bathroom, the floor swaying slightly as I weave through the crowd.

Tonight was exactly what I needed. It felt like a fresh start. I didn't feel like I was holding my tongue or trying to walk on eggshells around anything.

They don't know me, so it's easy to ignore all of the enormous decisions sitting in front of me and just be.

It's like a weight lifted.

As I wash my hands, I remind myself that everything I left in Vegas needs to be dealt with.

"Brielle?" A light female voice behind me says, and my eyes flash into the mirror.

A woman with platinum blonde hair and striking blue eyes stands behind me, and it only takes me a second to realize she's Awakened. The telltale glow I've come to notice gives her away.

I force a smile, turning myself around to face her, which only makes me dizzy.

Okay—definitely had too much to drink.

"Do I know you?" I ask, angling myself toward the door in the small space and trying to appear casual.

"Nope, but I know you," she says, moving her hand from behind her back to reveal a knife. "And you're going to walk right out of here with me quietly. Do you understand?"

"Not sure if I can do that, actually," I say, hoping my instincts are right. "See, I'm not here alone."

As I finish the sentence, the door pushes open, and I make my move, ducking behind a startled woman and back into the crowd. An arm wraps around my center, pinning me back into the wall and shielding me from the crowd. A single inhale tells me exactly who is holding me, and the fight in me releases, my arms looping his waist without a thought.

"Breathe, Firefly."

His whispered words hit my ears, and I realize my heart is racing, panic filling me.

"There's a woman in..."

"Shhhhh..." he leans closer to my ear. "I've got you. You're safe with me. Just breathe."

Just breathe?

I am breathing.

Am I breathing?

Shit.

His arms pull me into him, and he steers us to the back door, looking to any passerby like a couple off to finish our night.

The cold air outside hits my skin, and I inhale shakily, taking in the icy oxygen.

Cain releases me, giving me space to calm down, but the chill that hits me as soon as his body leaves mine only adds to my panic, and I step back into him, burying my face in his chest as tears begin to fall.

"I've got you. You're safe. Keep breathing. I've got you. You're safe..."

He repeats the phrases over and over, the soothing tone allowing me to focus on him, his words, his scent, his warmth, and even the rhythm of his heartbeat.

After a few minutes, I pull back, not releasing my arms but tipping my head up to look at him.

"Is it always like this in your world?" I whisper, knowing I can't survive a lifetime of looking over my shoulder, of constantly having to be on guard, ready for an attack.

"Not usually. You've just made an impression, and everyone wants to have you," he says, keeping his words light and gently kissing my forehead. My eyes close involuntarily at the act, and when they open, I see the doubt swirling in his.

"I don't want to spend my life having to be saved," I say, hating the way this new reality makes me feel helpless all the time.

"You've got a funny way of showing it, City girl," a smooth country drawl says from behind Cain, causing his hold on me to tighten.

I peek around Cain's body to see Ghost casually leaning against the bar wall. He's wearing all black, making his white hair and pale blue eyes even more pronounced.

"Yes, Casper, because I'm running around with a sign on my shirt that says 'kidnap me,'" I say, sarcasm dripping from my tone.

"Might as well be." He shrugs, continuing with a grin, "Told you yesterday people were after you, and yet still you are out gallivanting at restaurants and bars. Protecting you is a logistical nightmare. It's no wonder your 'kind of sort of maybe boy toy' over here had to bring a fully trained security team to handle the job."

"I didn't ask for any of this!" I snap, stepping around Cain's hold, causing him to shift his grip and place him behind me, hands still loosely hanging around my waist.

"And I thought you'd be watching my back. Some legend! Dante talked about you like you walk on water, but you ghosted me today! I guess that's the real way you got your name. Poof! You're gone when someone needs you!" By the end of the statement, I'm almost yelling, and Ghost's expression turns dark. For a moment, I feel bad as pain flashes across his face like I've physically smacked him, but the shaking of Cain's chest as he holds back laughter, pulls my attention away.

"Something funny, Mr. Mingan," I ask, raising an eyebrow and looking over my shoulder.

He clears his throat, amusement dancing in those stormy eyes.

"Nope. Sorry," he gets out, clearly holding back as he presses his lips together before looking back at Ghost.

"I've got her from here," Cain says, nodding at Ghost in a way that seems like a thank you.

CHAPTER 11

Ghost's eyes slide to mine, his eyebrow lifting and his head tilting just slightly, and I can almost hear the silent question.

'What'll it be, City?'

Is this what I want?

I nod, not trusting my voice as I make the decision.

The last few weeks have been stressful, and for one night, I want to turn off all the doubt and all the questions and stop running from how he makes me feel.

"I'll have someone grab her things," Cain says.

"No need. I'll drop them off," Ghost says, pulling something from his back pocket while walking up to me. He extends his arm, and I see my phone in his gloved hand. "It's clean, and I've added a few new safety measures so no one can track you," he adds.

"How do I know *you* aren't tracking me?" I ask, stopping his progress.

"You don't, and of course I am, just like your Mate is. Wouldn't want you getting yourself lost in the woods now, would we?" he says, a smile in his voice as he walks away.

He's what?

Cain tenses behind me, and I hear Ghost chuckle.

"Call if you need me, City," he waves behind.

"How? You want me to howl at the moon? I don't even have your number," I add, realizing he has all my stuff and I have no way to contact him.

"As amusing as that would be, I'm sure the contact I added on the phone will work just fine," he finishes before turning out of sight, leaving me feeling like an idiot.

Something about that man always has me irritated.

"Let's get your coat. You must be freezing out here," Cain says, wrapping his arm around me and guiding me back to the bar. My feet plant, stopping our progress.

"She's been taken care of. The bar is safe," he says, misreading my pause.

"Was he telling the truth? Are you tracking me?" I ask, my voice small.

We just started getting back to a good place.

"Yes and no. The pack has been tracking you since the night after the recording you took. I haven't used that access since you were taken, but we still can access it if you have your phone on you. Pres has everyone's phone in the system. It's for our safety and yours, but I swear, I have done exactly what I told you I would. I backed off. I gave you space," he finishes, and I can hear the desperation in his voice.

Stepping forward, I let my movement speak. I'm ready to move forward. Let go of the past. With this. With us.

I maneuver my way through the bar, catching Tristan's eye as I approach, and I see her gaze jump to the man at my back.

"Hey, I'm gonna head out. I will see you in the morning," I say, not introducing him or explaining my absence.

The glint in her eye tells me she's reading this situation, and she approves.

"Of course, sleep in a bit. We don't have our first meeting until ten." She winks at me, and I grab my coat from the back of the stool before heading toward the front door.

CHAPTER 11

When we reach the sidewalk, I pause—not knowing where he's staying or how he got here.

Pulling on my coat, I realize I'm exhausted. The anticipation of the day and the emotions of the night have left me drained, and the buzz I was sporting less than twenty minutes ago is completely gone.

"Which way, Candy Cain?" I say, turning back to look at him.

His eyes flash to mine, and my breath catches at their intensity. He pulls his phone out and types out a text message before responding to me.

"I thought I wasn't sweet enough for that nickname," he says, a sly smile forming on his face as he steps into me, his hands landing on my hips. His closeness forces me to tilt my head back, and I realize exactly how close his lips are to mine.

I lick my bottom lip in anticipation and lock eyes with him.

"I'd say saving me from a psycho with a knife would qualify as sweet," I reply, the words coming out breathy.

The door to the bar opens, and a man walks out, breaking the moment's tension and pulling Cain's attention. He drops a key fob into Cain's hand before heading back inside.

"I will always save you, Firefly. Always," he says, sincerity in his tone.

Every fiber of my being pulls me to him, and I stop fighting it. Lifting up onto my toes, I place my lips on his. The kiss is slow, sweet, and timid at first. My arms loop his neck, and he pulls my body flush to his. His tongue teases, and my lips part, allowing him entry.

His kiss is an apology, a promise, a vow, and I'm transported back to the day at the packhouse in the garden—all of the emotions rising within me.

His hand slides up, cupping my cheek and tipping my chin to give him more access. The sound of my moan is lost as he breaks from my lips and begins trailing kisses down my neck and then up my jaw and onto my cheeks.

It's only then I realize I'm crying. Emotions spilling out of me that I've held in for too many weeks.

He pulls back, holding my face in his hands with nothing but understanding in his eyes.

"Let's get you out of this cold," he says before placing one more kiss on the tip of my nose and turning me down the sidewalk toward the car.

I don't know if I'm ready to make all these life-changing decisions tonight, but I know how I feel, and whether I want to or not, I love Cain.

Chapter 12
Cain

My heart's racing, and it takes every ounce of self-control I have left to stop kissing her. My thumbs wipe away the streams of tears from her cheeks as her eyes, lit with their orange flames, stare at me with a million questions behind them. I wish I could answer every one of them. The uncertainty she feels is only slightly covered by the trust I see hiding within them.

I won't hurt you, Firefly. Never again.

The words don't come, and I hope she can read my mind; see the peace holding her brings me. My wolf hasn't been this calm since the last time I was inside her, and I plan to remind her of that very moment just as soon as we get out of this weather. Her nose is pink, and her breath comes out in small puffs.

"Let's get you out of this cold," I say as I kiss the top of her freckled nose, causing her to scrunch it in the most adorable way.

Her hand laces with mine as we find our way to the rental. Neither of us speaks as we fall into a comfortable stroll. It's as if any words spoken would pop the bubble this moment sits in. The idea that she wants to hold onto this feeling as much as I do brings a smile to my face.

I pull open her door and help her inside before walking around to the driver's side. Once the engine is on, I crank the heat to its maximum setting in an attempt to get her warmed up. As we drive back to my hotel, her eyes scan the city with a hint of awe that puts the slightest doubt in my stomach.

She loves it here.

Instead of focusing on it, I stuff the feeling deep down into the worry about it later category and pull into a parking spot.

"Wait here for just a second. I want to make sure we weren't followed," I say as she grabs her door handle.

"Oh, yeah. Okay," she responds, her jaw clenching as I see her remember the predicament she's in.

"Firefly," I say, placing my hand on her thigh and pulling her eyes to mine. "You're safe with me. Always," I finish, squeezing my hold before jumping out of the car.

Once outside, I lean into my wolf senses: listening, scenting the air, even scanning the lot for anything out of place. Once it's clear, I circle to Bri's side, pulling my phone out to text Carter.

> **Back at the hotel, no sign of trouble. The car's on the east side lot.**

CHAPTER 12

> **Got it. We will be back within the hour.**

Then I text Jess.

> **Report.**

> **Hotel is clear. The owner is pack council, so we're safe here. No competition staying on site. You're in 320 under your usual alias.**

I drop my phone back into my pocket and pull open her door. Her scent hits me immediately, and I close my eyes to hold onto it.

"Is everything okay?" she asks, her voice small as she climbs out, and I reopen my eyes.

"Yeah. I just miss you," I say, extending my hand for her to grab before guiding her to our room.

Jess checked us in under pseudonyms, so I walk up to the front desk, placing a polite smile on my face.

The woman behind the counter visibly brightens when her eyes hit me, and I pull Bri closer to my side on instinct.

"Welcome! Are you checking in?" she asks, focusing all her attention on me, and I feel Bri physically pull back.

"Why yes, my wife and I are," I say, releasing her hand and throwing my arm around her shoulders. I see the shock hit her face for a moment before she masks it and plays along.

"Of course," the woman says, finally glancing at Bri with a forced grin before placing her gaze solidly back on me and continuing. "Name?"

"Elliot Woods," I answer and feel Bri tense under my arm as the woman pulls me up in the computer.

"Of course, Mr. Woods. I just need to see an ID and take a credit card from you to put on file for the room," she continues, still keeping all her focus on me.

My wolf bristles at the disrespect she shows my Mate, and I clench my teeth, forcing the control it takes to hold back a growl.

I set the requested items on the counter while squeezing Bri's shoulder in an effort to relax her.

"Alright, Mr. Woods, you're all checked in. Breakfast is served in the main lobby from 6 am to 9 am daily, and coffee is always served in that room. Pool and spa are open from 10 am to 10 pm, and you will find additional towels in your suite. We have you in 320, up the elevator to the right. If you need anything at all, please don't hesitate to call down," she finishes and slides the electronic cards for our room along with a property map back across the counter.

I grab my identification, credit card, room keys, and paperwork before turning away, leaving the flirtatious attendant there with a nod. We walk silently. Bri's posture is stiff, and I'm sure her mind is full of new questions that pour out the minute the elevator door closes.

"Elliot Woods? Is Cain even your real name?" She steps out of my grasp, and the absence of her heat has me reaching for her again.

"Yes. My name is really Cain. Cain Arthur Mingan," I pull her back into me, tipping her chin so she can't look away. "You know who I am, Firefly. I've always been the real me when I'm with you."

Her eyes fall closed, and she exhales. The tension slips from her shoulders before she looks back at me.

"Arthur, huh?" she smiles, teasing me.

CHAPTER 12

"Caught that, did you... Yes, my dad always was a fan of the Knights of the Round Table. It took him months to convince my mom," I reply with a small laugh as the doors to the elevator open.

"Was a fan? Is he still.." she hesitates, dragging out the word.

"Still is, and he's still driving my mom crazy. They live in an RV and travel with the seasons. Mom complains that the heat in Vegas is just too much, so she spends time visiting family all over. Usually, they make it back for Thanksgiving and Christmas, but with everything going on, I asked them not to this year," I finish, realizing I haven't seen them since late April and wonder if I should have them come back for my birthday in a few weeks.

I'd love for them to meet Bri.

My Mate.

Mom's going to love her.

Opening the door to the suite, I guide Bri into the room. She takes in the space and paces toward the balcony, picking at her fingernails absently. I give her space, allowing her to find her bearings, savoring every minute I get to be in her presence.

"I'm sorry all this has kept you from seeing them. It sounds like you are close," she says, sincerity filling her voice while her eyes avoid mine.

"It's okay, Firefly. Everything will calm down, and they'll stop back in Vegas. I keep in touch with them. Mom even learned how to video call. Now I just need her to stop putting me to her ear." I laugh at the memory of the last phone call. Dad had to physically pull the device from her ear three times because she kept moving it.

I miss them.

The thought is quick but fills me with an underlying need to bring together the people I love.

"Maybe when they come down, you could meet them," I continue with a bit of hope leaking in as I sit on the end of the bed.

She stops her pacing, turning to look at me, and I can see she's examining me. Every part of me wishes I could read her mind in moments like these because her expression reveals only the questions she has bouncing around.

"I'd like that," she replies, a small smile pulling on the side of her mouth before she continues. "Can't say I'd want you to meet mine." She shrugs, rolling her eyes, and I call her on the lie she just slipped up on.

"I thought you told me they passed away?" I counter, my eyebrow raising to challenge her. The minute the words are out, I see her tense, and guilt fills me. My comment was meant to be playful, and the last thing I want is her back on the defensive. "It's okay, Firefly; I got a file on you before we met, remember? I know about your mom," I say, standing and walking over to her. I'm careful to move slowly, knowing my approach could cause her to pull away, but surprisingly, she lets me wrap her in my arms.

"She may still be breathing, but she was dead to me the minute she cost me Sammy." Her words lack emotion, and I know the years since the crash have hardened her heart toward her mother. Every fiber of my being wishes I could take away the pain.

"I'm so sorry, Firefly." My lips fall to her hair. My arms tighten around her as she stands there, fused to my chest like the missing piece to my puzzle.

CHAPTER 12

"It's fine. I mean, it's not, but there's nothing that can fix what happened. The accident changed me. Part of me died with my brother in that car, and I wouldn't be who I am if I hadn't had to overcome losing him and surviving the foster system."

"Why did they put you into the foster system instead of with your father?" I ask. Despite Presley's attempts to piece together her history, it's a question we have no answer for.

"They would have to know who he was. I don't know if they ever got an answer out of Elaine. She always lied to me, saying she never knew his name, only met him once, and couldn't ever find him again to tell him she was pregnant. At least that's what she told me the two times I asked. The only thing I know about him is that I have his eyes, which wasn't really surprising since hers were crystal blue, but she hated that they matched his. Makes me wonder what actually happened with them because you don't hate a one-night stand or carry that for years," she shrugs as she explains.

"Could be he just disappeared. We know he was the one who gave you the shifter gene because Elaine doesn't carry it. We checked her out once we found out who and what you are. She never said anything about where he was from? An accent? A team logo, nothing?" I ask, wondering if we could find him for her and give her a piece of her history back.

"Nope. Nothing. Honestly, until I found out I was Unawakened, I never really thought about him. I was more concerned with surviving and getting away from her. I've fought hard not to become her. I think Sammy would be proud of who I've become," she says, pulling back to look at me. Her eyes threaten tears, but the confidence in her declaration shows me how much she believes the words.

"How could he not be? You're strong, intelligent, driven, and you have compassion and empathy for everyone you meet. You not only survived that tragedy, you're thriving, and he's definitely keeping tabs on you from up with The Fates. Especially if he knows how much trouble you like to attract," I say, dropping a kiss on her nose.

She smiles.

"He always said I was too curious. Always asking why, never letting anything go," she adds, getting a faraway look in her eyes as she reminisces.

"So... you haven't changed that much," I say, taking her hit to my chest with a chuckle.

Our eyes meet, and heat fills the silence between us. I wait, allowing her to decide—to take the next step.

Tipping her chin, her lips reach for mine. The kiss is gentle, almost questioning, and I can feel her holding back. My arms pull her into me as I deepen it, allowing my feelings for her to pour into the kiss.

I need her to know she's it for me. I'm hers, and I'm not going anywhere. My tongue teases her bottom lip, and I bite down gently before she opens for me, giving in to the moment with a small moan.

The sound goes straight to my cock, and causes my heart to speed up. My hand slides up the back of her neck and into her hair, tugging it to tilt her head back, giving me more access. Her nails bite into the fabric at my back, and I realize we have far too much clothing on.

My hands slide down to her ass, and I lift her up, never breaking the kiss. Her legs wrap around me, and I turn to bring her to the bed, laying her down beneath me.

CHAPTER 12

"Is this what you want, Firefly? I will stop right now if it isn't, but if this is what you want, I need you to say it," I ask, breaking contact and panting. I know this is what I want and what my wolf wants, but I need to hear the words from her.

She nods, her eyes mirroring my lust-filled haze.

"Yes, I want this. I need you."

She barely finishes before my mouth is back on her, and I'm reaching for her shirt.

"God, I love you, Firefly. You're fucking perfect," I say, kissing the line down her jaw. She tenses, her eyes flying to mine, and I realize I've said the words out loud.

Shit.

"I mean, fuck. I'm sorry. I didn't mean for it to come out like that. Not that they aren't real. I mean every one of them, but I didn't want the first time to be like this." I drop my forehead to her chest, mad at myself for blurting out my feelings, knowing she's still trying to figure out hers.

"Cain..." she says quietly, and I try to put up my defenses, knowing what comes next.

I fucked this all up...again.

My head lifts, and I see tears pooling in her eyes.

No... No...No.

"Look, I..." I start trying to say anything to get back to who we were a minute ago.

"I love you too," she interrupts me. All the air leaves my lungs, and I'm not sure I heard her right.

"What? Say that again," I demand, shutting up this time and giving her all my attention.

"I love you too, Cain Arthur Mingan." She repeats, smiling as she adds my middle name. I'm stunned. "I have for a while, I've just been fighting myself. But I don't want to anymore. I love you," she finishes.

Her face mirrors the emotions, and I feel like my chest explodes. My lips smash into hers with every bit of emotion I have. It's no longer slow, sweet, or gentle but rather an outpouring of every bit of love I've held back over the last few weeks.

She matches my intensity and reaches for my shirt, her teeth tugging on my bottom lip as she pulls away to remove it.

"Off," she whispers, and I stand up, reluctantly releasing my grip from her to remove the garment. Just as it hits the floor, I'm interrupted.

Dante: We have a problem. LLC moved the timeline. They are there to take Brielle.

Cain: What do you mean "there"? In Vegas?

Dante: No. At your hotel. Downstairs. Carter is waiting with them in the lobby.

Cain: What the fuck? You don't actually expect me to hand her over to them...

"Cain.... You okay?" her voice pulls my attention back to her.

"Dante," I say, pointing to my head.

"Well, that's a new one... Can't say I've ever been cock blocked by mind messages from a best friend before," she says, her voice still sounding amused.

Dante: We don't have a choice.

Cain: You can't ask me to do this.

Dante: I'm not asking.

CHAPTER 12

"And... based on your face, this isn't good news," she adds, causing me to shake my head.

"The LLC wants to bring you in for questioning," I say, running my hand through my hair and trying to get my heart rate back under control.

Not now. Not when I finally have her back.

"Okay.... Dante said I might have to give a statement or something," she says, sitting up and adjusting her clothes.

"They're downstairs right now," I say, wincing as I see her shocked expression.

"Now?!? It's nearly midnight. I have work tomorrow. I can't go now. I don't even have my suitcase!" I almost laugh at the absurdity of the fact that she is heading into a literal wolf's den, and she's worried about her clothes.

"Ghost should have dropped it off at the front desk, and if he hasn't, I'll grab it before I get on our plane."

"I'll come with you," she says, standing up.

My fists clench as I fight my wolf.

"You can't. They'll have you on their plane to ensure no interference. The contract is still live," I say, hating the fact that I can't stay with her.

"You aren't going with me?" she asks, her face falling and fear filling it for the first time.

I walk to her, wrapping her into me.

"If there was any way I could stay with you, I would. I'll be there right behind you, and Dante will be flying in from Vegas on our other jet. You won't be alone for long."

"What about Ghost? Is he with the LLC? Is he going to be with me?" she asks, her voice only shaking a little.

"No, Firefly. He isn't. He won't be able to come with us, not that he would if he could. He hates the LLC."

"So I'm on my own," she says, and I realize she isn't saying these things to me—she's saying them to herself.

"Only for a few hours. Then, the entire pack council will be there to back you up, and Noah is the best lawyer around. He will find a way out of this. You can do this, Firefly. Don't say anything to anyone or let anyone touch you." I kiss her forehead, memorizing the way she feels in my arms, before grabbing her and taking her out of the room.

I swear if The Fates let anything happen to her...

Chapter 13
Bri

In the last three hours, I have felt every emotion imaginable: excited, entertained, happy, scared, angry, anxious, hopeful, loved, and now dread.

Hearing Cain tell me he loves me feels like a weight is lifted off my shoulders. We didn't have all the answers to what the future would be, but we love each other, and that is a solid start.

As we walk to the elevator, I replay his words. Don't talk to anyone. Don't let anyone touch me. Part of me wonders if that is just because he's possessive or if touching me gives them some kind of control, another question I'll have to ask later.

When we step inside, a thought occurs to me.

"Can't they use command on me?" I ask, trying to keep the fear out of my voice.

A growl rolls out from the back of his throat.

"Not if they want to live. Command is supposed to be used by Alphas to control their pack. Not to order people to do things against their will, but it does happen. Avoid looking anyone in the eye for too long. It could be seen as a challenge. I aim to get you in and out of there as quickly as possible. I will be with you anytime I am allowed."

His words reassure me as he squeezes my hand. The small gesture gives me the strength I need. I pull my shoulders back and exhale, letting out my nerves as the elevator door opens, and we step out into the lobby.

Cain steers me to our left to the waiting area, where three men and a woman are sitting in silence. Tension hangs in the air as we approach, pulling all of their attention.

Two of the men are in full suits. Due to the salt and pepper beards and the lines around their eyes, both appear to be in their forties. Their faces show no emotion, and they both rise as we approach, a short nod of acknowledgment to Cain, who tucks me behind him slightly.

The other two stand and walk to either side of us, the woman coming to my side and the man flanking Cain. Standing next to me, the woman looks petite, maybe five feet tall. Her jet-black hair is pulled back in a ponytail that's pin-straight and shines when it catches the light, and her face is kind without being especially friendly.

"Gentlemen," Cain says, his voice cold.

"Miss DelaCourt's presence is requested at headquarters," The older of the two says to Cain, ignoring the fact that I'm standing right here. "She will be taken to processing at central and held until the board decides her pack affiliation," he finishes.

CHAPTER 13

"Am I being arrested?" I ask, wondering how they have the authority to just take me. "Shouldn't I have a lawyer or a phone call or something?"

Irritation fills the man's face before he addresses Cain again.

"Your Alpha has been notified. His hearing will be held tomorrow at noon," he says, ignoring my question entirely and waving for his partner to take me.

"Understood," Cain says next to me before he steps closer to the man, all humor missing from his face. "We will cooperate with this request. However, know that if anyone touches her while in your care, I'll kill them. She's mine. My Mate. My Fated." The severity of his tone leaves no question that he's deadly serious, and, for a moment, all the fight leaves me as my heart flutters at his declaration.

Feminism: who is she? I belong to him.

The man appears surprised for a moment and looks at me for the first time before he schools his features and nods once before turning to leave.

Okay. Show time. I can do this.

Cain's lips lightly touch my forehead, and he squeezes my hand. When his eyes meet mine, I see he's struggling to let me go without him.

"I'll be fine, Candy Cain," I whisper, pulling a small smile.

"I love you, Firefly," he says, his intensity taking my breath away.

"I love you too, Candy Cain" I reply before turning to follow the man, his partner falling into step behind me.

***

Four hours later, I'm finally alone in my room. Well, alone-ish. A guard stands outside my door, so I'm not exactly by myself, but I'm not at liberty to leave either.

Neither of the men I left with spoke to me as we rode to the private airport or on the flight to Colorado. Once we landed, they escorted me to a hotel suite and left me with a guard posted up outside.

Quiet never seemed so loud. I wasn't sure if they weren't allowed to talk to me or if I had done something that led to the treatment, but they were about as far from friendly as you could get. I tried to ask questions, crack jokes, and even made faces at them, but they didn't react.

The next time either spoke was to explain to the guard standing at my door that no one was allowed in, and I wasn't allowed out.

I wish Cain were here, or even Ghost, well maybe more Snowball than Ghost.

Throwing myself onto the large bed, I consider my situation. My suitcase hasn't arrived, and I don't have my phone, the real one or the burner, and it's just after four in the morning. Part of me wonders how to explain my disappearance to Ethan and Tristan.

What will they do when I don't show up tomorrow?

It weighs on my heart to know that I'd blown such a fantastic opportunity. The company checked every box.

Well, all but one.

The one name still sitting on the 'move to Boston' cons list.

Cain.

Despite him telling me he would follow me anywhere, I know how hard it would be for him to leave his pack. They are his family.

Coming from a life without one, I couldn't live with myself if I took him away from them.

Not that it matters now.

No company is going to hire a candidate as flaky as I have been. At this point, I have to hope I can find another place where I can make my future.

If I have a future. As I drift off to sleep, my fears about being taken by Deacon Marlo slide back in, and the nightmares play on repeat. My screams echoing off the walls remind me how alone I really am.

Chapter 14
Dante

At five minutes to twelve, I walk into the courtroom with Noah at my side. We spent the whole flight discussing legal options and ramifications.

Not that we have many.

Our entire argument focuses on the fact that Brielle has spent her life in Las Vegas.

It's weak at best.

They won't likely care if she was raised in Antarctica. She hasn't been Awakened; we have no idea where her lineage comes from. Worse, Deacon has proof she was with his pack and that we took her out of his territory after killing his Second.

We have to hope that proximity is enough.

The courtroom is smaller than one available in the city. These are used for less significant pack disputes and hold only a dozen people when full. We've been assigned a special committee to oversee Marlo's claim,

CHAPTER 14

and we will be at a disadvantage since he works with the LLC members quarterly as our state representative.

A job my father held until his death.

The memory of him pulls at my heart, and I push the emotion away. I don't have time to feel his loss today. My best friend, Cain, needs me focused. My Second needs his Mate.

Straightening my shoulders, I note that Marlo is already seated at one of the two tables with an older man I've known as his lead counsel, Brian Concord. Both men stop talking as we enter, and we find our way to our seats at the table next to theirs.

"I must say I'm surprised you decided to waste your time coming all the way out here. This is merely a formality, Stone," Marlo's voice taunts.

"You seem awfully confident for a lying thief," I state, fighting to keep the anger out of my voice as I undo the button on my suit jacket.

"I think you have me mistaken for your father," he replies, making my blood boil.

Kill him.

My wolf pushes for control, and Marlo's eyes flash as a grin slides into place.

Fuck you, asshole.

Ever since he broke into our pack house on the day of my mother's funeral, I have hated him.

How could anyone try to kill an Alpha the day he lost his Fated?

He's pure evil, and had my dad not let him go to spare me seeing another death, Marlo would be dead, and I would have all of Nevada to rule.

He's lucky it wasn't me. I wouldn't have shown him mercy.

The doors behind the bench open, pulling our attention. Five committee members, two guards, and a court reporter enter, taking their seats above us, effectively cutting off our conversation.

I scan each, identifying four members immediately.

Doug Martin

Jonathan Barton

Oliver Horn

Mark Goodman

The fifth is the largest of the men. He appears to be almost 6'8" and probably 250 lbs with a full barrel chest. He's dressed casually in a deep blue shirt and jeans. His dark brown hair is knotted at the top of his head, and a full beard adorns his face.

My eyes flash to Noah, the mind-link message immediate.

Dante: Who is that?

Noah: No idea, not a sitting Alpha or Council Member.

Keeping my demeanor relaxed, I quickly glance at Marlo, noting that his expression remains disinterested as he twirls a pen.

"Good Afternoon Alphas. Counsels. We appreciate your timely response to our request for this hearing. After reviewing the evidence submitted, we decided this could be handled more quickly in person. To begin, would each committee member state their name and affiliation for the court record, after which we will have each party do the same," he finishes pointing to his left for the men to begin.

"Jonathan Barton, Alpha assigned to LLC Security oversight."

"Mark Goodman, Alpha for the Portland Pack, Oregon State LLC Representative."

CHAPTER 14

"Douglas Martin, Alpha for the Redding Pack, California State LLC Representative, Presiding member"

"Oliver Horn, Alpha assigned to Legal Oversight."

"Mo."

The man doesn't elaborate or provide any more information; he just leans back and casually crosses his arms.

"Let the record show the fifth member is Massimo Bjorn, here for interspecies transparency from the Colorado grizzly sleuth," Martin adds before pointing to Marlo to continue.

"Deacon Marlo, Reno Pack Alpha, Nevada State LLC Representative."

"Brian Concord, Reno Pack Attorney, Bar #15463."

"Noah Daniels, Vegas Pack Attorney, Bar #82917"

"Dante Stone, Vegas Pack Alpha."

After everyone is introduced, Martin opens the folder in front of him and begins the hearing.

"Let's begin. This is Marlo vs Stone, in the argument over ownership of one Unawakened female, Brielle DelaCourt. Both parties have completed written statements. I will start with you, Mr. Concord. Please explain your claim to the committee," he says, turning his attention to him.

"Thank you, Alpha Martin, esteemed committee. My client is requesting the immediate return of the Unawakened female, Brielle DelaCourt, to the Reno Pack territory. Her illegal removal from our territory last month is clearly the Vegas Pack's sick attempt to start a war between our territories after negotiations fell through last spring. We believe that, in addition to the blatant disregard for the LLC's strict border policy, and their deliberate attack on our pack, which resulted in the death of our Second, the Vegas Pack's actions should not only lead to the immediate return of *our* property, but also result in severe punitive repercussions, including not limited to the dissolution of their pack with all respective land, property, and territory rights reverting to the Reno Pack establishing a united single pack in Nevada," Concord states with pure seriousness in his delivery.

My jaw clenches, my teeth threatening to crack with the pressure it takes to keep from countering his statement.

He can have my pack over my dead body.

Noah: Stay calm. You're growling.

Dante: I will never hand over my pack to him. I'll kill him first.

Noah: Let's hope it doesn't come to that.

"You are making large accusations. What proof have you provided?" Horn asks, flipping through the papers in front of him.

"We have submitted photographs showing the female walking into our main business establishment of her own free will, photos of her meeting with our Second in his office requesting asylum, and video footage of her being loaded unconscious onto a private jet owned by VP Securities, a Vegas Pack front."

The atmosphere on the panel shifts as each member examines the evidence. Jonathan scrunches his face before asking his question.

"Who is the man in the photo entering with her?"

My breath catches for the briefest of seconds before Noah speaks up.

"Hudson Healy, Junior Enforcer for the Vegas Pack. He escorted Brielle to her meeting with the Reno Pack Second, Antonio Russo."

CHAPTER 14

Movement on the panel pulls my attention to another member.

"I don't see a statement from Mr. Healy in our files. Is he on site to be questioned?" Alpha Goodman asks Noah, his eyebrow lifting in irritation.

Great, he thinks we aren't prepared.

"Apologies, but Mr. Healy was also killed in the exchange. The Reno Pack's Second shot him," Noah states, letting the information hang in the air.

"So, of the three people at this apparent meeting, you are telling us that two happen to be dead? This doesn't feel like a coincidence," Oliver Horn says, disapproval written on his face.

"Mr. Daniels, the evidence provided appears to be rather damning against your pack. And without key witnesses to the exchange, we are not getting a clear picture of this situation," Martin states, and I take in the committee members.

Due to their alliance history, Horn and Barton will be on Marlo's side. Goodman's a wild card as a new addition to his LLC seat, and Mo has no skin in this game since he isn't even a wolf. Our best hope is that it goes two against two, but even then, Martin votes in the event of a tie between the other members, and unfortunately, I have no idea if he would go against Marlo.

They went through their Alpha retreat together with my dad.

Pain laces through me without any warning, and every part of me wishes he was still here.

He would know what to do.

"We will now hear your argument for claim," Martin continues, pulling me back to the hearing. Noah stands, adjusting his jacket before addressing them.

"Thank you, Alpha, committee members. Brielle DelaCourt has lived in our territory for her entire life. Due to the foster system, she never knew about her lineage or our rules until recently when one of our pack members identified her as both Unawakened and his Fated Mate." At those words, the four Alphas inhale, surprise evident on their faces when the words are left to linger.

Only Mo sits without any reaction, his face masking his opinions on either side. I also notice he hasn't looked at any of the papers in front of him; instead, he listens as each lawyer pleads their case.

"Due to her affiliation to our Second, Brielle was used in a blackmail scheme, the result of which ended with both a member of our pack and a member of the Reno pack being killed in the exchange. Ms. DelaCourt was severely injured and needed immediate medical attention. Her Fated Mate did what any of us would have and brought her to our pack facility to be taken care of, where she eventually healed. At no time did the Vegas Pack violate any territory restrictions as Ms. DelaCourt lives in our territory as does her Fated Mate," Noah says, allowing the committee time to consider our testimony before he continues.

"We have provided Ms. DelaCourt's University transcript, High school diploma, birth certificate, and medical records from the staff who fixed her after the exchange. We're requesting that the Reno Pack's claim be denied and the case be dropped in its entirety. It is clear she has resided within our territory her entire life. One trip up to Reno does nothing to change her residence, nor does it give their pack claim to her. They can say

CHAPTER 14

whatever they want about her reasons for being there. It changes nothing and has no way to be verified. Brielle DelaCourt is an Unawakened under the protection of the Vegas Wolf Pack until such a time as she can be officially Awakened and Mated."

"Why is she still Unawakened? Surely you realize this hearing wouldn't be necessary had this been completed?" Barton questions, unconvinced.

"Due to her upbringing, time was allotted for her to come to terms with the knowledge of her new reality. While allowing her to adjust, the event in question took place, which resulted in her being hospitalized for several days. During that time, the claim was filed by the Reno Pack, stating she belonged to them. In an effort to prevent retaliation, and in a show of good faith, we held off her Awakening until this case is concluded," Noah replies, confidence filling his tone.

Silence falls over the panel momentarily as they consider the arguments. Meanwhile, I'm fighting to keep a casual appearance as I scan each of their movements, hoping to glean some insight into how this will go.

Noah returns to his seat next to me, a slight nod his only communication as we wait them out.

"After hearing from both parties and reviewing the evidence, I will now turn this over to a vote for ownership," Martin begins before Goodman speaks again.

"Apologies for interrupting, but once you discovered Ms. DelaCourt, how come your pack never ascertained her lineage? Generally, It's pretty standard when an Unawakened is found that testing is used to reunite them with their home pack. Why wasn't this completed?"

Before I can even turn, Noah sends a quick mind-link.

Noah: How do you want me to play this?

Dante: Fated Mate bond trumps home pack and limited time.

He rises from his seat again, answering calmly.

"Brielle being discovered at nearly twenty-two years old was quite an anomaly. Most Unawakened are toddlers or young children, so reuniting them with their Awakened parents is necessary. In this case, however, the delayed discovery allowed our Second to not only identify her as an Unawakened but also as his Mate. Because the Fated Mate bond supersedes all others, finding her home pack took a backseat to revealing her new reality."

Goodman nods, returning his attention to the page in front of him as he speaks again.

"Well then, I believe we have another party to this claim. Her home pack deserves to know she exists and have a say in how this case should be determined," he finishes, turning to Alpha Martin expectantly.

"We can certainly perform a lineage test while she is here and see how that comes out," he responds, but his clenched jaw tells me he hoped to get this over with and voted on today.

The council appears satisfied with that response—well, all but Mo, who finally looks confused.

"Twenty-two? Why aren't you just asking the female which pack she wants to belong to or what happened?" he says, and for a moment, I want to smile at the obvious nature of his question.

Because they don't give a shit what any female has to say, especially not an Unawakened human female.

CHAPTER 14

"Mr. Bjorn, Unawakened are not allowed in these proceedings, and as she is unranked without a wolf, her Alpha would normally speak for her. Unfortunately, we have at least two who feel they have that right at the moment," Martin states.

"Not allowed?" he shakes his head before whispering under his breath. "Fucking wolves...." Clearing his throat, he continues. "Okay, well couldn't she be used to sort out what happened at the meeting? An adjudication to see what it was about?"

Irritation flits across Martin's face before he responds.

"Adjudicators are generally reserved for more important matters around here," he snaps before a deep growl rolls out of Mo, causing Martin to lean away physically. He shifts uncomfortably, shuffling his papers before continuing. "But I suppose we could see if one is available while we wait for the lineage bloodwork. We will check into an adjudicator and have her bloodwork pulled immediately. Let's reconvene tomorrow once the results are in. Does noon work for everyone?"

After waiting for a consensus, he closes his folder and quickly escapes the room while the rest of the panel begins to gather their own paperwork.

A full smile lifts on my face that I can no longer cover, and my eyes don't leave Massimo's oversized form until he catches my gaze. I nod thanks for his support, and he surprises me by double tapping the three fingers on his left hand under his eye. I freeze, recognizing the signal immediately.

Fucking Ghost.

At least I know he's an ally. I return the sign before rising from my seat to leave, Noah at my back.

Deacon's face looks far less amused than when we arrived, and I stop before crossing the aisle.

"You did a pretty good job at coming up with complete bullshit there. Impressive really. Sad it won't matter once the adjudicator sees that she never wanted to be a part of your pack in the first place."

I smile, arrogance rolling off me as I bask in this moment. In knowing I beat him at his own stupid game.

To my surprise, he doesn't look defeated. He isn't angry and doesn't even appear stressed. Instead, the side of his mouth tips up in a smirk, and he winks at me without a word before walking out of the courtroom.

Fuck.... What am I missing here?

Chapter 15
Bri

Sunlight dances against my skin as I wake to the sound of a male voice calling my name from the other side of the hotel door. A light knocking follows, pulling me completely from my nightmare-filled sleep. My eyes catch the clock on the nightstand. It's nearly one in the afternoon.

I can't remember the last time I'd slept this late.

Stretching, I roll myself out of bed, feeling thankful I'd put on the replacement clothes they brought me last night after my shower instead of stripping down naked and falling asleep. Reluctantly, I trudge to the door.

Coffee.

I need coffee.

Rising a bit on my toes, I look out the peephole to find my guard and a smaller man standing in the hall. The new arrival is just taller than me, with wire-rimmed glasses and a white lab coat. In his hand is an oversized aluminum suitcase that gives me pause.

Who is this guy?

"Miss DelaCourt, please open the door. We can hear you standing there."

Shit!

I forgot about that.

Sighing, I step back and pull the door open, not even attempting to hide the irritation on my face. Both men stare at me, faces neutral before the guard from yesterday speaks.

"This is Dr. Auguste Foret. He's here to take a sample of your blood," he says firmly, waving the man forward.

I retreat a step at his words, crossing my arms defensively.

"I don't think so," I reply, my voice stronger than I thought it would be, my eyes flying between them.

"Then I guess it's unfortunate that you don't have a choice. LLC orders. You can cooperate, or we can force you to cooperate. Which will it be, girl?" he sneers, appearing to enjoy the idea of forcing me into submission.

My jaw clenches, and I lock eyes with him, refusing to let this man make me feel helpless or small. He holds my gaze, the challenge apparent as we stand off.

I may not be able to take you, but Cain can, and will.

My eyebrow lifts as the silence fills the space between us.

"Enough, Tate. You can go," the doctor says, dismissing him as he walks farther into the room and over to the table.

CHAPTER 15

Tate growls at me, slowly shaking his head before returning to the hallway.

"You can sit over here. This will only take a minute," the doctor says as he unloads various items onto the table and pulls on a pair of medical gloves.

"Can you tell me what exactly I'm giving my blood for?" I ask, complying with his request to sit in hopes he will give me answers.

"I've been tasked with tracing your lineage. This blood will tell us where and who you came from," he says, rubbing alcohol on my arm before inserting the needle without so much as a warning.

I inhale through my teeth and look away. Both the idea that I'm going to find out who my biological father is and the pinch of the needle into my skin makes me dizzy, my stomach doing a little flip.

Breathe.

"And we're done," he says, removing the tube of blood, followed by the needle, and then positions a piece of gauze over the wound. Once it's in place, he bends my arm up at the elbow to hold it, and I instinctively place my fingers on top of it, keeping pressure as he labels the tube and sets it next to his bag.

"How long before we will know the results?" I ask, my eyes focused on the small red tube on the table.

"The committee will have my findings within the hour," he responds, packing everything back up.

"Thank you," I say to his back as he walks out of the room without another word.

***

About an hour later, there is a knock at the door. Immediately, I think it must be the blood test results, and I rush to open the door without even checking the hall.

To my surprise, it's not the doctor or anyone from the Vegas pack, but an exceptionally handsome man in a full black suit who I've never seen before. His hair is almost black and tied back in a man bun. His high cheekbones accent his almond-shaped eyes and perfectly straight nose.

Fuck.

"Can I help you?" I ask, looking over his shoulder, only to find he's alone in the hallway.

Where's Tate?

"I certainly hope so. I'm here for your adjudication, Ms. Dela-Court. May I come in?" he says, his British accent sliding off his tongue, making him even more attractive than before, which is saying something.

He stands there patiently, attempting to look nonthreatening, which only tells me I should be afraid.

Adjudication?

"Don't worry, I'm not here to hurt you. Just to verify your version of events," he says.

"Do you have some sort of identification? A badge or something?" I ask, knowing I have been too careless with my personal safety lately. Letting this man into my room seems like a mistake, especially considering the man who's been guarding my door all day is miraculously gone.

The man in the suit smiles. It's small and appears to be almost amused at the question.

CHAPTER 15

"I'm not sure secret agencies hand out identification; seeing as those things can be lost or taken, you're just going to have to take me at my word," he says, moving his hands out in an almost shrug.

Like hell I am.

"Or you could consider the fact that I could have killed you ten times over by now if that was my intention and allow me into your room before the mutt I told to take a walk returns."

My eyes bulge as his statement bounces around in my head despite his mouth never moving, and his eyes are now glowing a beautiful shade of purple.

What the fuck?

Was he using a mind-link?

"Not exactly. But similar."

You can read my mind?!

I shout the question in my mind, and he chuckles before me.

"Sort of. I'd be happy to explain if you would allow me inside so we can get to it," he says, this time out loud, and I bite my lip as I consider before waving him in.

He isn't wrong. He could have easily killed me.

I'm starting to think this whole being human thing isn't all it's cracked up to be.

I point to the chairs next to the table where I had my blood drawn an hour ago.

"I'd offer you something to drink, but I don't have anything here," I say, falling into the seat opposite the one I pointed at.

The man smirks before moving gracefully to the seat only slowing to unbutton his jacket before sitting and crossing his ankle over his knee.

Delight dances on his face as he silently observes me for a moment before speaking.

"I have to say it's been a long time since one of your kind had no idea about our species," he says, amusement apparent in his still purple irises.

"My kind? Do you mean an Unawakened?" I ask, not understanding.

He laughs again, and I feel a bit self-conscious at how he seems to be making fun of me.

"Look, I don't really appreciate you laughing at me. I've been told it's rare for someone like me to exist, that I should have been found a long time ago, and then I would know all of the rules of this world, but I wasn't, and I don't. If you need me to fill out some paperwork or something, I'm happy to, but if you plan to make me feel stupid for things I couldn't possibly know, you can leave," I say, crossing my arms defiantly.

"My apologies, Ms. DelaCourt. I never intended to make you feel this way; it's just... refreshing to see someone untarnished by the stories of our past. Let me start over. My name is Alexander, and I work with the LLC, utilizing my gifts for adjudication. I'm a vampire and can see things that have happened in people's minds." My jaw drops at the words, and I struggle to keep my heart rate even.

A fucking vampire.

Questions start flying through my mind at the thought, and he lifts his hand, signaling me to stop.

"I'm sure you have many questions, and I'm sure they will all be answered someday, but for today, I need to know about your role in

CHAPTER 15

the altercation between the Vegas and Reno packs. The special counsel is requesting I just pull the information from you, but it's not really my style, and I don't much like being given orders on how to do my job," he says almost conspiratorially.

"What do you need to know?" I ask, trying to keep my brain from thinking of the event, knowing he can hear those thoughts.

"How did you end up in the Second's office?" he asks, leaning back and casually throwing one of his arms over the back of the chair.

"I was kidnapped by one of the Vegas pack members and brought to the Reno pack to be used for blackmail," I say, locking down all other thoughts.

Purple fluffy clouds...

Purple fluffy clouds...

"So Vegas traded you to Reno and then stole you back?" he asks, confusion crossing his face.

"Kind of. Hudson, the guy who took me, was just trying to get his parents back. He thought if he could trade me to Reno, Dante could negotiate for my return."

"And did he?"

"Yeah, he made a deal for both Hudson's parents and me," I respond, my heart aching at the thought of the next question.

"So what went wrong? Because from where I'm sitting, Reno lost their Second, and Vegas lost one of their own. How did a human like you make it out unscathed?"

"I'd hardly say a brain contusion that required immediate surgery is 'unscathed,' but Deacon Marlo tried to bite me, which caused my... well... Mate? I guess. Anyway, Cain flipped out and charged him, causing everyone to fight. In the chaos, Big Tony tried to kill me. Hudson intervened, saving my life at the cost of his own, and the Vegas pack took out Big Tony, trying to save us both. Look, I never wanted to be a part of any of this. I don't belong to any pack. At least not yet," I say, losing a bit of bravado at the end.

"You must be rather important if both sides were willing to kill for you," he says, considering my words.

"I'm not important. I never have been, and if not for Ghost's prophecies about me being the stupid key, everyone probably would have realized that a long time ago," I say, irritation replacing the guilt.

Alexander tenses, his attention snapping into place at the mention of Ghost's name.

Damnit, I bet I wasn't supposed to say that.

"How do you know Ghost?" he asks, intensity filling his voice.

"I don't really," I say backtracking. "Hudson and I ran into him on the way to Reno," I finish, shrugging in an attempt at nonchalance.

He nods, and I hope that means he's moving on.

"So you were not contacting the Reno pack for protection?" he asks.

"Of course not," I say.

"And you are, in fact, not a member of the Vegas pack?" he questions further.

"Not yet," I say before continuing. "But I will be once I am allowed to be with Cain. Once I'm Awakened, I will choose Vegas," I state, confidence filling my tone.

CHAPTER 15

"It must be nice to believe you have a choice in such matters. Most like you do not," he says before standing up, causing me to flinch back instinctively.

"Apologies, I just need to verify your testimony. It won't hurt. I simply place my hands at your temples. I just need to see your time in Reno," he says, stepping toward me.

When his hands touch my temples, I'm transported back to the field on the day of the exchange. Goosebumps erupt over my arms as I feel the chill of the air from that day dance along my skin. My heart rate accelerates as we get closer to Deacon's arrival, and fear fills me in a way that reminds me of my nightmares.

"Calm down, Brielle. It's only a memory. It will play out exactly as it happened," he says in my mind just as I hear Hudson's words whispered into my ear from that day, telling me to calm down. I beg my head to turn to look at him one more time and see the face of the man who saved me, but of course, I don't. I stand there precisely as I had that day, waiting as my world is turned upside down.

The feel of Deacon's breath on my neck and the last moment of seeing Big Tony raise his gun has tears sliding down my cheeks. I don't even realize that Alexander has let go of my temples and moved away from me standing silently as I collect myself.

When I open my eyes to look at him, I see sympathy in his purple gaze, and for a moment, I wonder if vampires have the capacity for such emotions.

"I'm sorry you had to relive that. Thank you for verifying your testimony. I will ensure the report is given to the council," he states before buttoning his jacket and turning to leave.

I stay seated in the chair, exhaustion overtaking me as I feel the weight of Hudson's loss all over again.

When Alexander reaches the door, he stops, his head dropping before he exhales and turns around again.

"If I could ask you one thing, you mentioned finding Ghost. I've spent decades hoping to meet him. Could you tell me where you ran into him?" His words are full of sadness, and his expression looks almost hopeful as he waits for my response.

"I'm sorry, Alexander. I was kidnapped. I wasn't really privy to where we were." I say, clearing my mind again.

Purple fluffy clouds...

Purple fluffy clouds...

His head tilts just a fraction before nodding and turning to open the door.

"Loyalty is a rare quality in today's world. I'm glad it hasn't completely died out. Until next time, Brielle," he sends to my mind and closes the door behind him.

Well, shit.

Chapter 16
Dante

Returning to the courtroom the following morning feels like judgment day. Noah and I spent the evening working through each possibility, trying to understand why Marlo felt like he had won this.

Outside of the obvious that several sitting members were allied with him, we couldn't figure out how any of the information would fall in his favor.

That being said, I know how the LLC works, and if things go the way we think they will, we need a plan for every outcome. So we have one in place if this doesn't go our way today. We kept the details vague so adjudication wouldn't be a problem. Cain and Jess were already sitting on the hotel, ready to act.

Fates, I hope it doesn't come to that.

Could we win this war?

Shaking away the thought, I take my seat from yesterday. Noah and I are the first ones here, and the courtroom has an ominous feel. The silence echoes with the unknown, and I must pull back my wolf several times.

Marlo and his lawyer waltz in at exactly twelve. Neither looks our way or says anything and by the time they are seated, the council members are also filing in.

Judgment time.

My eyes scan each of their faces, hoping to see some sort of reaction, some sign of good or bad news, but each has their mask of professionalism securely in place. Once they are all settled, Martin begins.

"Good afternoon once again, gentlemen. Thank you for being here on time so we can get started. Yesterday, at the request of Mr. Bjorn, an adjudicator was sent to interview Ms. DelaCourt to determine her reason for being in the Reno Pack Second's Office. After a thorough questioning and verification, the report, located in front of you all, was completed. I will read those findings aloud for the record," he says before proceeding to read the official statement.

> I certify that the following statement is void of all opinion and states only facts given and verified by the witness, Brielle DelaCourt, by the adjudicator Alexander Kingsley on the 15th day of December in the year 2023.
>
> Brielle Delacourt was taken to Reno in a blackmail scheme in hopes of being used as leverage against the Vegas Pack. A trade was agreed upon, money exchanged, and

CHAPTER 16

> *a location set. During the exchange, Alpha Marlo attempted to Awaken Ms. DelaCourt, causing the Vegas Pack Second to attack in direct protection of her. During the scuffle, the Reno Pack Second, referred to by the witness as 'Big Tony,' legally Antonio Russo, attempted to shoot Ms. DelaCourt to prevent her from getting away. A Vegas Pack enforcer stepped in front of the bullet and was killed instantly.*
>
> *In the exchange of shots, the witness was taken to the ground, striking her head and knocking her unconscious.*
>
> *When questioned, the witness stated she had no affiliation with the Reno Pack and requested permission to return to her home in Vegas.*
>
> *All the above statements have been verified through the use of personal contact vivid replay by an authorized adjudicator.*
>
> *Alexander*

A blood-red signature at the bottom of the page certifies it as authentic and traceable to the vampire who adjudicated it.

Relief fills my chest as I think about how much this solidifies our case, and I intentionally school my expression so as not to give anything away.

Thank The Fates.

"It would appear, from this testimony, Alpha Marlo, that the Unawakened girl does not believe you have a claim to her. Under normal circumstances, based on the evidence presented, we would end this hearing in favor of the Vegas Pack. However, there was a second request submitted by Alpha Goodman inquiring about the witness's lineage, and the results of that test gave us a new pause."

With his statement completed, he passes out a new paper to each council member, leaving us to wonder how this new pack will affect the outcome.

One by one, eyes snap up, locking on Marlo and his lawyer in disbelief.

Dante: What pack is it?

My eyes slide over to Noah with the mind-link question, only to find he looks equally puzzled and gives me only a shrug. I turn my attention to the table across the aisle, but both members appear equally confused. After a long pause, Martin continues addressing the panel.

"As you all can see, this muddies the water on this case," Martin's attention slides back to Marlo's table as he says the words that knock the wind out of my chest. "Paternity links back to one Deacon Marlo, Reno Pack Alpha, with a 99.8% match."

Marlo pales as his hands hit the table, bracing himself. All sense of composure is erased as he processes the information that none of us can believe.

Deacon Marlo is Brielle's father.
Brielle's Home Pack is the Reno Pack.
Deacon just won.

CHAPTER 16

*Dante: Cain, get her out of there. **NOW!***

I send the mind-link as quickly as possible, infusing command to relay the urgency. All I can hope for now is that he can get her out before we're all trapped. As the silence hangs in the courtroom, I send one more mind-link.

Dante: Pres, prepare for war.

Chapter 17
Cain

My door is open, and I'm out of the car before Dante can even finish his message. Jess doesn't need me to say a word. Moments later, she's at my shoulder, matching my stride with a quiet confidence.

If Dante is calling a Hail Mary, the hearing must have somehow gone in Reno's favor. Knowing Deacon Marlo, he probably blackmailed a panel member or bribed them. His reputation proceeded him, and I'd never heard of an Alpha who had gone against him and won.

Or lived, usually.

Well, no one except Dante's dad, Marcus. He'd pushed back against Marlo and his pack over and over before his death.

Marcus Stone was a good Alpha, but more than that, he was a great man.

CHAPTER 17

As we approach the hotel door, my arm slides around Jess, and she curls her body into mine, looking up at me adoringly.

Showtime.

"Is that so? I would've taken you for the rom-com type," I say, forcing a calm flirtation into my voice.

"Oh no, I love scary movies. Monsters, masked bad guys, spooky abandoned houses. They really make you feel alive," she says, her voice animated, as we approach the check-in desk.

"I can think of a few ways to make you feel alive," I say, ensuring I'm loud enough for the receptionist and guard to overhear.

God, I hate this.

I have to physically push my wolf back, reminding him we need a way into this damn building, or I can't get to Bri. A throat clearing has me slowly taking my attention away from Jess, a sly smile pasted on my face.

"Can I help you two?" The man at check-in asks, his eyes bouncing from Jess to me.

"We'd like a room," I say to him as Jess blushes and tucks herself under my arm as if embarrassed.

"Of course, sir, do you have a reservation?"

"I don't, but any room will do if you know what I mean," I say deliberately, raking my eyes down Jess's petite frame with feigned interest.

Recognition flashes on the man's face, and he quickly gets us checked into an available room one floor away from Bri.

Bingo.

Grabbing the key, I turn Jess toward the elevator, giving the man a wave of thanks, keeping up the lust-filled appearance by dropping my mouth to just below her ear.

As soon as the doors close and we're alone, we separate. Jess throws her earpiece in and tests the connection to Pres. I do the same, making sure we can communicate through this mission.

The doors open on the third floor, and we both get out, moving swiftly down the hall. I slide the key into the slot and push inside when the light turns green.

"Ok, Pres, what do you need to access the camera systems?" I ask, hoping this will work.

"I'm working on brute-forcing the login to their surveillance system; it should only take me a few minutes. Once I'm in, I'll need to loop the camera feeds so the guards are watching old footage. I'll let you know when you're clear," she rattles off, and I use the time to send a mind-link to Dante.

Cain: We're in position at the hotel. We have three minutes to contact you. What's going on there?

Dante: The panel members stepped out to discuss. I should have a verdict shortly.

Cain: If there hasn't been a decision, why are we on plan b?

Dante: The lineage test came back. Deacon Marlo is Brielle's biological father.

Cain: No. Fucking. Way.

I growl, and Jess whips her head in my direction, tensing with uncertainty.

CHAPTER 17

Dante: He already has half the panel in his pocket. This gave them precisely the reason they needed to give her to him without looking shady.

Cain: What are the odds? Fucking Deacon Marlo. Did he know?

Dante: I don't think so. He hasn't spoken since the announcement, but his reaction was pure shock.

Cain: If we do this, there is no going back. I'm sorry to put you in this situation, but her worst fear is being returned to him. I swore I wouldn't let that happen.

Dante: We discussed this. I'm prepared to face the consequences head-on. When you get her clear, send Jess to the jet and disappear. We need to be in the air before they discover she's missing, and I can't know where you are. I'll reach out when we have a plan. Good luck.

He finishes, and I let the news settle.

How can I tell her the man who haunts her nightmares shares her DNA?

"Alright, She is in 416. You have one guard in the hall. Facial recognition IDs him as Tate Kent, Alpha assigned to the LLC on special projects since last May. So you can't kill him; he's too connected. Also, I scanned the building inhabitants just to cover our bases, and a Reno pack enforcer is registered on your floor in 322. This will need to be quiet and fast," she says before turning her communication to Jess.

"Once Cain has the guard down, you need to head to the west stairwell exit and disarm the emergency alarm on the door. I can talk you through the wiring. You both will have less than two minutes to get away from the building before the alarm will reset, causing it to go off."

As long as Bri cooperates and we don't have any surprise guests, we should be fine.

"How long until the jet is wheels up?" Jess asks

"Twenty-five minutes from now, so you two need to get moving. Cameras are set. Good luck. I'm here if you need me," she says, and my eyes meet Jess's.

"You ready?" I ask, my hand reaching for the door.

She nods, and we exit the room, heading for the stairs to the fourth floor. Once there, we open the door to the hallway in full view of Tate.

"Gotta hand it to you, though. It's not every day I get to make a grown man cry. Who knew I'd be consoling you through the movie?" Jess says, falling back into conversation.

"I wouldn't exactly call that crying. It was dusty in there," I counter.

"Say what you want. Those were tears," she adds, turning and shoving my shoulder. I let myself fall off balance and into the wall, using the distraction to see what Tate is doing as Jess giggles and saunters in front of him, leaving me behind a few steps.

His head follows her path, eyes scanning their way to her ass when I make my move.

My arm slides quickly around his neck, closing off his airway before he can make a sound. Jess turns back, pulling a small syringe from her sleeve, and inserts it into his neck before he can send off a mind-link, raising the alarm.

Seconds later, he's limp in my arms, and I carefully set him down against the wall before tapping on the door.

CHAPTER 17

"Tate's down," I whisper to Pres, giving Jess the go-ahead to move for the exit.

Jess is back through the stairwell door when Bri finally opens it, a smile forming immediately.

"Cain... what are you..." she starts before I step closer, interrupting her.

"We have to go. Grab what you need. We're leaving right now," I say, trying to force calm into my voice.

"Wait, why? What's happening? How did you..." It's then she sees Tate's limp form on the floor. Her eyes go wide, a gasp escaping her lips and causing her to gape. My hand reaches up, palm resting on her cheek to pull her focus back.

"I'll explain on the way, but we need to move now," I say, urgency slipping into my tone.

She closes her mouth with a large swallow and nods before stepping into the hall.

"I don't have anything to grab," she says in a shaky voice. I hear her pulse racing as her breath comes out in short huffs that signal she has begun to panic.

"Breathe. I've got you, Firefly," I whisper before dropping my hand and checking Tate's status. Still alive. Still knocked out.

Wrapping my arm around her waist, I close the door and steer her toward our exit. She falls into step with me, and we descend without issue.

As we hit the first floor, I see Jess leaning casually against the wall closest to the exit.

"Just in time. We have less than a minute," she relays before waving at Bri. "I'm Jess. Sorry to meet like this, but we need to move."

She tosses me the keys to the rental.

"It's parked to the left," she states, turning to leave.

"But how will you get..." she cuts me off before I can ask.

"Nyxon's outside. Good luck, Cain."

With that, she pushes the crash bar on the door, leading us into the back lot.

"Thanks, Jess," I say, sincerity in my voice.

My heart swells, knowing the risk my pack is taking for me. For my Mate.

I won't forget it.

We follow her out of the building and make a beeline for the car. I rush to open the passenger door, quickly tucking Bri in before sprinting to the other side. Dante's mind-link comes in just as I pull out of the space.

Dante: The panel ruled in favor of the Reno Pack 3-2. Marlo has been permitted to retrieve Brielle once the paperwork is completed this afternoon. Noah and I are headed for the jet. Did you get her out?

Cain: Leaving the hotel now. Jess is on her way with Nyxon.

Dante: Good. Pres should be sending you a location where you can swap out vehicles. Leave all your tech with the car, and we will get someone to retrieve it. I'll reach out when we have a plan or things settle down.

I can feel the tension in his voice, and guilt fills me.

This is on me. The pack's at risk because of me.

CHAPTER 17

Cain: I'm sorry for getting the pack mixed up; this is my responsibility.

Dante: It absolutely is. But never forget who we are. Pack First. We're family, and we will fight for our own. Keep your girl safe, and the rest will fall into place.

Cain: Thanks, D.

The echo of the hotel alarm blaring has me refocusing on our exit. I press my earpiece as I turn from the lot.

"Pres, where am I headed?" I ask, my eyes scanning the mirrors to ensure we aren't followed.

"Head southwest toward Dakota Ridge. I'll text you the address. When you get there, leave everything. Take the keys from the center console and disappear. They already know she's gone. Alerts will be out within the hour, so you need to go dark and stay dark until we fix this. D probably won't say it, but I will. We're at war now. We have no allies. Don't die. It would be a shame to go to all this trouble for nothing," Pres says, aiming for a bit of humor, but her tone gives her away.

She's worried.

"Got it, Thanks little P. Keep them safe for me while I'm gone," I say, using her old nickname in the hopes it will let her know that I care about her, too.

I turn off the earpiece and turn my attention to the road. Bri sits like a statue beside me, not saying a word, her eyes glued straight ahead.

Shit.

Instantly, I slow down, remembering her aversion to riding in cars.

"Sorry, Firefly. Do you want to drive? I can pull over," I ask, ensuring I keep both hands on the wheel despite wanting to reach out to her.

She will feel better if she can see I'm in complete control.

"It's okay. I'm fine; besides, I can't drive in the snow," she says quietly.

The white on her knuckles, as they grip the door handle, would probably disagree, but I make a concerted effort to keep all of my movements slow and steady so as to not make her anxiety worse.

My wolf paces beneath my skin, wanting to relieve her stress, calm her down, and take away her fear.

She's strong. She can do this.

"Talk to me, Firefly. Distract yourself from the ride. Tell me about the interview," I say, attempting to help.

"You mean the adjudication with the vampire? That was surprisingly fine," she says, and I hear the absurdity of that statement.

"They didn't hurt you, did they?" I ask, my head whipping to look her in the eyes before I see her tense and return my eyes to the road.

"No, he was surprisingly professional. Even after I offered him a drink, which, in hindsight, is laughable because he could have assumed I meant me. Not that I knew what he was then, but still, I imagine most people don't go around offering up their blood to them," she says, causing me to smile.

"You'd be surprised. Apparently, their venom has an aphrodisiac effect. Many become feeders just to feel the lust-filled high it gives them," I say, watching her jaw drop at the information.

CHAPTER 17

"Well, maybe I should have been more insistent with that drink," she quips, causing my wolf to come to the surface, my eyes flashing silver at her while a growl rumbles in my throat.

At that, she laughs, bringing the fire back into her eyes when she sees its effect on me.

"Careful, Firefly. You wouldn't want me starting a war with the vampires to keep them from laying a finger, or fang, on you because the only one who will be satisfying your needs is me," I say, lifting an eyebrow at her in a challenge, and for the first time in days I feel like we are getting back to who we were before Reno.

Now, we just need to stay alive.

Chapter 18
Dante

"Where is she?" Marlo's voice sounds like gravel over the line.

Well, that didn't take long.

"Lost her already, have you? Sounds like you're Father of the Year. How long has it been since she was put into your custody? An hour? Two? I mean, I guess it's a good thing she's already grown up because I can't imagine how she would have survived childhood under your 'careful' eye," I say, allowing my sarcasm to pour out.

"You will return her to me at once, Stone," he snarls.

"I wish I could help, but I don't have her. I left directly after the hearing. Important Alpha matters to handle back home. You understand that, though, right?" I say, enjoying every minute I get to play this game.

"I wonder if you will have such a cavalier attitude when you are kneeling before me to surrender your territory in exchange for your pack members' lives. You have 24 hours to return her, or I will ensure you have

CHAPTER 18

a nice reunion with *your* father, tick-tock..." The line disconnects, and I nearly crack the screen from the pressure of my grasp.

That motherfucker.

Once I release my grip and set the phone on the tray in front of me, I turn to Jess, who is staring at me from the other side of the aisle.

"You good boss?" she asks, forced lightness in her tone.

"Marlo is aware she is missing and believes we have her. Carter," I say, turning to the seat behind me to look at him. "Can you speak with Yelena and ensure we monitor the area closely? I wouldn't put it past him to shoot us out of the sky," I say before returning my gaze to Jess.

"Are you sure you want to return with us to Vegas? You finished your contract months ago, and from the looks of it, we are heading into a battle that has us outmanned and outgunned. I wouldn't hold it against you if you wanted to go back to your home pack," I say, hoping she sees the danger ahead.

Her eyes narrow, and her head tilts before she responds.

"Vegas is my home now. This pack is more my family than Boston ever was. Contract or not, I will fight to protect our Second and his Mate." Her tone is serious, and her words carry a sincerity that brings me pride.

We are family.

How many will die in this war? A war my father had been able to avoid for two decades.

Sorry, Dad.

My heart aches as I think of how he brought us together, taking over from Alpha Barton's lack of leadership and making us a united pack. Making sure everyone was included, trained, and cared for. His leadership made us strong, and despite trying to carry on his legacy, I've failed him.

I can't fail them too.

"I will do everything in my power to keep this from coming to that, but it's nice to know where you stand all the same," I say before retrieving my phone to call Pres.

"Hey, Boss," she answers, and I place the call on speaker.

"Any word?" I ask, not elaborating.

"Not since they switched vehicles and left their tech. Everett assured me that the car they are in now has no GPS tracking, but he was sure not to give me any other details, in case..." she answers, and the sound of her typing in the background comes through the line.

"And the LLC?" I ask, knowing from my phone call with Marlo that he is aware she's gone.

"I don't see any traffic on that yet, but I will let you know if they release anything," she replies.

"I need you monitoring anything you can. Have Keith take the public fronts, police, FBI, and local channels. We don't need a missing person report being the thing that finds them. Those should be safe for him to see,"

"Are you sure? Mason could probably handle that," she tentatively asks, questioning the directive, which gives me pause.

Pres is always a straight shooter; she speaks her mind. Why the hesitation?

"Is there some reason I should be worried about Keith's skills in this capacity or his allegiances?" I counter, opening the door for her to explain.

"Nope, he can do it. I will contact him and have him on it by the end of the hour," she says, her voice steady again.

Odd...

"Ok, let me know if anything, and I mean anything, changes," I say before disconnecting and dialing Quinn.

"Dante Stone's office. This is Quinn," she answers.

"Quinn, you know it's me. Why do you always answer like that?" I ask, grinning for the first time since the trial.

"Because it's my job to be professional, and it's my work phone. So yes, Mr. Stone, how can I help you?" Her snark reminds me so much of Pres, and I roll my eyes.

"I need you to call a full council meeting for tomorrow morning. Notify them they will remain on the property for the foreseeable future. Please make sure their on-site rooms are available. I also need full reports of our active pack members, their skill level rankings, and anything we have on Reno's numbers. I know we pulled this for a risk assessment in the Spring, but we need the most up-to-date information we can get." I pause giving her time to write down those directions before continuing.

"Please draft a message to all pack members notifying them to increase security around their property lines. Anyone who needs a more fortified position may come back to pack housing. They need to be ready for an attack. I will look the message over in the morning. Also, can you get me a list of our compromised pack members? Injured, disabled, pregnant, under 5, etc."

"Are we recalling our members who are serving other packs?" she asks, making me consider her question.

"Not yet, but we need to warn them. I don't want to shorthand our allies, especially since we are the ones who initiated this. Get that rolling, and let me know if anyone from the LLC reaches out," I say, intending to end our call, but her voice interrupts me.

"We received a call a few minutes ago, but you were in the air, so I figured I would notify you when you landed. Alpha Doug Martin requested you call him back. Immediately," she says, pausing for effect.

"Did he leave a reason?" I ask, fear building at what response they will have.

We planned for this.

"No, but when I refused to give him your personal phone number as he requested, he had a few choice words about my abilities. I'll spare you those, but just know he isn't happy with our customer service," she says, and I hear the smile in her voice.

One of the things I like most about Quinn is her no-nonsense attitude. She handles more clients and Alphas than I can count and doesn't break a sweat. It's always impressed me how she holds her own against those more powerful than her.

"Let's try not to pick fights with everyone today, but thank you for standing your ground. Let me know if it ever crosses a line, and I'll take care of it," I say, hoping she knows she doesn't have to take on these men alone.

"It wouldn't be a Wednesday if I haven't been called a bitch a few times," she says, and I can almost see her shrugging.

"It's Saturday," I correct her.

"Same thing. I'll get that started and see you when you land. Goodbye, Mr. Stone," she says, hanging up the phone.

There's so much to do.

CHAPTER 18

We need to be ready for anything because if there's one thing I know about Deacon Marlo, he doesn't bluff.

Chapter 19
Bri

You'd think I would be used to the surprises by now, and yet, every time I think I've found my new normal, I turn around, and my world flips again.

Cain showing up today while I waited for news about the case made me hopeful. I'd thought maybe we'd won, and he was taking me home.

Instead, we are riding in a beat-up Chevy pickup that's probably as old as I am.

At least the heater works.

The spacious cab keeps me from panicking now that I'm back in control of the anxiety, but Cain has been avoiding the big questions since he got me out of there.

CHAPTER 19

"Can you message Ghost? We need a safe house, and if anyone has a place we can hide out, it's him," he asks me, pulling the burner phone Ghost gave me out of his pocket and handing it over.

He'd taken it from me before I left with the men in suits yesterday, and I thought he left it with all of his technology back at the rental car.

"I thought we had to leave everything?" I ask, taking it from him.

"We did, but no one knows we have this one, and I know Ghost would never have a device that could be traced. So while he could probably find us, the people who we don't want on our tails, can't," he says, smiling to reassure me.

I guess that makes sense.

After turning it on, I pull up the contacts and see the ghost emoji, which both makes me grin and gives me pause.

"What's Ghost's real name?" I ask, realizing I'd never thought to ask before.

"I have no idea. I'm not sure anyone knows it. In his line of work, having a past means having weaknesses. I think he keeps his old identity hidden to protect himself and them," he shrugs with his response.

"That sounds lonely," I say, thinking back to the picture in his bag.

I wonder if he ever sees his sister or if that would endanger her.

Shaking away the thought, I send off a text.

> Hey Casper, we need a safe house.

> specifics?

> A safe one. One that no one knows about.

> **Yes, City. I'm aware of what it is. Where? For how long? How many people?**

"He needs to know where and for how long," I relay to Cain.

"Tell him we're in South Denver, and at least a week, maybe more."

> **Near South Denver, just two of us, at least a week.**

I copy and wait for his response.

> **K, give me a few**

"How do you know Ghost? Because based on how everyone talks about him, it seems like he should be the boogeyman, and yet Hudson, you, and Dante all seem like you are old friends," I ask to fill the silence while we wait.

"Honestly, I'm not sure anyone really knows him. We've heard rumors of other jobs he's completed, and we worked with him for several months on a pretty big mission in Detroit, but until he texted Dante about your kidnapping, we thought he died that night," he says with a faraway expression on his face.

"Why would you think that?" I ask, unsure how I would have survived if he hadn't reached out or followed me to Boston.

"The Detroit mission went sideways. After four months of intel, stakeouts, and surveillance, we were ready to take down the whole operation there. Everything was set, but someone gave us away, and a lot of people died because of it. The team working with us consisted of almost forty people in various capacities. Six are still alive, and five of us are only

CHAPTER 19

alive because of Ghost. He caused a distraction, giving himself up and leading everyone away. His sacrifice allowed us to escape. We didn't think he made it. Reports on both sides named him as one of those killed. So when people talk about him being a legend, he's earned that," he finishes, reverence in his voice.

Ghost's a hero.

Something inside me always knew he was one of the good guys, and not just because he was always saving me.

"Wow," I say, unsure how to respond when the phone vibrates in my hand. The message is only an address.

"Ghost gave us an address. It's in Colorado Springs. I'll look up directions," I say, changing the subject as I type in the information.

"We aren't too far from there, based on the signs I'm seeing. I'll stop at the next grocery store to grab some food and drinks to make it the week," Cain says as I send a quick response to Ghost.

> **Thanks, Snowball.**

> **Getting you out of trouble is becoming a full-time job, City**

> **Yeah, and I hear the pay and benefits are shit. You should quit.**

> **Tempting.**

I laugh, pulling Cain's attention, and his eyes flash to the phone.

"Apparently, keeping me out of trouble is a full-time job," I repeat Ghost's words to him with an eye roll.

"Well, he's certainly right about that," he says, and I backhand his arm in mock outrage.

"Hey, now, you two can both shove it. I never asked for a team of bodyguards. I just wanted to graduate, get a job, and live my life in peace," I say, realizing all of those things may be completely out of reach now.

I'm not even sure if I can graduate at this point.

The thought is jarring and pulls my mood back down.

"Firefly..." Cain says slowly, pulling my eyes back up to his as he pulls into a parking space.

"If you want those things, then you will have them. I will do my best to ensure you have the life you choose," he says, unbuckling his seatbelt and reaching for my chin. "You and me, Firefly. We're in this together, and I plan to spend the rest of my life making your list of dreams come true," he says before leaning down and capturing my mouth in a kiss.

I close my eyes, leaning into him and letting his declaration wash over me.

The rest of the world falls away, and for a moment, it's just Cain and I. No LLC. No wolf packs. Just the man who snuck his way past my defenses by showing up and protecting me at every turn.

I love him.

The words used to scare me, but now they comfort me. My future may not be crystal clear anymore, but my heart knows exactly what I want.

Tipping my chin up, I allow him more access. It causes him to respond with a growl before pulling back, my lip between his teeth in a gentle nip.

CHAPTER 19

"As much as I would like to pull you into my lap right here and fuck you until we can't see out these windows, we have to get to the safe house," he says, his eyes glowing silver as he calms his breath.

"Why do they do that?" I ask, holding his face near me as I examine them.

Pools of iridescent mercury.

"Do what, Firefly?" he asks, his brows dropping in confusion.

"Glow. They glow sometimes," I say, mesmerized.

"Oh, when my wolf threatens to take control, they shift," he explains, prompting more questions.

"So is your wolf separate from you, or an extension of you, or how does it work? Can you talk to him, or is he you?" I fire off the questions.

"It's hard to explain. He's me, but also, he's not me? I can hear what he needs or wants; he can feel when I need him to take over. His needs are separate from mine, but we live in the same body, so our goals have to align. When we aren't on the same page, it's hard to maintain control because he wants to take over," he says, trying to explain.

"So why did your wolf push to take over now?"

"You're his Mate. Or rather, your wolf is. He wants to Awaken you and claim her as his. Every time I'm with you, I'm pushing him back. It's a delicate balance of keeping him at bay while allowing you to make your own decisions," he says, kissing my forehead.

When he leans back, his eyes have returned to their smoky gray hue.

"Well then, I guess come on, you two. We have supplies to get," I say, a smile forming on my face as I unbuckle and jump out of the truck.

***

An hour later, we're parked outside a small cabin tucked a mile off the main road. The similarities to Ghost's cabin are startling, and I find myself paralyzed in my seat.

Cain notices my discomfort and reaches for my hand.

"Everything ok, Firefly?"

Of course not! I'm back in a cabin in the woods, albeit I'm much happier with this kidnapping than the last, but I still don't love the parallels.

"Yeah, fine. I just need a minute," I force out, trying to keep my breathing regular despite my anxiety rising.

"Talk to me," he says, dropping his voice and stroking the back of my hand with his thumb.

"Hudson took me to a cabin before meeting Big Tony," I whisper, not daring to look at him. Silence follows, and I try not to read into his pause.

"We can find another place to stay if this is too hard. I know you went through a lot in those two days, and I can't imagine how you kept it together, Firefly," he says, voicing nothing but reassurance in his tone.

I risk looking over at him only to find understanding in his expression. No judgment, no irritation. Just understanding.

It gives me the strength I need to get out of the truck.

"Thank you, Candy Cain, but I can do this," I say, unbuckling and opening my door. He's at my side of the truck before my feet hit the ground.

CHAPTER 19

"Hang on there, Firefly. I need to check the area first," he says, dropping a quick kiss on my head before jogging up to the cabin and doing a circle around the outside. He tests the front door and it opens without issue.

No locks?

I guess not a lot of people come out here.

He disappears inside for a minute before resurfacing and walking back to my side of the truck, shaking his head and rubbing his nose.

"Everything ok?" I ask, trying to read his face.

"Yeah, all clear, no tracks in the snow, and it doesn't appear anyone has been inside recently," he says before grabbing the bags from the truck bed.

"Then why the face? Is it a mess inside or something?" I ask, following behind him to help.

"No, it just smells odd. I can't quite place it," he says, handing me two bags of chips before taking all the other groceries himself.

Walking in the front door, I inhale, hoping to help identify the odor—only, there isn't one. At least not one you wouldn't expect to find in a place like this. It smells like the pine logs that make up the walls. It's a crisp, clean, woodsy scent that fits the space completely.

The whole cabin is open. There is a living room with a comfortable oversized couch, a small four-person dining table, and an outdated kitchen with a fridge that looks as old as me.

"It smells exactly like outside in here. How is that odd?" I ask, setting the chips on the table and taking in the cozy details of the place. Blankets are placed on the couch and in a basket by the fireplace, wood carvings decorate the mantle, and stunning animal art covers the walls.

This is like a storybook.

"Oh, I smell that too, but remember, my nose picks up things that yours doesn't," he says, unpacking the bags he carried in a single trip.

Add one more thing I can't do.

I can't keep myself from being kidnapped, I can't physically beat any of them, I can't even smell the way they can.

It hits me that no matter how long I fight, it will never be enough.

I will spend my life running, hiding, and waiting for the day when Cain, or Ghost, or Dante can't rush in and save the day.

I'm done letting this world scare me into submission.

I'm taking control.

Chapter 20
Cain

"Absolutely not!"

The words fly out of my mouth before I let her even finish her thought.

Yes!

My wolf perks up, hearing exactly the words he needs to try and fight me for control.

You shut up!

Not like this.

"Why not? You said I get to choose. I'm choosing," she says, her hands flying out dramatically.

"You can't just choose. Not like this. You're under duress! 'I want you to Awaken me.' Are you out of your mind, Firefly? This is a life-changing, can't go back kind of decision. You can't just say that while I'm putting away the guacamole like you're commenting on the weather!"

The fire in her eyes tells me she has no plan to let this go, and I have to physically look away from her to keep the parts of me and my wolf from jumping at the opportunity to make her ours.

When I finally look back at her, I see the sparkle that tells me all I need to know about what's coming.

Well, shit.

She stomps herself over to the table and picks up the burner phone as the pieces of her plan put themselves together, and I lunge.

"Oh, no, you don't!" I say, swiping the thing away from her seconds before she places the call.

"Why not? If you won't do it, Casper surely will! He wants me safe, for whatever fucking reason, so having me be Awakened makes his job a hell of a lot easier." The defiance she places in her jaw as she swipes at my hand, trying to get the phone back, has me wanting to punish her for even attempting to have someone else Awaken her.

Feigning right, I let her get just close enough, and I pull her into me, locking her body to mine. Her eyes slide up to mine, surprise and anger simmering beneath them.

"No one. And I mean, No. Fucking. One. is allowed to put their mouth on this," I drop a kiss on her shoulder. "Perfect," A kiss on the edge of her collarbone, sliding her oversized hoodie to the side. "Fucking." A kiss right above the fluttering pulse at her throat. "Skin," I say, nipping lightly at her jaw before slamming my lips onto hers without any hesitation.

CHAPTER 20

The sound of her moan hits my ears as she opens, allowing my tongue to delve deeper and taking me right back to the moment in the cab of the truck. Reaching down, my hands slide across the curve of her ass, and I lift her, placing her on top of the table before me.

My teeth dig into her lip, and I pull on it before leaning away, wanting to fully take her in.

"In case I haven't made it crystal fucking clear, Firefly. You. Are. Mine." I pause for effect before continuing, enjoying the light panting coming from her and seeing the pure arousal on her face. "Maybe you just need to be reminded," I growl out before grabbing the bottom of her hoodie and pulling it along with her shirt over her head in one fell swoop. My lips reclaim hers while I reach around her to unhook her bra.

Her hands tug my shirt out of the way before unbuttoning my jeans and dropping my zipper, distracting me from the bra hooks.

Fuck.

I'm so hard my cock pushes onto her hand before the zipper gets to the bottom, and she wraps her fingers around it, gripping me over the thin fabric of my boxer briefs. It takes everything I have not to explode right then.

"Naked. Now."

The order is quick before I tear my shirt over my head, and my lips start trailing kisses down her neck to her shoulder, sliding the bra strap off as I go. Her soft whimper hits my ears just as the undergarment springs free, revealing her already-taut nipples.

Absolutely perfect.

Before I can even complete the thought, my thumbs slide under the fabric, gripping the top of her leggings and tugging them off with a single pull.

I pause momentarily, admiring the look of her splayed out for me on this table like my very own last supper.

My eyes meet hers, and I can see the lust in her gaze as she pants with need.

"You're beautiful like this, Firefly. Naked, on display, dripping for me," I say, sinking to my knees, my tongue tasting its way up her glistening center. I can't hold back the moan that spills out as I get to taste her again.

It's been too fucking long.

My arms grip around her thighs, holding my head between them as I suck on her clit lightly in a hurried rhythm. I don't have time to ease her into this; the precum is already soaking its way through my boxers.

I adjust my grip on her, dropping my arm to allow me the freedom to tease her with my fingers. Slowly, I slide one inside her, curling it and applying pressure before I slide it back out again, and repeat the process before I add an additional finger. Her gasp has me pulling my mouth off her and leaning back to glance up to see her.

She's a vision.

Her head is thrown back, her back arched, and her chest pulsating with each rapid breath. I drag my tongue along the inside of her thigh before returning to her now swollen clit. Flicking it gently.

"Damn, you taste amazing. I'd say they should bottle it, but I'd kill anyone who tried," I state, dragging my teeth across the creamy skin

CHAPTER 20

and nibbling my way back, never stopping my assault with my fingers. In. Curl. Out. In. Curl. Out.

"God, I'm so close," she says, her voice barely above a whisper.

"What did I say about you calling me that, Firefly?"

My lips drop back to her, sucking in her clit with less care and thrusting my fingers at a more hurried pace before she can even respond.

Three. Two. One.

The sight of her falling over the edge and the sound of her crying out is almost enough to have me lose my control. My wolf sits just beyond the wall I'm holding up, and the feel of her walls clenching my fingers and the taste of her orgasm on my tongue has me almost handing him the ability to claim her. To make her ours.

Not yet.

She asked for it!

Not yet.

My fingers slow, and I release her clit, peppering light kisses up her leg and standing to continue onto her hip.

All mine.

By the time I make it back up her throat, I freeze, pulling back in a silent question. Her eyelids part, barely opening as she searches my own.

"I need you inside me, Cain. Please." She leans forward, moving her arms around my neck as I kiss her, loving the fact that I know she can taste herself on my tongue and that it causes her no hesitation.

"As you wish," I say with a grin, remembering the line from that pirate movie she talked about during one of our study sessions.

Without removing my lips, my hands quickly slide my jeans and boxers the rest of the way off, freeing my cock from its cotton prison.

I pull her forward, scooting her to the edge of the table, and I line myself up at her entrance. Taking my time so I can feel every inch of her, I slowly fill her, inch by inch, and allowing her to adjust to the size difference between my two fingers.

"You take me so well, Firefly. It's like the Fates made this cunt just for me," I pause, seating myself fully within her and leaning to nip at her ear before continuing. "Think they'll be mad if I destroy it right here on the kitchen table? Huh? Let's find out," I finish before wrapping my arms around her and squeezing her ass cheeks to go just a little deeper. Her intake is all the encouragement I need, and I'm sliding out and slamming back into her, her legs twisting themselves around my hips as she clings to me.

That's my girl.

I'm so transfixed by the moment that I forget to hold back, and it only takes me four pumps before I can no longer hold back. My eyes open, flashing to her to see how close she is, and the vein in her neck has me dropping my thumb to her clit, circling with enough pressure to send us both into oblivion. Stars burst in front of my eyes as I fill her. The warmth of our climaxes and the pulsing of her walls around me are the only things I feel as my heart rate returns to normal and the world comes back into focus.

"Okay, I guess I'm yours," she says, her voice playful.

"You guess? You *guess*? Sounds like you need round two," I say before picking her up, throwing her over my shoulder, and carrying her toward the bedroom with the sound of her laughter bouncing off the hall.

Chapter 21
Bri

A shower and two more orgasms later, I'm starving, and knowing I'm a mess in the kitchen, Cain is currently scrambling eggs in nothing but an apron that reads 'Paws off my grill.'

That man can certainly make anything look good, and even the thought has me craving him again. The ache between my legs quickly squashes that thought.

Nope. Too sore.

The smell of peppers and onions floats in the air, and my stomach growls in anticipation. There is a peaceful silence between us that feels comfortable despite the fact that I know we need to talk. Something had to have gone wrong.

Here we are: In a safehouse cabin in the middle of Colorado, hiding from a supernatural legal corporation who wants to send me to Reno with a complete psychopath.

You know, just another Saturday.

"Want this in a tortilla or just on the plate?" he asks, pulling one down from the cupboard.

"Tortilla, please. A burrito sounds amazing. Was there any hot sauce in the fridge?" I ask, not remembering if I had seen any in there earlier when we finished putting everything away.

"Unfortunately, no, but I may have seen some salsa I could add," he says, turning to pull it out and put everything together.

When he slides the plate in front of me, I dive right in, not waiting for it to cool down, and regretting it immediately as the cheese he'd added burns the top of my mouth.

Ouch.

The eggs are perfectly cooked, and the combination of flavors makes me moan and dance a little in my seat.

His chuckle draws my attention, and I raise an eyebrow at him, challenging him to make fun of me to my face before chomping down another bite.

Shit. Still hot.

"Slow down there, Firefly. No one is going to take it from you." His words hold the same humor I see dancing in his eyes.

"Well, with my luck, I'll be rushed off somewhere before I get a chance to eat it," I say with a smile once I've swallowed, causing his face to fall serious. My hand reaches for his on instinct.

"I was kidding, mostly. It has been a lot to take in, but honestly, I think I'm doing okay. I've accepted that my life is never going back to what it was, and that's okay because I will get to move forward and have a new life with you. And let's be honest here: the idea that I have a cool

CHAPTER 21

wolfy alter ego has me excited to let her loose. It will be nice to feel strong for a change." I squeeze his hand before returning to my food.

"Before we get back on to the subject of you being Awakened, which, for the record, I still think is too soon to make a decision about, I promised you no more secrets, and I intend to keep that promise now that we are safely off the grid."

At his tone, I brace myself, wondering what the LLC did to make him jump to removing me from their custody behind their backs.

"Why did you have to take me out of there?" I ask, voicing the question that had rolled around in my brain for most of the drive here.

What were we running from? Is he going to get Dante in trouble? Are we running from Dante?

He levels his eyes on mine, reading me as he chooses his words.

"The LLC hearing yesterday came down to a split panel. Half of them sided with Marlo. The other two didn't know where to fall, so they posed questions that led to your adjudication and DNA tests," he says, helping me understand more of what was playing out around me.

"When they returned today," he says, slowing down and sighing before continuing, anger rising in his voice. "They said that the DNA came back showing that Deacon Marlo is your biological father."

Time stops.

The air leaves my lungs, and I feel as if I've been punched in the stomach.

No.

No. It's not possible.

How?

Cain keeps talking, but I only hear fragments as my mind spins out of control with questions.

"...not sure how he messed with the results..."

"...will get to the bottom of..."

"Dante has his lawyer..."

I close my eyes, trying to regain my focus on his words.

"How sure are they that he is my father?" I ask, my throat causing my words to sound croaked and strained.

"He didn't say."

"Could they have switched them?" I continue, needing something to hold onto to keep the panic away. My grip on Cain's hand turns my knuckles white, and I focus on his thumb, which rubs back and forth on top of it.

"I'm not sure, Firefly," he says, his voice almost sad, causing me to look up at him.

"Can we call Dante and see?" I question, hoping more details will help me understand this news.

"I could mind-link him, but it's probably unsafe to call. Right now, they don't know who has you. So the pack is safe. If they adjudicate Dante, he knows nothing but that I got you out. He has no details on where we are staying, so they can't use him to find us."

At this moment, I realize how good Cain is at his job. His calm tone and thorough answers tell me he's in complete control of what he's doing.

"What do we do if the news is true?" I verbalize the dark thought.

I don't want to be related to that monster.

CHAPTER 21

The man who played a part in my kidnapping, traded me like cattle, and then ensured that I would be killed, all before realizing what I was and trying to force me to be Awakened before I even knew what that meant fully.

He's a man full of darkness, and just the thought that part of who I am comes from him makes me want to get back in the shower and scrub until my skin comes off.

His evil could be a part of who I am.

Cain's eyes search mine as he tries to find the words to answer my questions.

"I can reach out to Dante tomorrow for more details, but I think we need to get to bed for tonight. Are you done eating?" he asks, standing and reaching for my mostly empty plate.

My stomach clenches, thinking about the fact that all these years, I've wondered who my real dad was. I'd pictured him picking me up from school and teaching me how to ride a bike. I'd spent years hoping she would tell him about me.

I was only alone because he didn't know. If my father knew I existed, he would take me away from her.

The childhood lie came easily. I could make him whoever I wanted, and in my imagination, he was a good man who just didn't know about me.

I guess that fantasy is shattered now.

Deacon Marlo isn't a good man. He's the worst kind of man.

Cain's arms encircle me before I even realize he's come back from cleaning up the dishes.

"We will find out the truth, Firefly. I promise you we will," he says, nothing but confidence in his voice.

"What if that is the truth?" I ask, wondering how, in a world of so many people, it could be possible.

"We'll cross that bridge when we come to it. For now, you need sleep. Let's get you to bed," he says, kissing my forehead before lifting me like I weigh nothing and carrying me back to the room.

My mind spins with questions, trying to prepare myself for the possible outcomes, but one question just won't quiet down. Dante had told me Deacon Marlo had been Alpha of the Reno Pack for almost four decades.

What the hell was Deacon Marlo doing in Vegas's territory twenty-three years ago?

Chapter 22
Dante

Whatever I expected the fallout to be, this was worse. In the last twelve hours, I've spoken to every Alpha on the West Coast, trying to explain our situation. Unfortunately, most packs want nothing to do with getting on the wrong side of the LLC.

Doug Martin has left more than a few messages with Quinn requesting I return for questioning.

They've done everything short of sending someone here to take me back despite my story staying consistent.

- I don't know where my Second is.

- I've tried reaching him, but he's blocking the link.

- No, my pack has nothing to do with the kidnapping of the Unawakened female, nor are we assisting in harboring her.

While every one of those is true as spoken, there is definitely a gray area. I made sure any plans Cain made for our Hail Mary went through allies in the area, and I specifically left to go to bed, so I wasn't privy to those discussions and, as such, couldn't be adjudicated against him.

I just need a little help from The Fates on this one.

You brought them together; now, keep this from tearing my pack apart.

The rhythm of my nervous tapping keeps me from losing it and allowing my wolf to lead us through this instead.

I can't remember the last time I'd gone this long without shifting and letting him have control.

Soon.

Since returning home yesterday evening, I have messaged every member of our pack, local and serving with allies, to let them know the truth about our situation.

We're under investigation for disregarding the LLC verdict, violating our cease-fire treaty with Reno, and preparing for a war.

Several members indicated they would be returning within the week. Cain's parents included.

Even with the increase in members, I'm not sure it will be enough to hold our territory.

The coffee cup being placed before me pulls my attention to Quinn, who I hadn't even heard enter my office.

"I'm starting to think you don't sleep because I'm very sure you sent me home at midnight, and the alarm system alerted me that it was turned off around five this morning, something that has never happened.

CHAPTER 22

I didn't even know you knew the code," she says, placing the toasted bagel from her other hand next to the coffee.

Her voice is aiming for cheery but falls short, and I notice the circles under her eyes as she grabs the documents I'd signed earlier off my desk.

The last few months have been hard on us all, and I know I should say something, but I pull on my Alpha bond with her instead.

Fear comes through the strongest, confusion, and an undertone of trust.

She's worried, but she believes in me.

I don't even believe in me right now.

Over the last five years, I've prided myself on running this pack the way my dad did. By finding people I could trust, leaning on their good judgment and my own while building alliances with the surrounding packs based on loyalty.

I'd never broken my word. I'd come to their aid when requested. Shared resources, technology, and pack members, and after twenty-seven phone calls, I now know that while they won't be joining Deacon, none of them will stand by us either if there is a fight.

Fucking cowards.

I stop my tapping and reach for the coffee, which I know will be my favorite dark roast brewed at the strongest setting and left black. I don't bother testing the temperature because I know Quinn has already ensured it is cool enough to drink. When we first started working together, I'd burned myself several times before she'd given up on telling me it was hot and just brought it to me once it was drinkable.

"Can you try contacting my aunt again, please? They have double the resources we do. We need them," I say, returning my attention to the spreadsheet on my center screen.

"Of course, she should be available by now. Her Second mentioned an Awakening ceremony they conducted had gone long," she replies, turning to head back to her office.

Before she reaches the door, I call out to her again.

"It's your birthday," I say, aiming for a lighter tone.

She scrunches her eyebrows, confusion evident on her face.

"Umm, no, actually..." she starts before I interrupt her.

"The alarm code. It's your birthday. I remember you setting it to that a few years ago when I forgot it and last-minute scheduled all-day meetings that I needed you in. The next day, I recall you saying something about 'I guess you don't get to forget it now, do you?'" I say, copying her inflection and smiling at her.

Surprise flashes across her face before her sass returns.

"Well, I guess it worked because you haven't missed it since," she says before walking out.

Hopefully, neither of us miss the next one.

Damn. How can I protect them all?

My phone rings a few minutes later, and I know that Quinn has gotten Aunt Juliet on the phone.

"Stone," I answer.

"Now I thought you knew better than to get mixed up with those litigious assholes," she says, and I soak up the familiarity of her voice.

CHAPTER 22

I haven't seen her since the funeral, and my heart aches when I think about how broken we both were. I don't even remember if we actually spoke after.

I should have been better about staying in touch.

"How bad is it, nephew?" she says without hesitation.

"Worse than the odds were in Detroit," I say, and I catch an audible gasp at my honesty.

"What can we do to help?" she asks, a calm seriousness entering her voice.

"If we've got any shot at holding our territory long enough to appeal the case, we need manpower. Currently, I've got just under two thousand shifters that can fight, with a few dozen more returning within the week. I can hold a perimeter around the city with my forces, but if anyone is injured or killed in the first onslaught, I don't have replacements."

"Two thousand is solid. Reno can't have that many up there?" she says, almost posing it as a question.

"Their pack will only have a portion of our number, but they have alliances in Utah, California, and Arizona that will side with them, and they have the LLC on their side, so it's possible they will also supply pack members for this fight, since they won't listen to reason," I say anger building.

Brielle is Cain's Mate.

They never should have considered anything else.

All I can hope is that they will hear our request quickly before Deacon Marlo tears my pack apart.

"Let me run some numbers and see what we can afford to send you while keeping our territory protected. I'll call you back this afternoon with more information."

"Thanks, Auntie J. I appreciate it more than you know," I say, emotion filling my voice.

"It may be pack first, but I'll never turn my back on my blood or my favorite nephew," she says, her tone lightening.

"I'm your only nephew," I point out.

"I guess that makes you my least favorite nephew, too," she says with a laugh before disconnecting with promises to call as soon as possible.

The weight on my shoulders lightens slightly, knowing she will come through, and I send a quick thank you to my dad for raising Presley and me to put family first.

He always knew what was best.

I wish he were here to help me through this.

At that thought I reach for my top desk drawer, retrieving the key to the hidden compartment built into the file cabinet on my left. Standing, I remove the false back and unlock the hinged door beyond, grabbing the journal from inside before closing it and covering it back up.

I'd found the keys two months after taking over the pack. It had taken weeks longer to find what they opened, but when I had, I'd spent hours pouring over its contents.

An old ledger with a list of names and dollar amounts.

A black book with contacts listed under odd aliases.

A journal with entries written in my dad's handwriting.

CHAPTER 22

My finger traces slowly over the engraved cover before opening the leather jacket. I flip absently through the pages before reaching the last entry.

It's dated six weeks before the accident.

> *"9/2018 - Completed 827. Asset recovered—one injury. No fatalities. Need to resupply Hendrix. Sparks meet in October."*

The words still mean absolutely nothing to me. No one in our pack or alliances goes by that name. None of his council members knew anything about it. I've looked through every record I can find for the date listed, and it always comes up empty. Even I can't seem to recall where I was that day to try to remember what he was doing.

Why didn't you tell me about any of this, Dad? What does it all mean?

Looking at the journal leaves me with more questions than answers, which are the things I came here to find.

How do I win this war, Dad? How do I keep everyone safe?

I slam the book closed, frustration bubbling within me, threatening my control, before I let out a breath and focus on what I can control.

Dante: Council meeting, noon. I need everyone there.

Pack First.

That's what he taught me, so that's where we start.

Chapter 23

Bri

Waking up this morning, I feel the weight of Cain's arm wrapped around me. His firm chest pressed flush against my back allows me to feel the steady rhythm of his heartbeat.

Home.

The thought may have terrified me weeks ago, but now, there is a comfort in knowing I belong somewhere, that I belong with him.

Every fiber of my being knows it to be true, and as I lay listening to the steady pounding, I find myself entirely at ease.

His scent is present in every breath I take, and I can't recall ever sleeping more soundly. No nightmares. No memories. Just rest. Part of me wonders if most people sleep like this all the time.

I'd never had that luxury.

Between Elaine coming home at all hours of the night with random men, foster homes where I couldn't trust the other kids or the adults, and then as an adult who has been kidnapped and nearly trafficked, relaxing is not in my wheelhouse.

Maybe it can be.

Maybe in a world where I'm Awakened, where Cain is by my side, and where I have a wolf to help protect myself from the scum in this world.

Cain's arms squeeze tightly around me, and I feel his lips on the back of my shoulder.

"Morning, Firefly," he says, his voice gravel-filled.

"Pretty sure it's more like afternoon," I say, squinting at the curtains, which only allow a few rays to break through the gap at the center, but by the shadows, the sun is pretty high up.

"Then I guess you don't want breakfast," he says, but his playful tone reveals his intention.

"I didn't say that. Coffee would be amazing. Eggs and bacon would be great, too," I say, rolling myself to face him. "That is if you're offering," I finish and press my lips to his, holding the moment a bit longer than usual.

I could get used to this.

"Keep this up, and I might just have you for breakfast," he says, nipping at my ear before untangling himself from me.

"If there were already coffee, that would certainly sound appealing," I say, snuggling into the spot he vacated and basking in his scent.

The sound of his chuckling echoes off the hallway as he walks out to the main living area and into the kitchen. Pans clanging on the stove and water running lull me back to a snooze-filled sleep until the sizzling of bacon hits my ears along with its mouthwatering aroma.

Rolling over, I walk myself into the bathroom, taking a few minutes to use the restroom and freshen up with the tooth and hair brush we bought yesterday. When I feel a bit more human, I saunter out to join him, pausing only to grab his t-shirt from the day before.

Walking over to the small table outside the open kitchen reminds me of the last time we had breakfast together in my apartment. It's like that moment is frozen in my memory as the 'us' before. Before Hudson took me. Before Deacon tried to Awaken me. Before I found out the truth, everyone had been hiding from me.

While I know we will never be those people again, part of me wants the normalcy we had in those moments as I made pancakes from a box and talked about plans for the day.

Could we have that again?

"Scrambled, alright?" he says over his shoulder as the steam wafts up in front of him.

"Perfect," I say, scanning the counter for the coffee maker I'd seen yesterday and seeing it already sitting with a full pot.

Nectar of the Gods.

I make a bee-line for it, pulling down two mugs from the cupboard above and filling them both. I grab milk and a few heaping spoonfuls of sugar to add to mine, and I leave Cain's black, just the disgusting way he likes it.

Walking back to the table with both mugs in my hands, I see him placing the eggs onto plates with bacon and buttered toast, and my heart melts at how very domestic it all feels.

"Hear anything from Dante today?" I ask as he sets a plate in front of me.

CHAPTER 23

"No, he hasn't reached out. He won't unless he has to. It's not safe if they know where we are, so I've been keeping my shields up, so I would only feel his request; not his message. But none have come through. I'm hoping no news is good news," he says before taking a bite.

"Are the LLC going to punish them for me leaving?" I ask, not sure how Cain taking me away yesterday left things. He had mentioned that the LLC had officially ruled 3-2 that I should be returned to the Reno Pack, and my DNA puts them as my "home pack" despite me never knowing anything about them.

"That's what they are working through right now. The LLC doesn't take kindly to insubordination, and me taking you instead of allowing you to be handed over will certainly ruffle some feathers. We just have to hope Dante can negotiate a trade with Marlo," he says, his jaw clenching as his wheels turn.

"And if he can't?" I say, scooping a bite of eggs into my mouth.

"Then we will be at war with Reno. They'll attack, and they'll have the LLC's backing," Cain says, leveling his eyes on me with concern. "Dante will do whatever he can to avoid that."

"How?"

"Well, the last night there, we discussed some options with our attorney, Noah Daniels. He plans to appeal the decision on the grounds of bias," he says, shoveling his last bite of eggs into his mouth before continuing. "We hope that will give us a better chance at a fairer group to plead our case to. We need people who understand that your situation is unique, and because of that, allowing you to be with your Mate rather than your home pack is the correct choice."

"Will it be hard to convince them?"

"It shouldn't be. Shifters believe heavily in The Fates and their will to choose the paths we walk. The best way I can explain it is as if it were a religion. They are like God, and our Fated Mates are the soul mates that are chosen for us. Most of us never find our Mates. So when we do, that bond stands over all others. The problem is because you aren't Awakened, and aren't Mated to me, we don't have the marks. It would be impossible for them to separate us if they could see we were Mated. None of our kind would make the decision to split up Fated Mates. We just have to hope whoever presides over the appeal can see reason." He shrugs, idly chewing on the last few bites of his bacon strip.

He's silent for a while after that, and I take the time to finish my breakfast, pondering how I can make this right for everyone. When he grabs my empty plate, I lock eyes with him, hoping he will listen to my plan.

"You need to Awaken me." I pause for emphasis, watching his eyes widen in surprise, and the fight crawls back into him. I lift my hand, silencing him so I can continue.

"It's the only way they will see reason. You said it yourself: if they could see the marks, they wouldn't have a choice but to allow us to be together. So we force their hand." I finish confidence infusing my tone.

It's the only way he will stop hunting me.

It's the only way to keep Dante's pack safe.

Cain's pack.

And someday, my pack.

"It isn't that simple, Firefly," he says, sitting down and leaving the plates in front of him. His shoulders hunch with the heavy weight he's been carrying, and I need him to explain it to me.

CHAPTER 23

"Why not?" I ask, confidence wavering as I see the pain in his eyes.

"Because you can't take it back. Once you are Awakened there is no way to take it back. It's forever," he says, adding emphasis to the word.

"I understand that. I've made my choice. I'd rather embrace this life than spend the rest of it running, scared and weak," I counter, shouting back at him now and standing myself up.

"You've never been weak! But it isn't just about embracing your wolf. Awakening you won't give you the mark. That comes from being Mated, and I will not force you into that," he finishes, anger resonating through his voice.

"You aren't forcing me. I'm asking you to!" I exclaim, frustration boiling under my skin as I slam my hands onto the table before me.

"You don't understand what you are asking for; you couldn't possibly," he says, fists clenching while he tries to hold his temper.

"Then explain it to me. Tell me everything. Let me decide!"

He pushes back from the table in a swift movement, causing me to lean away instinctively, stepping backward until I hit the wall with my heel.

My heart races as he pins me there, arms caging me on either side. His eyes are wild and glowing again, but I find that rather than being afraid, I feel safe. I know at the core of my being that he would never hurt me, so I stand my ground, not looking away as he seethes in front of me.

"Mates are permanent. They cannot be undone; they cannot be traded or altered. What you are asking for is more than marriage. It's a bond that ties our lives together. Our futures would be eternally intertwined."

He slowly sets his forehead on mine, his eyes closing in defeat as I process what he has said.

It cannot be undone.

Permanent.

"Oh," I force out finally, reality hitting me as the sting of rejection starts to slide over my skin.

He doesn't want me forever.

I'm a fool.

The pain that floods me takes me right back to the hospital room. The moment I realized that everything was a lie. A lie I let myself fall for again.

I'm not his forever.

I close my eyes as tears begin to slide down my cheeks. Hoping to hide them, I turn my head down and away from him—anything to keep him from seeing me break.

His hand moves from the wall, gripping my chin roughly as he turns my face to him.

"Look at me, Firefly," he says to my closed eyes. A whimper escapes my throat at the sound of the name, and I wish I could disappear, evaporate into thin air, so I don't have to feel this moment.

His voice shouldn't be able to affect me this much. He just told me he didn't want to be tied to me forever, and I'm a puddle on the floor with a single touch.

I'm pathetic.

Thumbs swipe away the streams of silent tears as I try to find the strength to look at him again.

"We will find a way through this. I promise you that I will do everything in my power to protect you," he says, nothing but sincerity in his tone.

"Why?" I ask, finding my voice.

"Why what, Firefly?"

"Why risk your pack, your family, for me when you don't want to be with me? Why?" I ask, finally opening my eyes to find his no longer glowing and confusion flashing across his face.

"Don't want to be with you? What are you talking about? I only want to be with you. *You* are my whole world, Firefly. I would give up my life if it meant allowing you to have the life that you wanted." His eyes search mine, sadness replacing the confusion. "Is that what you think? That I don't want to be your Mate? That I don't want to be tied to you forever?"

"You're the one who is saying no," I state, trying to keep the quiver out of my voice.

"For you. Firefly. I'm saying no for you. We're just getting back to the good place we were in before Hudson," he pauses, grimacing at the mention of his fallen pack mate. "You just started to let me back in. I don't want you to feel pressured into deciding this out of fear or obligation. I want you to choose this life. I want you to choose us. I want you to choose me. I need you to choose me." Tears form in his storm-gray eyes, and I see his restraint for the first time.

Why do I always jump to the worst possible conclusion?

He has always shown me this side of him. He's never wavered, never faltered, but the moment he said something I perceived incorrectly, I assumed the most destructive intent.

"This is me choosing you," I say, placing my hand on his cheek and mirroring his motions of wiping away the streams that are falling.

His eyes search mine. What they are looking for, I don't know, but I stand still, holding his gaze, knowing with every part of myself that my words are true.

I choose him.

I choose us.

Forever.

Chapter 24
Bri

I'm not exactly sure what I was expecting when I told him to Awaken me, but a living room floor covered in couch cushions and pillows wasn't it.

"Is all this really necessary?" I ask, watching him move the cushions and pillows just so, before flipping them.

"I don't know how long you will be out, and I want you to be comfortable until you wake up," he says, not looking at me but continuing to mumble a list off under his breath.

It had taken another hour of discussing everything before he finally agreed I was ready. We'd talked about my career, or at least the idea of it, kids, pack life, and his role and obligations should we stay in Vegas.

I'd asked every question I hadn't gotten to or had thought of since my chat with Dante, and he answered every one with care.

I'm ready.

And now he was fluffing pillows on the floor and pacing around shifting things.

"I think this will be just fine. You said you will be behind me to catch me when I pass out. You can lay me down carefully and go about your day," I say, pushing more confidence into my voice than I felt.

"I will absolutely not be going about my day! I will sit right here until you wake up so I can get you to shift as soon as possible. We will do this exactly how it is supposed to be done, only I'm not the Alpha of the pack, and you aren't ten," he finished, his complexion waning as worry lines his features.

Stepping close to him, I place my hand on his chest just over his heart, pulling his eyes to me.

"I'm going to be fine, Candy Cain. You said it yourself: your friend Jake's Awakening happened at eighteen, well after puberty, and he had no issues. You're going to say the words, bite me with your magic 'make a wolf' venom, and I'm going to take a nap for a few hours. Easy peasy. When I wake up, we can both meet my wolf," I say, smiling at the idea.

This definitely wasn't on my Bingo card for this year.

Silver flashes in his eyes, and I know at least one of them is excited by the prospect. I giggle at him as I see him fighting for control.

"Do you think my eyes will glow silver, too?" I ask, stepping back and pulling off his shirt so I'm standing in front of him completely bare.

"Not a chance, Firefly. I'd bet orange or copper based on their color," he says, his voice full of gravel as he takes his time enjoying the view.

"That how you looked at Jake too?" I quip, raising an eyebrow at him, causing a growl to roll out.

"Usually, initiates wear a robe," he says, wrapping his arms around me and kissing his way down my throat. "But I'm definitely seeing the potential of taking that particular piece away for today," he finishes, dragging his teeth across my collarbone.

God, this man is intoxicating.

My body melts into him, allowing him to linger another moment before physically stepping back. Reaching around him, I grab the oversized robe from the back of the couch and pull it on.

"No distracting me with sex," I say, mocking frustration because damn if I don't want him again.

Plenty of time for that after I alter every cell in my body.

The thought is sobering, and I take a minute to let myself remember how I feel in this body. I stretch my fingers in and out, roll my head to loosen my neck, and even jump in place.

This is me.

What will it feel like?

"I'm going to write down the words so I don't mess them up," Cain says, leaving the living area and heading back into the room quickly before returning with a pen and paper. "I've seen hundreds of Awakenings, but I've always been the witness, Dante or his dad... Shit! We need a witness," he says, returning his attention to me.

"Well, unless a ground squirrel is going to count, I don't think anyone else is out here, and we can't exactly pull someone off the street in town. Could we just pretend we have one?" I ask, nerves bundling low in my stomach at the thought of having to wait even longer.

I'd made my decision.

I'm ready.

"No. I will not cut corners with this. I will not do anything that could be seen as outside the tradition because it could be used against us later." Determination is set in his jaw, and my heart drops.

Not today. It's not going to be today.

"How long would it take to get someone here to be a witness," I ask, curling myself into the large recliner. He stops writing and looks up at me instead.

"We can't let anyone know where we are, Firefly. If anyone knows, the LLC will come to take you before we can even complete the transition." His shoulders fall, and he sets down the pen he is holding.

"I forgot about that," I say, my voice low and sad. Maybe Ghost knows someone in the area he can trust?" I say, sparking another idea. "Wait... Ghost! Can he be the witness? He already knows where we are!" I say excitedly as the plan forms in my mind. He can meet us here. Cain can perform the Awakening, and everything will work out."

I wonder how far away he is or if he is on another secret 'I'm not going to tell anyone' mission.

Standing, I walk over to the phone plugged into the outlet by the table and text him.

> Where are you, Casper?

As I wait for his response, I try to settle my heart rate, which is now racing as I anticipate his response. Hoping he is close and can make it today or tomorrow at the latest. We need to finish this so that we can get the Vegas pack out of the trouble we've put them in.

CHAPTER 24

The phone vibrates in my hand, his message popping up.

> **In trouble again already, City?**

> **Listen 'next to be' Nearly-Headless Nick, just answer the question!**

> **Well, since you asked so nicely…**

> **Pretty, please?**

> **I'm tanning on a beach in the Maldives**

> **Ghost…. I'm serious. I need you here. Where are you?**

> **Last time I checked, I didn't work for you, and I just did you a favor less than 24 hours ago. Your IOU list is getting a little long.**

> **I need a witness.**

> **Getting married already? I guess your 'kind of sort of maybe boyfriend' finally got his shit together. Mazeltov. Find someone else.**

> **I'm not getting married! Do you take anything seriously?**

> **Not if I can help it**

> **I need a witness to my Awakening. You're the only one who knows where we are.**

And finally, she finds the words.

> **Can you help me or not?**

> **When?**

> **Today.**

> **Wish I could, but like I said, I'm on the beach**

I nearly throw the phone at the wall in my frustration.

> **Wouldn't me being Awakened make me staying alive easier on you?**

> **Not sure if easier is the right word.**

Before I can clap back, the phone rings in my hand.

"You must have a pretty good reception on that beach to make calls!" I say as an answer, anger causing my cheeks to heat.

"Modern technology is funny that way. Put me on speaker," he says, his whiskey voice more serious. I do as he asks, turning to see Cain still sitting on the couch with the list in front of him.

"Okay, you are on," I say, irritation leaking into my tone.

"Cain, this phone has an encryption block on it. You'll need to remove it and download Signal. Once it's verified, video call me. You have an hour before I have somewhere I need to be. We can do the first half, and I will call back once I'm clear to complete it. Sound good?" he says in a polite and professional voice.

Sure, be nice to him but be an asshole to me.

"Block have a passcode?" Cain asks.

"Yep, 063019," he says before disconnecting.

CHAPTER 24

Cain is frozen in his spot, eyes locked on the phone in my hand.

"Do you know how to do that?" I ask him, walking over to the couch, my hand outstretched.

Please let this work.

He shakes his head, eyes coming back into focus before he takes the offering.

"Yeah, I can do it. Normally, Pres handles most of this stuff, but I had to learn while she was away. Mason, the guy who used to have her job, has a family, so we couldn't call him up at all hours of the night," he explains, screens changing under his fingertips.

"How long will it take?" I ask, picking at my nails to keep myself from pacing around the room.

"A few minutes. It will need to complete an update and a hard restart, but we should be good soon," he says, his focus never leaving the device. "Do me a favor and grab two water bottles from the fridge. We might need them."

Nodding, I walk into the kitchen, happy to have something to do to fill the time.

It's going to happen.

I'm ready for this.

God, I hope I'm ready for this.

When I return, the screen has a loading ring with 87% showing. I hand the water bottles to him, and he opens one before returning it to me.

"Drink. Shifting the first few times will take all of your strength," he says, concern evident in his tone.

We are doing this.

I'm becoming a wolf shifter.

I'm ready for this.

What the actual fuck! I am not ready for this. Who could ever be ready for this?!?!

The room sways, causing my knees to buckle, and I nearly sink to the floor, but before I do, Cain's strong arms loop my waist, supporting me.

"Breathe, Firefly," he whispers into my hair, and I focus on his voice.

Fucking panic attacks are for the birds.

I focus on his even breathing and calm mine to match. I focus on the warmth of his embrace, allowing it to take away the chill of fear coursing through me.

"Will Awakening me get rid of these?" I ask, finding my voice.

"No. It won't change who you are like that. This is a part of you," his words don't comfort me.

"I want to be strong enough to not have them. I wanted this to fix me," I whisper, fully back in control.

"You aren't broken, Firefly. You feel emotions deeply because of everything you've had to overcome. It's not a weakness to be able to feel. It's a strength, one most people will never be able to understand. Your heart is the most beautiful thing about you."

His words hang in the air, and I find myself speechless.

He sees me.

"I'm ready," I say, vocalizing the words I'd spent the last hour trying to convince myself were true.

I'm ready.

Chapter 25
Cain

*F**ucking focus!*

You've seen this done a million times.

I chastise myself, hoping the argument will take away the overwhelming mix of emotions I feel.

I've never done this.

Not fucking once.

And I'm terrified I'm going to fuck it up. Part of me wishes I could reach out to Dante and ask him how I'll know when I've given enough of the venom. Is there a chance it will be too much? Could it kill her?

I wouldn't survive if I lost her.

I couldn't if I was the reason.

Not everyone completed the ceremony, though it was exceptionally rare. Sometimes, the DNA wouldn't take the change from the venom, and instead, it killed off the cells in the body. It hadn't happened in our pack in my lifetime, but I'd heard of packs losing their kids.

I can't even imagine.

Fates, watch over us.

The prayer is one of many I've sent up over the last few weeks. Leaning into my faith in them is the only thing that keeps me from losing it most days.

They brought her to me.

They wouldn't take her away... would they?

They couldn't. It would be too cruel.

Releasing the air trapped in my lungs, I pick up the paper I've just finished and raise my eyes to the girl who has become my entire world.

She's picking at her nails absently while I watch her mentally have a conversation completely in her head. Her expression gives away absolutely everything, and watching her eyebrows dance animatedly, I can tell she's still arguing with Ghost.

Their banter is comical and reminds me of Dante and Pres. It's a similar dynamic. I can't even feel jealous because I see the lack of sexual tension behind their snarky comments. Her eyes light differently when he pisses her off than when she looks at me.

It's probably the only reason I've never tried to kill him.

That and I'm not sure I could.

He's a tough son of a bitch, and we've always been on the same side, so I've never had a reason to challenge his wolf with mine.

Hopefully, we keep it that way.

CHAPTER 25

Reaching for the phone, I see we are all set for the call.

"Firefly," I start. "It's time."

The way she jumps slightly at the sound of my voice tells me she forgot I was sitting over here, and when her eyes hit mine, the tension is back in her shoulders.

Pulling my chest up, I push every ounce of confidence that I can into my eyes.

She needs me to be strong for both of us. So that's exactly what I will be.

We've got this Firefly.

She stands a quick nod of her head before her jaw lifts, and I see her swallow, closing her eyes briefly before exhaling and opening them again with a newfound strength.

Fates, she's beautiful.

Clearing my throat, I type the number for Ghost and wait the two rings it takes for him to answer.

"Mingan," he says, answering the phone in a location that is very clearly not the beach.

"Ghost," I reply before turning the camera to Bri, who gives an irritated wave.

"Hello, Stay Puft Marshmallow Man."

"Ah, City, a white robe, how becoming. Sure we aren't getting married?" he replies, and I turn the camera back toward me with a growl.

He puts both hands up in a sign of surrender, but the grin on his face doesn't budge.

I'm surprised I can see him. He's in a dark, industrial-looking room, and he's in full tactical gear.

"Are you sure you're good to do this now?" I ask, wondering if he's on location for a mission.

"Wasn't really given a save the date for this shindig. I'm forty minutes to shift change, so as long as you don't stretch it out, I should be fine," he says, checking a small laptop connected at his right.

"Shift change? You're at work?" she asks before thinking better of it. "Oh, 'work'. You must be annoyingly stalking someone who didn't ask for your help."

"Interesting how you get to complain about that solely because I 'annoyingly stalked someone who didn't ask for it.' he replies, and I try to keep the smile off my face as she clenches her jaw.

He isn't wrong.

"Okay, then I will put you over here," I say, walking the phone to the mantle over the fireplace so he can see and hear the ceremony and I can have my hands free.

Turning my back to the camera, I square my shoulders, locking eyes with her.

Ready?

I silently ask, and I wait for the dip of her chin.

Showtime.

"Kneel," I say, announcing the word and pointing in front of me. She obeys without a word, and my dick hardens at the way she follows my orders without resistance and looks up at me from beneath her lashes.

Fuck me.

"You come before us, one of the chosen. Destined by The Fates to walk this Earth as both woman and beast. Today, you have the choice to embrace that future or deny your birthright. This choice cannot be

CHAPTER 25

changed, and once spoken, is final. What is your choice?" I say the words, enunciating each to avoid stumbling over them.

She pauses, remembering the response she needs to say before lifting her chin and speaking.

"I choose to follow the path The Fates have set before me."

My wolf surges with pride at her response, and I have to force him back before continuing.

"As is your birthright, we bear witness to your Awakening. Rise."

I walk behind her as she stands, gently pulling the robe off her left shoulder. One hand slides securely around her waist, and the other pulls her chin to the side, exposing her throat and shoulder more.

Mine.

My wolf growls as I whisper quietly in her ear.

"I love you, Firefly."

Placing my lips to her neck, I feel her tense as I lightly kiss the fluttering heartbeat there before gliding down to her shoulder. Then, without pause, I bite down.

Heat fills my mouth as my teeth shift, and the copper taste of her blood envelops me. Instinct takes over, and I follow its command, my bite deepening as I feel the burn of the venom release. A faint whimper hits my ears, but I'm too far gone to acknowledge it.

Just as quickly as it came, the burn subsides, and I release my bite, gasping for air as I hold Bri's weight against me.

Shit. Is she ok?

Leaning into my wolf hearing, I find the muffled patter of her heartbeat, and relief fills me.

My Firefly.

So far, so good.

Laying her down, I arrange the cushions around her before grabbing the first aid kit I'd pulled from under the kitchen sink. With a light hand, I clean the bite mark, removing the blood and excess venom from her skin, watching the punctures for any sign of healing.

Slow clapping behind me makes me stand ready to fight before I realize Ghost is still on the camera phone on the mantle.

"Looked like you'd done it a hundred times," he says, with no hint of sarcasm in his tone but rather a bit of reverence, which is unlike him.

Ceremony and tradition aren't his things.

"Thank you for witnessing today. I realize we have asked a lot of you in the last few weeks," I say, trying to find the words to convey my respect and gratitude.

"It was my honor. She's a pistol, and I don't envy you having to put up with her stubbornness for the rest of time, but know she is your strength, your sword. Your job now is to be her shield. Protect her light," he says.

The severity of the words hangs in the air, and I look back down at her, lying peacefully, almost as if asleep.

She's always been my light.

"I will," I say, meaning every promise the words carry. "She will be out for a while. Most Awakenings I've seen take at least an hour. Take care of your mission and call back once you're clear, and Ghost, be careful." The words feel right coming out, despite the fact that they are the last ones I said to him before he gave himself up to save Dante.

"Always am," he says, and I speak again before he hangs up.

CHAPTER 25

"Why the block code? On the phone, why'd you use that day?" I ask, needing to know why a day that cost so many their lives would be used on her phone.

It's a moment before he answers.

"I touched him. Dante, I mean. It wasn't intentional, but we were getting our final gear on, and the truck hit a pothole. I reached out to steady him before I even thought about it," he says, shrugging as the pieces fall into place in my mind.

He knew.

Before we ever started. He knew what would happen.

Fuck.

"Thank you," I say, trying to form words. "For saving him. For saving us all."

"Some things are bigger than all of us," he says just as movement at my feet pulls my attention.

No.

It's too soon.

Chapter 26
Bri

The sound of muffled voices slowly pulls me back to awareness. The burning sensation that enveloped me with his bite had me seeing stars before there was only darkness. Every nerve in my body felt singed by the lava that erupted in my veins. Fire consumed me, and at its peak, only pain existed.

Once the darkness took over, there was peace. Silence that felt like renewal as healing followed the burn like a salve.

"Firefly?" Cain's voice is closer now, and I can almost feel the proximity of his hand before it touches me. His palm connects lightly with my cheek.

My eyes sluggishly peel themselves open, and the first thing I register is the concern etched into his forehead.

Oh no... what's wrong?

CHAPTER 26

"How long was I down?" I ask, rolling my shoulders to find them not stiff or tight but reactive as I sit up.

Cain's eyes are examining and dissecting every inch of me. His eyes stop on the flesh of my shoulder where he bit me.

"How do you feel?" he says quickly, his voice so low it's almost a whisper.

"Fine, I think?" I reply, starting to worry. "Did something happen while I was out?" I attempt to look down at my shoulder, and I don't see anything that would cause alarm. The bite mark left by his teeth is now just a faded pink.

That's normal, right? Rapid healing and all that.

"Cain… you're scaring me. Say something," I put both hands on his face and pull his eyes to mine. Fear radiates from him, and I see sweat forming on his brow.

Mate.

The voice feels foreign and tickles at the back of my skull.

"Welcome to the Vegas Pack, Brielle DelaCourt. Pack Member 9878. Initiated by Cain Mingan," a voice from over Cain's shoulder says pulling my attention, and I realize Ghost is back on the phone.

"Thanks," I say, leaning around Cain. "How'd your 'beach' mission go?" I ask, taking my hands off Cain's face to make air quotes.

"I'll let you know when I do it. Always knew you were impatient; just never really realized how stubborn that part of you was, City. Well, I'll leave you to it," he says before giving a two-fingered salute and disconnecting from the call.

Bri: What's wrong?

Cain's eyes bulge, and his jaw drops at my question.

Cain: Can you hear me?

Bri: Of course, I can...

It's then I realize I'm staring at his face, and his lips haven't moved.

Bri: Holy Fuck, I'm talking into your head!

Cain: Shouting, really, but yeah...

"Sorry!" I say out loud, my hands covering my lips despite not using them to shout.

"It's ok. Managing that will come later. We need to get you to shift," he says, his concern returning to his expression.

"Okay, how do I do that?" I ask, wondering if I'm unaware of some new button inside me.

"You have to give control to your wolf. Can you feel or hear her in your head?" he asks.

Hello?

Are you in here?

Mate.

Shit!

I nod. My eyes showing the surprise I feel hearing her again.

"You have to let her take charge," he says, trying to encourage me.

Let her take control.

Sure.

No Problem.

Squeezing my eyes shut, I concentrate on letting her in.

Okay, you're on.

Anytime...

I open one eye, looking around.

CHAPTER 26

Nothing

Work with me here.

Kind of hard to take control when you won't move.

Move? It's my body! Where am I supposed to go?

Away.

Well, I'm trying!

"Just breathe, Firefly. It's a little like falling asleep. Clear your mind and relax," Cain says, the words making complete sense but not helping at all.

"I'm trying," I say through clenched teeth. Not relaxed. Not calm.

Just give up control. Just let go.

I'm waiting.

Well, you could try to force your way in. I've seen Cain's wolf do it. Can't you do that?

Do you think you would still be in charge if I could?

His hands slide slowly up my arms, grounding me in the moment and forcing me to focus on his touch.

"Do you want me to help you? I could try command," he offers.

"I guess it couldn't hurt," I say, shrugging.

Since I can't do it on my own.

"Okay, **shift**," he says, command entering his voice.

And just like that, darkness.

Chapter 27
Cain

She shifted.

The relief that fills me is instant.

In all my years, I'd never seen, Hell, I'd never even heard of anyone responding to the shift that fast. Most transitions took anywhere from one to three hours.

I don't think she was out even ten minutes.

More like eight.

Eight. Fucking. Minutes.

Dante took almost sixty minutes, and I took about the same, but eight minutes. It had to be a record.

It also was the scariest moment I've had since I thought she'd taken a bullet on that field.

CHAPTER 27

When I thought I'd lost her forever.

In the few minutes since watching her initial struggle to shift, that fear has only intensified.

Had I done something wrong?

Not given her enough?

The mind-link after helped ease some of my worry but didn't completely remove it.

It wasn't until her eyes flashed copper that I could finally relax. Once the command takes hold, she shifts seamlessly, and her wolf is beautiful.

With fur that's chocolate brown and freckled patches of black, she stands taller than most female wolves.

You're stunning.

I send in a mind-link to her when the glow of her eyes finally meets mine.

Bri: Mate.

She responds, and I know her wolf is pushing her out. She will learn to remain aware once she's done this more, but I would bet she won't remember any of her time shifted today.

My wolf pushes for control, and I allow him to speak to her.

Mate.

Very original, buddy.

His growl has me throwing my hands up in surrender as I pull off my shirt, wanting to run with her.

Before I shift, I open the cabin door, letting her out into the sunshine. Her movements are tentative as if she's testing her ability. Her coat shines in the sun, and my heart soars as I watch her scent the area.

The cold hits my skin, and I close the door behind me before allowing him to take over.

Once I'm shifted, I reach out, tugging on our bond and feeling her excitement.

Cain: Come on, Mate. Let's see how fast you are.

I send before taking off at a jog, hoping she will chase me.

The sound of her paws breaking the icy snow behind me tells me she does. Staying mainly on the path, I try to keep the route simple and steady, not pushing the pace to see how she does.

She falls into my rhythm, matching me stride for stride before overtaking me just a few minutes in and pushing the pace. Before she can get around me, I nip at her flank playfully and then allow her to lead.

She's fast.

Agile, graceful, and surefooted, but damn if I'm not struggling to keep up.

Bri: Should I slow down for you? You're breathing a little heavy there, big guy.

Cain: I'm fine

I respond, not liking how difficult maintaining her pace has become.

Bri: Of course, you are.

Her mind-link comes through just as she darts off the path and disappears.

Shit.

Nearly missing where she cut off the trail, I slide into a nearby trunk before having to regain my feet.

CHAPTER 27

For the next thirty minutes, we play a large game of tag: me catching her before taking off. Her coming around to catch me. By the time we find our way back to the path, I'm panting and grinning from ear to ear.

My girl is perfect.

It's the most entertaining run I've had in years, and despite feeling like my legs might literally give out at any second, I can't wait to do it again.

When I reach the porch, I shift back, grab my shorts from where I left them, and turn to wait for her to do the same.

She circles the yard before lying down in a pool of sunlight in the front.

Watching her wolf brings me a sense of pride I've never experienced, and I don't think I could be more grateful that The Fates made her mine.

My Fated Mate.

My Firefly.

My Forever.

When I see that she's going to lay out for a while, I head inside to grab her some warm clothes and pull out a hoodie for myself. Before returning outside, I brew another pot of coffee and start the fire in the living room.

She's still basking in the yard when I come back out, and part of me wants to let her stay there, feeling out this part of her. The other part of me knows she needs to eat, and the longer she stays shifted the harder it will be for her to come back to me.

Cain: Time to come back inside before you freeze to death.

Bri: I can't even feel the cold.

Cain: Be that as it may, you need food and rest. It's been a big day.

Bri: Maybe later.

Cain: Come on. You need to shift back.

Bri: No

She replies, standing to face me. Challenge shining in fiery eyes.

Her defiance is both infuriating and hot, and I fight to keep myself from forcing her hand.

Cain: Mate...

Bri: She had twenty-two years. I think she can give me a few.

Cain: That is not how this works. You don't get to have complete control over her. It should be a partnership—a team.

Bri: Well it looks like she put me in coach, and I'm ready to play.

The second she says it, I swear she raises her eyebrow exactly like Bri does, and my patience dissolves.

Cain: **Shift Back**

The command flows out of me, and I step closer to her. Her head tilts, and she casually lays herself down, paws crossing in the front.

Holy shit.

Bri: Funny how genetics work.

She's a fucking Alpha.

More than that, she's stronger than me.

***

Four hours later, she's still a wolf, and I'm pulling my hair out.

CHAPTER 27

She can't stay like this.

Can she stay like this?

Has anyone ever gotten stuck?

I reach back through every memory I have, and the few that have taken a while to shift have always been forced to through the use of command.

Well, that didn't fucking work!

Every fiber of my being wants to reach out to Dante, tell him what's going on. Find a solution. Hopefully before she actually freezes to death.

Thankfully, she's stayed close to the cabin, not venturing off into the woods again, but somethings got to give.

Setting my pride aside, I pick up the phone and call Ghost.

Maybe he has some idea I haven't thought of.

"I wonder if I'm going to need to increase my plan. All these calls are adding up," he says when he picks up.

"Apologies. We have a problem," I say, keeping my eyes on her as she paces the front area.

"You mean you have a problem," he retorts with a laugh. "What's going on?"

"I can't get her back," I say, defeat evident in my voice.

"You lost her?"

"No, I didn't lose her. I can't get her to shift back!" I say, irritated.

"So use command to force her," he says, like its the most obvious solution.

"Oh my gosh, what a great idea! Why didn't I think of that? Oh, wait! I fucking already tried. Her wolf basically laughed at my attempt," I say, anger flowing from me.

Silence follows my statement for several moments before uncontrolled laughter rolls out of him.

Oh, he thinks this is funny.

"Not sure your laughter is helping here," I state, glaring at the phone.

Catching his breath, he responds.

"Ha, I'm sorry, but the fact that you thought she wasn't going to be even more stubborn as a wolf is hilarious. Have you met her?" Laughter again. "Whew, thank you. I needed that after the night I've had."

"Happy to help... Now, do you have any useful suggestions?" I ask.

"You could knock her out with something. Subconscious her is much easier to deal with," he says, humor still evident in his tone.

"I'm not knocking her out," I say, rolling my eyes at the thought.

"Then your only option is food. The only time she ever shuts up or stops being snarky is when she eats. Lure her back with food. She especially likes chili," he says before disconnecting the call.

Food... It's not the worst idea.

Chapter 28

Bri

My first thought that filters through is how cold I am. The second is how good it smells.

My stomach growls.

Opening my eyes, I realize I'm naked on the porch.

What the fuck?

Covering my lady bits, I stand up and lose my footing immediately.

Ouch.

My legs are killing me.

In fact, every part of me hurts.

Going in for my second try, I place my foot carefully before putting my weight on it and find that I can focus enough to make it to the door.

Which is locked.

Son of a bitch!

I knock hard, nearly SWAT team pounding by the time Cain opens it, allowing the room's heat to float out.

Dear lord, I need inside.

"How could you leave me out here?!?" I shout, pushing him to the side as I tenderly move to the couch with the largest blanket. Once I'm burrito'd , I turn back glaring at him waiting for an answer.

"Oh, I tried to get you to come inside. I asked nicely. I was reasonable. I used command. Your wolf found it very entertaining to defy anything I ask of her," he says, frustration showing on his expression.

"Oh," I say, not understanding why she wouldn't listen.

He's not our boss.

He's our Mate.

True, but he doesn't control us.

My eyes grow wide at her attitude.

Well, shit.

"Sorry," I say realizing what he's been dealing with.

"It's fine. Dinner is ready if you want some," he says, nodding to the pot on the stove.

Yes!

My stomach growls in answer before my words can catch up and concern etches itself on Cain's face.

"Yes, please," I say, watching him walk to the stove and scoop what smells like heaven into a bowl.

He sprinkles cheese and onions on top before grabbing a spoon and walking it over to me.

"Aren't you having any?" I ask, taking the bowl from him.

CHAPTER 28

"I ate. An hour ago," he says before grabbing a pile of clothes that are sitting on the table by the door. "I tried to get you these so that you wouldn't be cold, but you wouldn't shift."

"Thank you," I say, spooning the chili into my mouth.

Good.

It's not as tasty as Ghost's, but it's still satisfying.

I eat the entire bowl in under five minutes and lift it back toward him in silent question.

He returns to the stove, doles out another serving, and then returns it to me. He moves my legs off the couch and sits himself down in their place before draping them back over him.

His body heat adds to the warmth under the covers, and I moan at the comfort it provides.

"Do you remember any of it, Firefly?" he asks, his hands slowly rubbing my feet in a way that makes me melt.

"The ceremony, yes. Waking up from it, yes, but after that, it was like taking a nap and coming back from a coma with every one of my muscles screaming at me," I say, trying to put into words the empty darkness.

"It will get easier. Each time you shift, it will become more natural," he says, a smile lifting one side of his face. "Your wolf is quite the force. She's big."

"Just what every girl wants to hear," I say, swatting him.

"She beautiful, Firefly. Fast, agile, her instincts are spot on, and she has your fiery eyes," he finishes.

He looks at me, and the rest of the world falls away. I can see the love in his stare, and it makes me feel worthy.

"Thank you," I choke out. Not sure where all of the emotion is coming from.

"You had me worried when you woke up so fast. I thought for sure I'd messed something up, but when you finally let go and shifted. Your wolf knew exactly what she was doing," he says, a smile on his face.

"How long was I down for? An hour?" I ask, genuinely curious because it certainly felt short on my end, but I had nothing to compare it to other than the stories he'd told me.

"Eight minutes, Firefly. You were only out for eight minutes. I've never heard of anyone waking up that fast. Ever. It shows how strong your wolf is and how ready she is to be released. It made me wonder if it was because you were Awakened so late that your transition was faster, but Jake took just under two hours to wake up from his, and he was eighteen, so it can't be that," he says, his voice trailing off in thought.

My wolf is strong.

We're strong.

Her voice startles me, and I ask the question I'd been avoiding since he told me he couldn't get me to shift.

"How strong are we? Am I an Alpha?" I ask, looking away from him to brace myself for the answer.

"Stronger than me, Firefly. Your wolf can refuse my command. So yeah, you're an Alpha and a damn strong one at that," he says, and I chance a look at him, relieved when all I see is pride emanating from his stare.

"Is that okay?" I ask, holding his gaze. "Me being an Alpha? Does it change anything for you?"

CHAPTER 28

"More than okay, Firefly. I've always told you how strong I think you are. Even without your wolf, it's one of the things I love about you. Having a badass wolf only makes me feel better about how stubborn you are and your tendency to get yourself into trouble," he says, his smile back as he picks fun at me.

I'm an Alpha.

I'm strong.

I'd like to think I have something to do with both of those things, but feel free to take all the credit.

My wolf says, and I can hear her rolling her eyes.

Sorry. You know what I mean. I'm strong because of you.

That's more like it.

"Is she sassing you, too?" he asks me, a chuckle in his voice.

"Yep, but honestly, would you expect anything less? You said it yourself: she's a part of me. I'd be giving me shit, too," I say, relaxed for the first time.

"Let's get you showered and off to sleep. You've had a long day," he says, kissing my forehead and scooping me into his arms. Snuggling into his embrace, I inhale his scent, relishing the way it always brings me peace.

Our shower is efficient. Cain takes his time soaping and massaging my sore body before washing my hair while I stand under the warm stream, half in a daze. When I'm deemed clean, he wraps me in an oversized fluffy towel and escorts me into the bedroom. I pull on some underwear and one of his t-shirts and crawl into the bed.

Sleep takes me before my head even hits the pillow, and I spend the night dreaming about the woods, lying in the sun's rays, and chasing a particular black-furred wolf with metallic silver eyes.

Chapter 29
Dante

Silence hangs in the air as the council considers the information I've given them. Where we usually have seven members, only five are present today. With Cain being off the grid and Jake on special assignment watching over Bri's roommate, Liv, I feel like we're operating as a skeleton crew, and it makes me nervous about the impending war.

"Any ideas?" I ask, opening the floor up and scanning from Pres to Erik before sliding my gaze across the table to Elijah and James. Erik speaks first.

"Do we need a full perimeter for the city, or can we focus our protection on our assets? Feels like we are wasting personnel with teams patrolling open desert that is meaningless in the grand scheme of things," he says, his eyes scouring the personnel document in front of him.

"We could back off and focus our intentions on more of our properties, but then we have gaps, and we have pack members all over the city. I can't ask them all to leave their homes for an unforeseen amount of time. Patrolling the perimeter, keeping tabs on all highways into the city, and using Pres's extensive drone collection to monitor areas farther outside the perimeter seem like the best ways to identify if they are moving in. Additionally, we can't attack them in the city. The fight will have to happen away from human eyes. Too many cameras exist, and the last thing we need is a wolf shifter battle being live-streamed to the world." I finish, realizing the last war didn't have these additional complications.

"If this goes that far, I'll be jamming most electronics as a precaution. That being said, shouldn't we be looking for ways to negotiate a new peace treaty rather than preparing for a war we have a very, and I mean very, slim chance of winning?" Presley asks, concern evident in her tone and tension firmly placed in her posture.

"I can't see Marlo being willing to negotiate anymore. He lost his Second; then we took Brielle even after he won her from the LLC. If the feud between him and our father was tense, ours has made it even more tenuous. He has no reason to want to trust us, and while his entire case for Brielle was bullshit, it was our anonymous tip that got his original Second thrown in jail, and then we got the replacement shot. It's not exactly a platform of peace," I say, feeling even more frustrated and wishing Cain was here with ideas.

"Everyone has a price. We just have to find what he's willing to trade for besides all of our territory," Pres says, typing something into her computer.

"Any word on resources? Packs who will help?" Erik asks, looking from me at Elijah and James.

CHAPTER 29

"None of our allied packs believe that the Reno Pack should have been awarded the Unawakened girl, and yet, they won't support us because the LLC is involved," Elijah says, and James nods in agreement.

That's what I found when I reached out as well.

"The only pack willing to assist is my aunt's pack in New Mexico. She is currently working on numbers to see how many shifters she can send. So we have our numbers, which Quinn ran most of last night and this morning, and we have 1,926 able-bodied, plus whatever they can contribute," I say, supplying Erik with our totals.

"Do we know how many Reno has?" Erik asks as a follow-up.

I shake my head, preparing to answer him, but James pipes in with a response.

"I spoke with a friend of mine from one of the northern California packs, and apparently, his son was sent to work with the Reno Pack last spring. According to him, they have close to a thousand active wolves, and that's not considering any they could pull in for this now that the LLC has basically blacklisted us," he says.

"Deacon Marlo also has his fingers in several different less-than-legal ventures and has familial ties to the Amatos, who we know have resources they could send," Elijah adds.

Shit. I'd forgotten about their ties with the Miami pack.

That's part of what got us into this in the first place.

Dante: Quinn, I need to meet with David Healy asap

Quinn: I will reach out. Any reason I should tell him?

Dante: No, just that it's urgent; try to get him in here before two today.

Quinn: You got it, boss, but remember you have an in-person meeting with a client from Resort World at 1:00 p.m. and a video call scheduled with Doug Martin at 1:30 p.m.

Dante: I'll have to be fast, or he will have to wait, but it needs to be today.

Looking down at my watch, I see I only have about fifteen minutes before I need to head to the client meeting, so I turn to Presley.

"It won't matter how many resources he has; ours must be better. Pres, where are we with the motion sensor grids?" I ask, hoping she's made some headway.

"We are sourcing what we can, but based on our current inventory, we should be able to cover about 70% of the areas you highlighted in your request. If we have another week, we probably could get that number closer to 95%, but then the placement teams would be working around the clock to get them set up, and we still need a way to monitor and power every grid. I'm playing with a few other options, but it will be more about getting power to the grids than the technology itself. We know it works, but for how long is the question. I only have four on my team, and that's a lot of responsibility to place on us working twelve-hour shifts with no days off," she says, grimacing at the admission.

Only four? How is that possible?

She must read the question on my face, so she elaborates.

"Green team has twelve members, but eight of them are human contractors we can't pull for this due to… well, the obvious reasons that they can't know," she says, clarifying.

Shit, she's right. We will need to expand the shifter side of our green team fast.

CHAPTER 29

"Erik, do you have anyone who can be moved to the green team?" I ask, watching as Presley's expression changes.

She hand-picked her team members, and I've allowed it since she returned from college because I wanted her to have something that was truly hers. But we don't have time to be picky—not anymore.

Dante: You need people to watch screens temporarily. Anyone could fill this role.

I send the mind-link while Erik rattles off a few names he thinks would be a good fit.

Pres: Most of the black or red team members couldn't plug in a computer if it had picture instructions.

My laughter at her snark pulls everyone's attention, and I have to clear my throat before allowing him to finish.

"Pick four more so each green team member can shadow them until they know what's going on. Additionally, can you pull two of Jake's teams together for installation? Pres will need to brief them and be at each grid to ensure functionality, but we must start tonight. Pres, brief your team about their responsibilities with this and hand off any client-side stuff to your other eight members. We can't share resources right now, so whoever is most competent needs to lead them. I need you 100% on this." She nods, but I see her wheels turning and her hesitation.

"James and Elijah, please work with Quinn to prep temporary housing for our returning members and find us another location that we can use as a secondary safe location should the need arise. Erik, reach out to Jake when he becomes available. You will need to work through your recruits and put them into teams for patrolling. We are increasing all of our security starting right now." I stand before finishing.

"I have complete faith that we have every ability to beat them should this come to that, but my priority will always be protecting the lives of our people, so I am looking for ways around this. There is a full-pack meeting in the large auditorium tomorrow night. Let's have our plan locked in before then. Let me know if you need anything," I say, grabbing the folder of documents from the meeting and striding out of the room.

Before I return to my office, footsteps behind me tell me exactly who is following me, and I leave the door open, knowing she will follow me in.

"What is it, P?" I ask as I turn and sit down in my chair.

"Keith is the best brain I have on the human side—honestly, on either side—but I also know he's new and has been tangled up with Marlo before, so I'm wondering if I should trust him with leading the client side," she says slowly, sitting in the chair opposite me.

Something about her feels off, and I pull on the bond to read more into her emotions. Fear is there, but so is guilt, and something I can't quite put my finger on. We're all scared of what's to come, and I know she is still holding onto the guilt for her role in starting this ball rolling, but it's something else.

As she sits there, concern etched on her face, it hits me.

She's in all black. She has no headphones on. Nothing about her is loud or obnoxious. It may be the most understated I have seen her since our dad's funeral, and for a moment, my heart aches that she's lost herself.

"Tell me what this really is about?" I ask, hoping she will give me something. "Because you have excellent intuition, and you never like my advice when I give my two cents," I say, keeping my tone neutral.

"Well, because usually, your advice sucks," she says, forcing snark that doesn't entirely land. "But also because I keep messing up, and I'm worried my intuition is off, I don't want to do something else that could hurt the pack the way I did with Brielle," she says, looking down at her fingernails as I hear the emotion reach her throat.

"That wasn't your fault. Cain's told you, and so have I. Hudson would have found another time, at school or work, to grab her if it hadn't been then. We got lucky getting her back because of Marlo's absence at the initial trade. You can't keep blaming yourself for this."

"Easier said than done, but, either way, I need your thoughts on Keith. Do you think he can be trusted?" she asks, and her eyes look up again.

"I do. I wouldn't have offered him the position or forced you to put him on the team. He shows strong loyalty, has never wavered on his intention with us, and you said it yourself: he's the best brain you've got. Trust him with this. If I'm wrong, it's on me, but I need you to focus on keeping the rest of us safe. Can I count on you?" I ask, knowing without a shadow of a doubt that Presley would never allow anyone in our pack to be harmed if she could help it.

"You know you can. I'll have the coverage maps to you by the end of the day and will send the first teams at nightfall," she says, standing and turning to walk out of the room.

"Oh, and D. You will keep them safe. I know you will," she says before exiting the room, leaving me with the confidence I need to get through this.

From her lips to the Fates ears...

Chapter 30
Cain

Falling asleep with her in my arms is by far the most peace I have felt in the last few months. It's as if a stillness has settled over me, and I can finally breathe. She's mine. She's here. She's Awakened.

Mate.

Now, if we could get that, too, life would be perfect.

We'd discussed what Mating would be like, and I explained how it works, but with yesterday's stress, I didn't need another thing to worry about. I needed her safe. Seeing her shift was like watching art come to life before my eyes.

Her wolf is every bit as sassy and strong as she is, but she's more. More dominant. More protective of her. More merciless.

She needs that.

CHAPTER 30

A small moan floats from her as she tugs the blanket closer to her, wiggling to resecure her feet.

My lips fall to her neck, peppering featherlight touches down the creamy column. Her heart rate accelerates, and her chin tilts, giving me more access.

"Good morning, Firefly," I whisper into her ear, nibbling around it and dragging my teeth down the lobe before moving her hair out of the way to further enjoy teasing her.

"Not sure it's all the way morning yet, but ok," she says, a small smile forming on her face. She still hasn't opened her eyes, but the way her ass is now grinding itself against me tells me she's ready for a wake-up call.

My hands explore her body, sliding over the curve of her hip and tracing along the hem of the thong she put on before bed. I dance my fingertips just inside the fabric, and the sharp inhale she gives urges me on.

"How do you feel?" I ask her, skimming my knuckles down the inside of her thigh and appreciating the way she opens for me as I do.

"Amazing. I feel amazing," she says, her words breathy as she arches, hoping to get my hand to where she wants it.

"Not sore?" I ask, opening my hand before grabbing and squeezing her inner thigh. Kisses still landing on her shoulder and onto her collarbone.

She nods her response, whimpering a little at the pressure of my grip.

"Good, because I want to bury myself inside you, and I don't plan on being gentle about it. Roll over. On all fours," I order, loving how quickly she responds to me.

Once she's set, elbows and knees holding her in position, I slowly pull the thong off, intentionally not touching her center.

Not yet.

Staring down at her glistening pussy, perched up for me, is almost too perfect, and my cock strains against the thin fabric of the boxers I have on. I stand, dropping them to the floor and sliding my eyes over every inch of exposed skin on her body.

Mine.

Mate.

A growl escapes me, and she whips her head back, locking eyes with mine. For an instant, hers flash orange, the coppery glow giving confirmation to my wolf.

Her eyebrow lifts, and she shakes her ass at me in invitation.

"Damn, you're beautiful, Firefly," I say, climbing behind her; I lay myself down and pull her hips to sit her directly over my face as she squeals with the unexpected move.

I lick up the side of her thigh, biting at the meat of her leg.

"Jesus, Cain..." she moans.

Releasing my bite with a chuckle, I lick straight up her center, enjoying the salty flavor of her need on my tongue. Once I reach her clit, I suck it into my mouth, swirling my tongue around it.

She sinks lower, attempting to get more friction from my face, and my hands move to rock her against me, urging her to take what she wants.

CHAPTER 30

After a minute, she finds her rhythm, and I reach up to slide two fingers inside her, matching her pace with the pumps.

When she falls apart, her walls clamp down on my fingers, and she collapses on top of me.

I could die happy just like this.

"That's my good girl," I praise, sliding my fingers out and sucking them clean.

She's panting, and I've never seen a more beautiful creature than my girl when she completely falls apart. Skin flush, sweat glistening, eyes dazed.

Mine.

Mate.

I move her off of me and set myself up behind her. Her knees are barely holding her up, so I give her a moment to catch her breath, and I fist my cock, stroking it slowly.

Once I no longer see the shaking, I line myself with her center, and I slide the head of my cock into her folds, enjoying the way my precum mixes with her orgasm in a shimmering display.

Inch by inch, I push my cock into her, feeling her slowly relent and allow me inside.

Fucking perfect.

"You were made for my cock," I say, barely containing the gravel in my voice.

Sliding back out, I squeeze her hips and use them as anchors as I slam back in, finding my own rhythm.

Reaching out, I fist the back of her hair, sliding my hand from the base of her neck and pulling her up with my grip. She tenses, gripping my cock even tighter with the reaction.

"Grab the headboard," I demand, releasing my grip and moving us closer so she can sit up more.

I pull the t-shirt she's wearing off and wrap my arms around her, gripping her breasts possessively and pulling her body to mine. I restart my thrusts, which are slower now from this angle. She's nearly in my lap, and I love her weight against me as we build together.

I slide my arm down the planes of her stomach and play with her enlarged and over-sensitive clit.

"Yes, Cain, oh my god, yes," she pants, losing her paces and melting into me.

Mate.

Mine.

"Tell me who you belong to, Firefly," I whisper into her ear.

"Yo..uh..ou," she pants, unable to form the word.

My fingers squeeze on her clit, freezing their movement just as I stop pumping into her.

"Try again," I taunt.

"You, I belong to you," she says, sounding out of breath as she lays her head back on my chest.

"Look at me," "I order, moving her off me to turn her around. Her chest slides down mine as she seats herself back onto my cock, her legs wrapping my waist.

CHAPTER 30

My hands land on her ass, and I pull her closer to me, feeling her heartbeat on my skin. I build into a steady rhythm. Never looking away from her eyes as I push us both to our limits. The edge dangling so close.

"I love you Brielle DelaCourt. I belong to you—mind, body, and soul. I am yours, forever." I say, staring into her fire-flecked eyes, knowing every word is true.

"I love you too, Cain. I'm yours. Forever," It's all I need to hear before my climax hits, and I feel my wolf take over my eyes flashing, teeth shifting, and I bite into her left shoulder just as I feel the piercing of my flesh from her bite.

MATE.

Chapter 31
Bri

*M*ATE. My orgasm explodes through me as my wolf forces to the surface. Instinct takes over, and I find myself biting into his flesh, heat filling my mouth as his blood leaks into me.

He's fucking delicious.

Mate.

Every cell in my body is connected to him, static spiraling around each nerve. My essence pours into him as I take his into me, becoming one as our bond anchors itself in the very fiber of our DNA. Our heartbeats sync, matching in cadence as we become intricately woven together.

My skin crackles with electric energy, and it feels as if every nerve has been touched by lightning.

Deep within me, I feel his thoughts, emotions, and even his memories flash before my eyes. His Awakening, Meeting Dante, graduation, his parents moving away, Marcus's death, and even the day he met me all snap into my mind as if I'd lived them.

The last memory that flows into my consciousness is a vision of me. My cheeks are flush, my forehead gleaming with sweat from the last orgasm he gave, and my eyes are glowing in a burnt orange hue.

Seeing myself through his eyes has me gasping.

Stunning.

Is this how he sees me?

My gasp releases the bite and, with it, seals our connection. Warmth envelops me, and I feel the skin on my shoulder begin to knit back together.

When my breath finally evens, I lean back to see the damage I'd done to his shoulder, only to find that instead of open sores and blood stains, his flesh is now intricately decorated in glowing silver lines so vivid they appear to be moving in his skin. The pattern begins with three stars where my bottom teeth punctured, and from those stars, lightning charges in every direction over his shoulder, in between his other tattoos at the top of his arm, and down the entirety of his back.

My fingers are drawn to it like a magnet. Delicately, they slide over the hundreds of branches, and I can feel the touch on my skin as they glide.

Mate.

When I glance at him, I see he's also staring at my shoulder. The same three stars sit at the top of my back, and silver lightning spreads off in every direction, just like it does on his.

They match.

Our Mate Marks.

Cain's lips drop, and he individually kisses each star before turning and placing a final kiss on my lips.

"I love you," he whispers, not needing to say the words because I can feel them thrumming through me.

"I love you too, Candy Cain," I respond, melting into him. The satisfaction of feeling genuinely whole for the first time brings a sense of peace I've never known—the missing part of my puzzle.

"I told you that you would be mine," he says, snark filling his tone as he rolls me to my back and drops a kiss on my nose. "The first time I kissed you in that parking lot outside Dante's car, I said I would have you, and look at us now. You're mine."

The way my heart soars at the term has me closing my eyes to bask in the feeling.

I'm his.

"Let's go get cleaned up," he finishes, pushing himself off me as he stands, pivoting to the bathroom.

Bri: Well, with this view, there is definitely no buyer's remorse.

Cain: Buyer's remorse? Firefly, is that all I am? An object for you to own and play with?

Bri: Maybe

Cain: Good, come play with me in the shower

He sends in the mind-link and looks over his shoulder, a Cheshire smile spreading across his face before he strides off to turn on the water.

It's as if my whole body is smiling, and I can feel his love for me radiating over the bond. The connection is like being plugged directly into his emotions; the fact that they mirror mine only intensifies the feeling.

CHAPTER 31

I crawl my way over to the edge of the bed to follow him as another mind-link comes through.

Dante: Welcome to the Vegas Pack, Brielle, and congratulations on your wolf.

Holy shit.

Having Cain's voice in my head is one thing, but the way Dante's message came through without any sign startles me.

When the vampire did it, I felt him kind of sliding around in there first.

Cain pokes his head out of the bathroom, concern etched in his features and worry running along the bond.

"I guess I'm connected to Dante now, too," I say, pointing to my head in explanation. I feel his relief wash over him.

Bri: Thanks, boss errr... Alpha?

Dante: Dante is fine. You don't work for me, so outside of official pack functions, we can stay on a first-name basis. Are you two okay?

"Careful, he can feel your emotions too if you don't shield them from him," he says, returning to the bathroom.

Bri: We're fine. Any news from the LLC? Are they mad at Cain?

I ask him because I don't think stealing a person from the LLC's custody is a small thing.

Dante: We're working on it. We should have an appeal date soon. Please worry about keeping you two safe. I'll reach out when I know more.

With his last message, I head into the bathroom, questions weaving themselves together in my mind as I join Cain under the steamy spray.

I have to fix this.

We can't hide here forever while others fight this battle for me. It's time we go on offense, and I'm ready to play their game. Brielle DelaCourt, Alpha, is off the bench.

Chapter 32
Dante

The sensation of a new pack member's bond being tied to me is not new. I've Awakened hundreds of wolves as Alpha and recruited even more, but I've never had it take me unaware.

Love, joy, and overwhelming peace course across the connection, and I must brace myself on the desk for a moment.

She doesn't know how to shield herself yet, so the feelings flow into me as if I were feeling them myself.

Way to go, Cain.

I send off a mind-link welcoming her and checking in before returning to my email and confirming the date and time for the appeal I'd worked out with Alpha Martin.

Two days.

Knowing they are Mated helps our case, but I wonder if it will matter to Deacon now that he knows she's his daughter.

War has always been inevitable.

We just need to make it until the LLC no longer has us blacklisted, and then we can utilize our allies without them being afraid of legal ramifications.

We can hold our own for two more days.

Flying out of my territory, even to sort things out, leaves a bad taste in my mouth, and I'm struggling with the idea of leaving my pack vulnerable.

Would he attack while I'm gone?

Of course, he would.

What better time to launch an assault than when he knows both myself and Cain are out of the area, so there are two fewer Alphas he'd need to defeat?

In terms of war strategizing, it's a solid plan for him, so I need to find a way to ensure their safety.

The light knock on my door pulls my attention, and I see Quinn standing there.

"Mr. Healy is here," she says, pointing to the waiting area. "Are you ready for him?"

"Yes, please, send him in, and Quinn, can you contact Noah and let him know we have an appeal date? I'll forward you the information for my calendar as well," I ask, closing a few of the documents on my screens as David walks in.

"I appreciate you coming in so quickly, David," I say, extending my hand to invite him to sit.

"No problem at all, Alpha Stone. Your assistant said you needed some information about Luca Amato," he says as he sits.

CHAPTER 32

"Yes, recent events have led to some turbulence between the Reno Pack and ourselves. We believe an attack is likely in the next few days, and I was wondering if you had any information about what resources the Miami pack may be able to supply them," I say, not wanting to be too open about our position but also needing very specific intel from him.

"Well, I'm not sure how useful I can be. We were only officially part of the pack for a few months, and neither of us had wolves strong enough to be of interest to them. Had I not," he pauses, looking at the floor momentarily before clearing his throat and continuing. "Hmph, had I not gotten mixed up with my debts, I don't know that I would have ever had a conversation with him outside of our recruitment."

David fidgets in his seat, obviously embarrassed about the whole situation and his role in it.

"I understand, David, and I'm not here to judge you, but anything you could tell me would help," I urge, hoping he can remember something.

"I know they handle a lot of the drug trade in the area, and while they had me detained, I heard one of the enforcers talking about a shipment they were receiving. Something about a new development in one of their internal projects. I don't remember its name, but he said it was like steroids, but it was for your wolf. I guess Amato had been testing it on his enforcers, and it was enhancing them," he says, his voice gaining enthusiasm as he speaks.

A steroid drug for wolves?

Fucking perfect.

Super soldiers.

If they were testing them on their own pack, I have no doubt that by now, they could be shipping them to other packs, including Reno.

"Did you hear anything about the new development in that drug or any details? Side effects? Duration?" I question, trying to keep my voice even despite the dread creeping through me.

"Sorry, nothing about that. He just kept complaining that it wore off too quickly, and he hoped they found a way to make it permanent," he said, shrugging.

"Ok. Thank you. Anything else you remember? How many wolves they have or technology?" I probe.

"At my recruitment into the pack, I was pack member 45, 804. I'd never heard of a pack having so many, and I remember saying so. One of the other recruits mentioned the pack was only about a third that size, probably close to 18,000 active wolves. So I'd guess they could send thousands." he says, frowning.

Thousands?

Thousands of drugged-up super soldiers.

Could it get any worse?

He stands, signifying the end of the information he has to offer.

"I know it's probably not the news you were hoping for, but I know you will find a way through this. You have your dad's moral compass. You'd never allow people like that to win," he says before bowing his head slightly and exiting my office.

I may not allow it, but I have no idea how the hell I'm going to stop it from happening. Especially now.

Dante: Pres, I need you in my office. Now.

CHAPTER 32

I'm not bothering with pleasantries. There isn't time for them. We need solutions, we need options, we need my dad.

My heart sinks, knowing I'm not him.

A few minutes later, she walks in. No music is playing, and her pink cat-eared headphones are absent from her outfit.

She falls into the chair rather than just sitting in it and opens her laptop before looking up at me expectantly.

"Well, hello to you too," I say, trying for humor but missing the mark.

"You summoned, I'm here. What can I do?" she asks, exhaustion evident on her face.

Before I answer her, I pull on my bond with her and clench my jaw when I feel her shield blocking me.

"If you want to know how I'm feeling, you could just ask," she says, irritation seeping into her tone.

"Sorry, Pres. You've just been well, not yourself lately," I say as an explanation.

"We're about to be at war, D. That doesn't exactly feel like unicorns and rainbows from where I'm sitting. Our shipment of motion sensors we added yesterday has been delayed, and the order I attempted to add on after the meeting today won't be shipped for another week at the earliest. And if that wasn't enough, you should have seen the smug look on stupid Keith's face when I asked him to oversee our client division. You're lucky I didn't punch his perfectly straight dumb nose, or we'd probably have a lawsuit pending too," she finishes with a huff, and it's nice to see a bit of her fire come back, even if it is through violence directed at an employee.

"Well, thank you for controlling yourself. I'll be sure to have Quinn send over a gold star for your efforts in that regard. As for the shipment, we will figure it out. Let's focus on what we can control. I need information on a drug the Amatos are running," I say, shifting from big brother to Alpha.

Her attention drops to her lap, and she begins clicking and typing.

"What's it called?" she asks.

"I don't know," I reply, her fingers slow as she looks up.

"Can I know what it does?" she continues, squinting her eyes as if I'm intentionally being obtuse to make her life hard.

"The description I was given was 'steroids for wolves,' and apparently, there's been a new development in it," I say, giving her the only information I have.

She looks back down, and her typing resumes. Her head nods, and she scans the various pages she's been running through. I sit watching her, not wanting to interrupt her flow, when she stops, purses her lips, and pulls them to one side.

"So, at first glance, there isn't much activity for Maimi at all, which is suspicious by itself since it's such a large city with a huge wolf presence. But digging a bit deeper, I found a discussion post that may be relevant. It's focused on something called F-4110N, and it's vague but mentions that someone is looking for more because it wears off more quickly with each use. That wouldn't usually cause any reason for suspicion, but one of the replies mentions a new development in the formula which allows for twelve-hour boosts."

She pauses, tilts her head, and then types again.

"That could be anything. Why would that point to the Amatos?" I ask, and she looks up at me.

"The Amatos are the only game in town, and the name of the drug is bugging me. I haven't heard of it before, and it's literally nowhere on any server," she says.

"F-4110N? It could just be a random lot number," I say.

"It could, but do me a favor, maybe have Elijah and James reach out about it," she says. I grab a pen from my desk drawer and write it on a piece of paper so I can pass it along. The minute I put it down, I see it.

F4110N

Fallon.

"Pres," I say, realizing.

She looks up at me, seeing the word written out, and her eyes become saucers.

"This isn't good. If this new drug came from anything related to the Fallon Project, then we know exactly who the players are. If they are working with Marlo, we have even bigger problems with this war," she says, her eyes turning distant as she starts imaging all the ways this could go wrong.

"I need as much information on this as you can find. Spend the next few hours digging. We will need to meet with the council again tonight. This changes things," I say as Pres stands and strides out of my office without another word.

Dante: Quinn, I need you to get Ghost on the line and then call the council. I need them back here for a meeting at 8 p.m.

Quinn: Ok, what about Jake? Does he need to come in?

I think for a moment, knowing he's watching over Brielle's roommate, and while I don't believe the LLC would use her as bait, I know Marlo will without hesitation.

Dante: Reach out and see if he can get away. We won't leave her vulnerable, but if she's somewhere safe or somewhere we can put someone else on her, have him come in.

Quinn: I'll take care of it. Thai or Mexican for dinner?

Dante: Mexican, and get enough for everyone. Have it in the conference room for the meeting. Thanks for thinking about food.

I send it before returning to my screens. I have five hours to devise a plan to fight thousands of super soldiers.

Should be a piece of cake.

Fates help us all.

Chapter 33
Cain

Our new connection is both the weirdest feeling I've ever had and the most natural. My protective side loves knowing exactly how she is feeling and being able to discern how far away she is. The ability to mind-link with her means that most of our morning is spent in literal silence while we talk about all kinds of things.

My wolf feels settled for the first time in months, and there is a strength simmering across the bond. I can sense her wolf reaching for mine and know we will be a force together.

Flipping the grilled cheese in the pan, I feel the heaviness of the conversation we need to have and know the words must be spoken out loud.

"So, have you decided whether you want to stay in Vegas?" I ask, desperately aiming for nonchalance and trying to shield my feelings from her.

"I thought that was obvious with my choice to be Awakened and Mated to you," she says, confusion showing in her scrunched brow.

"Not sure it was obvious. I told you I would follow you wherever you wanted to go. I didn't know if Boston was still something you wanted," I say, plating her food and walking it over to her.

My grilled cheese is no match for Presley's, but it's edible.

"Even if Boston was still an option, which I doubt it is as 'flaky' as I've been already. I can't imagine taking you away from your family. The pack is your family. I feel it when I think of them because I've lived those memories, too. We can't abandon them, especially now that I'm the reason the whole pack is in trouble with the LLC," she says, guilt sliding out of her.

"You aren't the reason for that. I am. I broke the law taking you out of there, and don't get me wrong, I would do it again in a heartbeat, but it definitely left Dante in a tight spot. I'm sure there are warrants out for me by now," I say, not wanting to hide the truth from her. When we decide to leave here, I will have consequences to make amends for, with the LLC and with the pack.

"Warrants? Like you could go to jail? Is there wolf jail?" she asks, panic slipping into her voice.

"There are, in fact, confinement facilities, and we can be put there, but for something like this, I doubt that would be the punishment. I embarrassed them by taking you; they will want to save face somehow. We will cross that bridge when we come to it. What I'm most worried

CHAPTER 33

about is the pack. With Marlo being given authority over you and me breaking that, he will have the freedom to retaliate against the pack. He could start a war," I say, the gravity of that sitting heavy on my heart.

"Can Dante beat him? In a war, I mean," she asks, rubbing her hand on my arm to soothe some of my growing worry.

"One on one, sure. Dante is strong and younger, but Marlo has one of the strongest wolves of his generation. So it wouldn't be easy, but I think he could win. Pack against pack, I don't know. Most of our alliances wouldn't be willing to join us in a war if we are on the wrong side of the LLC. Marlo's allies won't have that problem, so he will have more resources than we do. He also isn't known for being a law-abiding citizen, so where we would try to preserve the lives of the innocent, he wouldn't have such compunction. He's not a good man, and he works with even more bad men. We would lose hundreds if not thousands of wolves trying to fight him." I finish, anger filling me at the idea.

We could be losing them right now.

No, Dante would have called for me.

Wouldn't he?

Bri: We need to protect them. We need to stop this.

She sends directly into my mind.

How?

Cain: I'm not sure we can. If we join them, the LLC will come for me, bringing even more problems.

Bri: We can't let the pack sacrifice themselves for us if we won't even show up to protect them.

Cain: I understand that. I don't want anyone dying for me.

Bri: Can we talk to the LLC? Can we go to them directly to plead our case? We're Mates; you said that matters to them. Maybe they will understand and change the ruling. Then Marlo won't have a reason to attack. Or if he does, at least we will have allies to fight with.

I'm unsure when the conversation went from speaking to mind-link, but the transition was so smooth that I didn't even notice we'd changed.

Her idea isn't bad. Going straight back there and revealing the Mate Marks proves her right to be with me. They couldn't ignore it if it were in front of them.

"You want to turn ourselves in to the LLC without knowing the consequences?" I ask, pride filling me at her resilience. Her willingness to do what's right. Her belief in justice.

"If it can save the pack from war, I think it's our only choice. I don't want to spend my life running. Not anymore," she says, pushing her now empty plate away from her. I'm not sure when she ate it, but her sandwich is gone, and she stands waiting for my answer.

"I will run with you to the ends of the Earth, or I will stand by your side and fight until my last breath. My choice will always be you, Firefly. So, if you want to take on the LLC, we can leave tonight," I say, meaning every word.

"My whole life has been about running away from the pain. I need that pain to mean something. Not only that, I want to start causing some," she says, grabbing the discarded plate and walking to the kitchen.

"Then we fight back. We take our power back. We protect what's ours," I reply, understanding that the LLC won't change their minds easily, but knowing if anyone can make them see reason, it's her.

CHAPTER 33

Ready or not... here we go...

Chapter 34
Dante

"What are the chances they have this new drug?" Erik asks Presley.

"Honestly, there is no way to know for sure, but the Healys were in Florida two months ago, and it was already being pushed to the enforcers there. It's likely been shopped around to the packs, and we aren't seeing much traffic on it because of the supply chain. It's not dealer to user. It's pack leadership to pack leadership. They don't need to advertise when full packs are their target audience," she says, switching the slide in her presentation.

"But how come this is the first we are hearing of it?" Elijah asks, voicing the same question I have.

Why is this available right now when we might be going to war?

"Again, we don't know, but if I were to venture a guess, they don't have an unlimited supply. If they can't make large quantities, they would prioritize the conversations they would have selling it. But that's

CHAPTER 34

a guess. Every other drug I see on their sites, I've been hearing about for years. This one is brand new. So new, local dealers have no idea about it," she says, her eyes flashing to mine.

Dante: Local dealers? Please tell me you haven't been talking to drug dealers...

Pres: How am I supposed to get information about drugs without talking to people in that world? Stop worrying; it was all handled online, so I covered my tracks. I just needed to know what they know.

Dante: Fuck, Pres, you are supposed to do virtual research, not communicate with the thugs of that world.

Pres: I don't know if you know this, but most criminals don't like to post about their illegal activities. Vanishing discussion boards are a safe space to talk shop for them. At least I didn't meet anyone in real life.

"Can we share with the class?" Erik says, humor in his voice as he tries to pull us out of our mind-link argument.

"Dante's mad I reached out to dealers. It was unavoidable. Anyway, I have the first team heading out after this meeting to place grids one through eight. The goal is to be done by sunrise. Thank you for the additional team members. I think we can make them work," Pres says to him before sitting down and turning the meeting back to me.

"Grids one through eight cover the area immediately surrounding the north end of the I-15?" I ask, confirming I'm reading her map correctly, and she nods. "Do we have teams watching over those areas as the sensors are placed?" I continue turning the question to Erik.

"Jake established two teams to assist with security and placement. My teams will be further out, ensuring no interference. We should be covered with shifts for the next forty-eight hours. Then it will get dicey as the sensors cover more area," he replies.

"We should have reinforcements about then, so hopefully, the timing works out. New Mexico is sending four hundred to start and another four at the end of the weekend. We just need to make it until then." I state, knowing it still might not be enough.

"Can they send a personnel list so we can work out a schedule before they arrive?" Erik asks.

"I'll have it to you in the morning," I answer before sighing and saying what I need to say.

"This will not be an easy fight. We've known this was possible for a decade, but we always believed we would have our allies on our side. Without them, we are at a considerable disadvantage. The LLC has scheduled our appeal for Wednesday afternoon, but I can't, in good conscience, leave the territory unprotected. Without Cain here, it's too much of a risk. I'll be sending Noah to the appeal on my behalf. My hope is that Marlo will go, which will delay his attack, but I have a feeling he will use that time to push into the territory," I pause for emphasis.

"We will lose people in this fight—our people. I can't prevent every death. All I can do is prepare us. We have a full-pack meeting tomorrow night. I need all of the council members standing with me. The pack needs to know we are doing this together. Win or lose, I will fight to keep men like Deacon Marlo from taking control of the state. My father believed in this pack. This is our time to prove we deserve that belief," I say, making eye contact with each of them when Quinn interrupts with a mind-link.

Quinn: The LLC just called. They have Cain in custody.

CHAPTER 34

Shit!

Dante: How?

Quinn: They wouldn't say. He said it was a courtesy call to inform us they'd arrested our Second.

Dante: Noah, I need you now! Pack a bag. You're headed back to Colorado tonight.

Noah: Yes, Alpha.

My pause has everyone on edge, and I push back from the table.

"Apologies, I need to go. The LLC has arrested Cain. He's in their custody. Pres, can you pull up the arrest record and see what they are charging him with, and then meet me in my office? I will see you all at the meeting tomorrow. Make sure we are ready. Pack First," I say, placing my hand over my heart.

They mirror the movement.

"Pack First," they say in unison, and we all exit the conference room.

Fuck.

Dante: What the fuck happened? How did you get caught? Where are you?

I send to Cain, attempting to push the mind-link through.

No response. Either they drugged him, or he's unconscious, and knowing his wolf, I would bet on both.

What a shit show.

Dante: What happened? You were supposed to be hiding out.

Turning into my office, I flag Quinn to follow me.

Bri: They separated us. I'm being detained for a Reno pack representative. Cain's been charged with witness tampering, abduction, and failure to obey. They won't let me speak to anyone. They won't listen to me.

Dante: You're a female. They will only listen to him, and he's being charged. Hang tight. I'm sending legal to get you both out of this.

Quinn stands ready, a notebook in her hand.

"I need you to draft an email to Doug Martin asking him to hold Ms. DelaCourt in their custody until the appeal. She cannot—I repeat—can not go to Reno. It would cost us everything," I say as Presley walks in. And get Yelena ready. They need to leave immediately," I say before turning to Pres.

Quinn hugs her and whispers something in her ear before departing to complete my requests.

"What does the record say?" I ask, losing a bit of my control and slamming my fist into the desk, causing Presley to jump.

"He's being charged. The court date is Thursday. It looks like trumped-up charges, but unfortunately, they could stick. None of them are wrong," she says, and I rub my palms down my face, attempting to regain composure.

"What the fuck else are you going to throw at me, huh?" I shout at the ceiling, imagining The Fates up there, just adding problems to my life.

My elbows hit the table and I hold my face in my hands.

"We are going to lose everything. We can't win," I whisper so quietly I don't think she can hear the words.

"How can I help?" Her voice is small, and I still jump when I hear it.

CHAPTER 34

"You can't. No one can. Deacon Marlo wants my territory, my Second's Mate, my demise. He won't stop until he gets it, and everything falls apart every time I try to get ahead. We're going to lose Pres. We can't win this war with everything stacked against us," I pause, never looking at her.

I've never felt more defeated in my life. No allies, no second, not enough resources,

"Dad trusted me to keep them safe, and I can't. I can't do this," I finish and let myself wallow in this feeling for a moment.

"Dad was right to trust in you. You have been an excellent Alpha since he passed. These are unprecedented circumstances, and I think if he were here, he would choose to stand up and fight. You're not alone, D. You don't have to do this all by yourself. We are here and ready to fight by your side. Have some faith in us," she says, and I look up into her eyes, which match our mother's, and see conviction there.

"I'm leading them to their death," I say, pain settling in my chest.

"Not if I have anything to say about it," she responds, and I can feel the resolve running through her.

"It's too late; the bad guys will win," I say, trying to prepare her.

"Dad used to say the only difference between good and bad men is the reason they fight. We fight to save our pack. He fights for power. If we are still breathing, there is still time to find a way. We just need to change his reason," she says before walking out of my office, looking more like herself than I have seen in days.

It's nice to see her fire, but I know that the only thing Deacon Marlo has ever wanted was control of our pack. He said as much the day of my mother's funeral, and now, twenty-two years later, he's coming to collect on his threat.

Chapter 35
Bri

This has been a shitshow ever since we arrived.

We didn't make it three steps into the headquarters building before enforcers threw silver handcuffs on Cain and took him away.

My treatment wasn't much better, but I've been placed in an interview room.

So much for fighting this together.

Bri: Are you ok?

I send, feeling for him through the bond.

It's been hours, and no one has come to talk to me. My connection to Cain has been muted somehow, and my wolf is starting to worry.

He's fine.

Then why isn't he answering?

My inner argument is cut short when two men walk into the room.

I don't recognize either of them from the last time I was here, and I feel my wolf at the ready.

That's new.

"Ms. DelaCourt, I'm Enforcer Jones, and this is Alpha Martin. We're here to take your statement," the man says, addressing the second man with a deference that makes me realize he is the superior of the two.

Jones appears to be in his early thirties, over 6' tall, with ash blonde hair and deep-set brown eyes. A dusting of facial hair lines his jaw, which appears to give him a more rugged appearance but does nothing to take away his boyish good looks. In contrast, Martin is older, in his early sixties at least, and a shorter, burlier man who reminds me of one of the dwarves from Lord of the Rings, though he is of average height, around 5'9. His wild, auburn hair is barely tamed by the tie at the base of his neck, and his beard nearly reaches his navel.

What an odd pair!

"My statement?" I ask, not hiding my surprise while doing my best to remain calm.

"Yes, ma'am," he says, sitting at the table across from me.

"Am I being charged with something?" I ask, more worried than before.

"No, ma'am. You're the primary witness in another case. We just need your version of things," he says politely.

"What other case?" I question, my eyes bouncing between the men seated before me.

"We aren't at liberty to discuss that, but would you be willing to answer a few questions for us?"

"I'm not sure I should be answering questions," I say reluctantly.

CHAPTER 35

"Ms. DelaCourt, Brielle, can I call you Brielle?" he asks, prompting my nod before continuing. "We just want to get to the bottom of everything that happened the last time you were here. Can you tell us about that?" he inquires, pulling out a small notebook and a pen from his jacket.

Bri: I'm being questioned about Cain taking me. Should I ask for a lawyer or something?

Dante: Stall any way you can. Noah should be there any minute. I sent him as soon as I heard. You can ask, but they aren't required to give you one. Normal laws don't apply here.

"Umm, a little, I guess. I was in a hotel. I'm not sure what one; I don't remember anything having a logo on it." I say, pitching up my voice and giving intentionally vague and off-topic information.

"We are aware of your accommodations. Can you tell us about them after your arrival?" he pushes, holding a polite expression despite it not reaching his eyes.

I note that the other man has done nothing but stare at me. He hasn't said a word.

"Oh, sorry, yes, well, once I was here, a man was stationed at my door. He didn't speak to me or tell me his name, but he was outside the door, just guarding the hallway. I tried making faces at him, you know, like you do with the British Guards?" I paused, expecting a nod or agreement, but I got neither as Enforcer Jones's eyebrows came together.

"Maybe that's not as common as I think it is, but anyway, he just stood there, not talking, looking like a statue in the hall. I'm surprised he didn't attract more attention. You'd think other hotel guests would wonder what he was guarding, like maybe someone famous. Being from

Vegas, I know that happens all the time there. When I was seventeen, my roommate Liv and I snuck into the Bellagio on the Strip; you know that one. It's the one with the huge fountain, anyway; she was sure that The Weeknd was staying there, and we rode in the elevator going floor to floor,"

"Ms. DelaCourt," he interrupts, irritation filling his tone as he drops the attempt to be friendly by calling me my first name. "If you could focus on the question," he finishes.

"Of course, sorry. When I'm nervous, I ramble; it's a bad habit I got from my mom," I say, knowing that the LLC is already aware of who my dad is.

A fucking evil asshole, that's who.

"So, about your question, I was just at the hotel. I didn't have my phone or my luggage because they picked me up in the middle of the night while I was on a recruitment trip from the marketing firm in Boston. They specialize in sustainability within product disbursement, which is a focus of mine in school, so I was really hoping I would be able to make a good impression. I guess probably not anymore since I had to leave without a word. Well, maybe I can find a way to explain it to them. Come up with some reason. Obviously, not the real reason, you know, but like a sick relative or something? I can't exactly explain that a supernatural governing body of werewolves took me in for questioning about a battle between packs, am I right?" I pause hoping one will speak up, but neither does.

My eyes scan back and forth between them, my expression as pleasant as I can make it.

CHAPTER 35

"I did it again, didn't I? Dang it. Okay. You asked about my time here. Well, I remember a doctor coming to see me. I mean, I assume he was a doctor? Now that I think about it, I realize I never really had him show me any credentials. Wow, how stupid! He could have been anyone off the street, and I let him stick needles in me and take my blood for who knows what! Do you know if he was a doctor? Like a real one?" I ask, feigning concern.

"Dr. Foret is a real doctor," Jones says, his tone even, his eyes desperately trying not to roll.

"Are you sure? Because there are a lot of people who claim to be doctors but really aren't, like Dr. Seuss, Dr. Zhivago, Dr. Dre, heck, I don't even think Dr. Phil is a real doctor anymore!" I exclaim, causing Martin to sign and clench his teeth.

Ah, finally, here is some reaction from that guy.

"Ms. DelaCourt, he is a real doctor. Can we please continue, possibly without all of the theatrics?" Jones says, nearly gritting his teeth.

"Of course, I'm sorry. It's just a lot to take in and everything, what with being kidnapped, nearly killed, having brain surgery, surviving only to be picked up and carted off again. It's just been a long couple of weeks, you know, and I'm not sure I've had the time to really process everything," I start to tear up, using a technique I'd learned from Liv in middle school to get out of trouble with our male teachers.

"Sorry," I sniff before continuing my charade. " So it's good to know he was a real doctor, at least because the last thing I need is another secret coming to light," I say.

Jones looks uncomfortable now, and Alpha Martin seems irritated that he has to sit through this.

"It's understandable that you would be stressed, ma'am. Can you tell us what happened after the DNA test?" he asks, urging me to do so.

"Of course, after the doctor left, it was a little while before another man showed up. This one came alone and sent the guard away," I say, giving some accurate detail so that it seems less forced when I go on my next tangent.

"What was the man's name?" Jones asks pen at the ready.

"Alex? I think. He was mesmerizing like he walked right off the pages of a magazine. I've never met anyone with purple eyes before, and I'm not usually a fan of purple. Growing up the way I did, I was always more of a black-loving girl. I don't think I would own a single thing that was brightly colored if it weren't for Liv. She insists that colors keep people from thinking I'm a serial killer, which is crazy because, at least from what I've seen, most serial killers don't look the part. In fact, I don't think I've ever heard of a serial killer who was goth or emo. They are always just the picture of normal, or at least that's what everybody says when they find out," I prattle on.

The slamming of a fist causes me to gasp in fake dismay.

"Enough!" Martin shouts, staring me down. "Stop wasting our time with nonsense. **Tell us about Mingan taking you!**" he demands, infusing his words with command. My wolf rushes to the surface, no longer content with sitting in the background.

My vision sharpens, and I instinctively know my eyes are glowing just like Cain's.

Without removing my stare from his, I lean back in the chair, crossing my arms over my chest.

"Didn't anyone teach you it's not polite to shout at a woman? Even less polite to try to use command to get your way. Unless you would like your throat removed from your body, you will not try that again," I say, allowing the words to flow from my wolf to him.

His jaw drops, and his eyes bulge. It's comical how surprised he is, and I bask in the moment before attempting to use command for myself.

Just as I open my mouth to speak the words, the door opens, pulling everyone's attention.

"Apologies for being late. As I wasn't notified that one of my clients was in custody and another was being questioned, it took longer to get here than usual. That being said, this interview is over. Any further questions will be directed through me at an assigned deposition," he says, turning to me. Brielle, if you would come with me, please," he finishes.

"You can't just take her!" Martin shouts, standing in his outrage at how the whole situation unraveled.

"Unless she is under arrest for breaking the Lycan Constitutional Code, I'm very sure I can," he says, ushering me out the door without another word.

"Impeccable timing," I say as we walk down the hall.

"Sometimes the Fates are looking out for us. Let's go find your Mate," he says, and we walk back to the front office with a newfound purpose.

Chapter 36
Cain

It's nearly morning when one of the enforcer guards comes to get me. I haven't been released from the silver cuffs since they arrested me last night, and the skin underneath them is burned and blistered. Apparently, locking me in a silver cage wasn't enough.

Honestly, it probably wasn't.

They had muted my wolf with the same serum we give wolves in interrogation to keep them from accessing their wolves and mind-linking with their Alphas, effectively keeping me from contacting not only Dante but Bri, too.

I could still feel her through the bond, but none of my messages penetrated the medical block.

She was safe, so I sat tight and didn't fight anyone.

CHAPTER 36

Even as this guard walked me to the interview rooms, I kept myself in control.

My wolf was fighting it.

I felt him slowly pushing back through, which meant I'd be able to send messages soon.

Stupid of them not to redose me this morning. I'm not only an Alpha but one with a Fated Mate, which only added to my strength and ability. My guess is this dose usually lasted twenty-four hours, and I'd only been here about ten.

The closer we get to the room, the more I feel her. She's close. I chance sending a mind-link message to her.

Cain: You doing ok, Firefly?

Surprise and relief flood the bond, and I smile at her reaction.

Bri: Yeah, Noah and I are just waiting. They said they were getting you. I can feel you getting closer. How come you didn't answer me last night?

Her question pulls at me, and I wish we had more time to discuss how this would go.

Cain: They muted my wolf and my abilities, so I was less of a threat. It's wearing off now.

Bri: Did they hurt you? I couldn't feel you at all. I was worried.

Cain: No, just stuck me in a cell for the night.

The guard opens a door, and I know, without even entering, that she is inside. As soon as I enter, Noah springs from his chair.

"You still have him in cuffs!?! Remove them at once!" He demands, horror evident in his voice as he yells at the man escorting me.

"Apologies, counselor, I haven't got the keys. I'll send for them and have one of the prosecutors bring them," he says, dipping his head in a polite farewell before leaving through the same door we'd entered.

My eyes never leave hers as I stare, reconnecting with her and finding peace, knowing she is perfectly fine.

I take a seat on her right and lean over to kiss her, capturing her mouth with mine in a possessive exchange. Her moan echoes through the mind-link, and I have to physically push my wrists into the silver to force myself to stop.

When I pull back, her eyes are slow to open, and she smiles knowingly.

She can feel how much I missed her. How much I want her.

Cain: Forever, Firefly.

Bri: Forever.

She responds, her voice breathy even in my head, and I take her hand in both of mine, careful to keep the cuffs from touching her skin.

"I'm sorry it took us so long to pull you out. They were giving me the run around since there are two court dates now," Noah says, sliding into the open chair next to me. "Have they questioned or adjudicated you at all?" he asks, noting the cuffs in the leather-bound notebook before him.

"No, just had me locked up and dosed with a block," I say, not looking at him. "What's this meeting for?" I ask, not entirely sure why a special council for my criminal misbehavior isn't seeing us.

"Not sure. I tried to get your hearing moved up to today, but they wouldn't budge on it; then I went and retrieved Brielle, and suddenly,

CHAPTER 36

the council wants this negotiated first," he says, shrugging and drawing his brows together to show his confusion.

"What are my chances?" I ask, knowing they've added some inflated charges because I'd hurt their pride when I took her.

She's my fucking Mate.

Let's hope it's a defense that is strong enough.

"Well, on the witness tampering, you could get anything from probation to six months of hard time. The abduction charge can be anything from five to ten years, depending on the person's determination of whether it's aggravated or not, and failure to obey is most likely a slap on the wrist to a penance of community service, six months to a year," he rattles off, not adding any emotion to the information.

That's one thing about Noah. He is always collected. I've never met anyone who has held their patience more, and he has had to go through it with our pack over the years.

As Bri considers what that would mean for us, I feel the tension running over the bond, and I rub slow circles into her hands.

Cain: It's okay, Firefly. We knew this was a risk. None of these things will be the maximum sentence. Breathe.

She exhales, but her stress stays firmly seated on her shoulders.

Before I can ask my next question, I hear footsteps in the hall and center myself, pulling my mask on to keep my emotions to myself.

The door opens, and three men walk in. I don't recognize any of them but I feel my Mate tense and feel the anger she has simmering.

Cain: Talk to me.

Bri: The one with the long beard. He tried to use command on me earlier.

She sends, and I bite the inside of my cheek to keep a growl from escaping.

Cain: Tried?

Bri: uh huh. I guess I'm stronger than he is, too.

She sends it, and I feel her pride. It matches mine, and my need to defend her dissipates, knowing that having him not be able to force her was its own kind of humiliation.

Cain: That's my girl.

The three men sit across from us, setting down a series of documents and folders on the table before the man at the center begins.

"Mr. Daniels, Mr. Mingan, Ms. DelaCourt," he begins, and I interrupt him.

"It's Mrs. Mingan," I correct, and nod for him to continue as I feel the surprise and subsequent joy that comes from her.

Cain: I guess we should have discussed that too.

Bri: No need. I've never been attached to her last name. I'd be proud to be a Mingan.

Her reply has my heart fluttering.

"Oh, apologies. I wasn't aware you'd had your Mating ceremony," the man says, turning to Noah. "Has their Mating paperwork been filed?" he asks, flipping through documents as if trying to locate it.

"Not yet; I've been busy with the more… pressing legal action and planned to submit them before returning to Vegas," he says, not allowing the question to rattle him. "However, before we continue, can you please remove my client's cuffs? He is no threat to you. He turned himself in willingly and has been nothing but cooperative," Noah says, crossing the fingers of his hands together and placing them in front of him, waiting.

CHAPTER 36

The man nods, and the bearded man stands, producing a key from his pocket. I extend my hands to him, hating that I must release my hold on hers, even if only for a moment. A growl escapes her throat when he grabs my arm, causing him to pause before tentatively continuing.

Once he's seated, the man in the middle continues while I rub my sore wrists.

"We asked you here today to clear up some misconceptions and hopefully be able to set the record straight. We understand that sometimes these things need a second look, and with the new information we received, we would like to discuss some options going forward. My name is Oliver Horn, and I am assigned to the legal oversight committee here at the LLC. This is Alpha Douglas Martin, one of the committee members for the hearing that was just conducted, and this is Attorney Evan Hasting, legal counsel for your criminal charges."

He reaches for a document and picks it up to be read aloud.

"Cain Mingan is being charged with one count of witness tampering, one count of abduction in the second degree, and one count of failure to obey," he finishes setting down the document.

"Now we can agree that we may have been too hasty in our judgment regarding the placement of Ms. Dela... oh, Mrs. Mingan. Our laws clearly state that Fated Mate bonds trump pack affiliations. The gray area of this case was that she was neither Awakened nor Mated at the time of the hearing. That is no longer the case, and as such, we are willing to reverse our decision regarding her home pack. Hasting here will write up the overturned motion today and submit it to official records before the end of business." He tips his head to the younger man in the suit on his left, who nods in agreement.

"So the Reno Pack no longer has control over her?" Noah clarifies.

"That is correct," he says, and I see the bearded man on the left bristle in irritation. My hand finds hers again, and I give it a squeeze, knowing the future of the Vegas Pack and the war was her biggest concern aside from me going to jail.

"Where does this leave the criminal charges? If you agree that she was his to take all along, are those being dropped too?" Noah questions.

"Not exactly," he says, pulling a small stack of papers out and sliding them across the table for Noah to look at while he continues.

"Mr. Mingan still broke the law. His decisions came while orders were in place. We have avenues for appeal, and they should have been taken. However, we also understand that he may not have been thinking clearly when he believed his Mate was in danger of being taken by another pack, so we are willing to offer him a deal. It is outlined in the document before you. We believe it is more than fair considering the alternative. Take a few minutes to confer, and let the guard know when you've decided. This deal is good for the next thirty minutes. Then it's off the table, and we will proceed with all of the charges in court." He stands, prompting the other two men to follow suit, and they file out of the room without another word.

Noah reads the document silently for a few minutes before setting it down and explaining the terms.

"All I can do is advise you on what happens if you do or don't take the deal, but let me start with the fact that I think it's very fair. The LLC is offering to drop the abduction charges completely and only charge you with witness tampering and failure to obey. Additionally, they are willing to limit the punishment for each offense to six months of community

CHAPTER 36

service. Meaning you would only have to complete a year of service. They have also outlined a position that Brielle can fill here in Colorado in the... sustainability marketing?" he says, unsure if the term is correct.

My chest releases the air held there, and relief fills me.

No jail time away from her

Just community service for a year.

She gets to stay with me.

"So I just need to, like, clean up parks and pick up trash for a year, and I'm done?" I ask, knowing this is the best we could have hoped for under the circumstances.

I feel Bri's hope filling the bond as I wait for Noah to explain more fully.

"Usually, it would be something like that; however, they have added an addendum to the community service," his tone turns more serious.

"They are offering you the community service under the condition that it be carried out as a special assignment working directly for the LLC here in Colorado," he says.

"Doing what?" I ask.

"High-priority enforcement, detection, and elimination," he says.

Well, shit.

"What does that mean?" Bri says out loud, not knowing who to direct the question to, fear filling her as her eyes bounce between us.

"It means I would be tasked with catching, eliminating, or guarding the most dangerous criminals on the planet. They want my wolf. They want me to be their weapon," I say.

Bri: So, like, what Ghost does?

Cain: No, Firefly. Ghost gets to choose his targets. I wouldn't. I would be assigned to take the job, and if I were to breach their deal, all of the charges would be back, and I could go to jail for years.

Bri: I don't like this.

Cain: Neither do I, but what choice do we have?

Bri: They've blackmailed you into this. How can a system be set up like this?

Cain: The LLC has been flawed for a long time. Marcus, Dante's dad, was trying to fix it when he worked with them.

Bri: Maybe this is our chance to fix it from the inside?

Cain: It will be dangerous, Firefly.

Bri: Not if we do it together. You said it yourself: Packs like Marlo's need to learn to follow the rules. What if we use this time to tear it down from the inside? They want to use us; let's use them right back.

When my eyes meet hers, I see the determination there. She wants to make a difference, to regain her control. Maybe this is the best way to do just that.

Cain: To the end of the Earth by your side.

Bri: We bear our scars together.

"Make the deal," I say to Noah before grabbing her cheeks in my hands and setting my forehead on hers.

Cain: Forever.

Bri: Forever.

The End.

Epilogue
Dante

After rolling around for hours trying to turn off my brain, I'd finally exhausted myself to the point of sleeping.

Noah: Apologies for waking you up, but I have news.

Dante: Call. I'll answer.

Stretching my arms over my head, I glance at the clock to see it's just after seven in the morning—three hours of sleep.

Not nearly enough.

My phone rings on my nightstand, and I grab it, put it on speaker, and lay it on my bare chest.

I need some good news.

"Go ahead, Noah," I say, my voice sounding like gravel from the lack of sleep.

"LLC offered Cain a plea bargain for his charges, and he is signing the paperwork now. They've agreed to overturn the motion from the hearing and reinstate Brielle to our pack," he says, making me sit up in bed and causing my phone to fall.

"Why? Why would they overturn the ruling before the appeal, and what was the plea bargain?" I say, fully awake now.

"Cain has to work off his community service for the next year with the LLC in Colorado," he pauses before saying the bad news. "As an HP Enforcer."

Well, shit.

Not only am I losing my Second for an entire year, but HP Enforcers have the highest death rate of any job in the LLC.

I could lose my best friend altogether.

"Why would he agree to this?" I ask, anger building in me.

"It was this, or they threw the book at him, and they have all the evidence they need for the charges against him because he did them," Noah says, making complete sense while also making my head spin.

A deal with the Devil.

How do we fix this?

"Has Marlo been notified of the new ruling?" I ask, wondering what this means for the impending war.

"Paperwork will be filed this afternoon, so I don't think so," he responds.

"Thank you for letting me know. Get everything tied up there and get home. Hopefully, we will have a negotiation set up for a new peace treaty in the coming weeks," I say, trying to find the light in this situation.

The LLC is no longer against us. We have allies again.

EPILOGUE

"Oh, and Noah, Thank you for taking care of everything. I know I've asked a lot of you these last few weeks," I say, meaning every word.

"Pack First. It's what we do," he says before hanging up.

Yes. Yes, it is.

Dante: Quinn, you up?

Quinn: Always. Who needs sleep? What do you need?

She sends back, trying to cover the sleepy tone but failing as she yawns.

Dante: Take today off. The LLC has given us a reprieve. You need a break. I'll see you tomorrow.

Quinn: We have so much to do.

Dante: It will all be there tomorrow. Rest. That's an order.

I send, not infusing my voice with command. She will listen without it.

***

Later that night

Sitting in my office, I'm scrolling through emails that need to be answered when I see the one I have been waiting for hit my inbox.

It's official. It's been overturned.

My hand moves to the phone on my desk, and I put it on the speaker, wanting to capture both sides on the recording system I have wired in my office.

He answers on the second ring.

"Baby Stone," he says, no emotion sliding into his voice.

"Marlo, I just got the news. I'm sorry to hear about the loss. I guess she wasn't yours after all," I say, smiling, not the least bit sorry.

"You may not know this yet, but you have no idea what belongs to me," his voice is calm, and it bothers me that I'm not getting the reaction I wanted.

"I know that Vegas will never belong to you," I say, confidence filling my tone.

"Perhaps not, but I have my sights on other things. Sometimes losing what you want most, shows you what you truly need," he says, disconnecting the call before I can respond.

What the actual fuck?

The thought is barely out when I feel it.

The painful severing of a bond breaking away, and then nothing.

Emptiness.

Presley's gone.

Reader's Note
Remember I love you

Okay, so I know you're mad at me... but all I promised was a HEA for our main couple, and you got that! If you had just stopped reading at "The End" you wouldn't be here and we would be hunky-dory. You are really the one to blame. But, because I know how hard it is to wait on the edge, here is the prologue for Fate Encoded to give you some relief. Don't say I didn't warn you...

Fate Encoded
Presley

Everyone has a weakness.

An addiction, a vice, something that they need in order to survive. All you have to do is find that thing, and you've got them.

The only problem is I've been looking into Deacon Marlo for the last few weeks, and I can't fucking find anything I can use.

Now, I'm generally not the 'try to blackmail' people type, but when my family is threatened, there isn't anything I won't do. I've even juggled the idea of going to Reno and challenging him for his seat.

Dante would kill me.

Probably even before Marlo did.

My wolf is strong, fast, and able to take on just about anyone I come across, but I've heard the stories about Marlo.

I can't help anyone if I'm dead.

An alert pops up on the vanish board I'm scanning, and I open it to find a new message from Imin, another drifter on these sites. I've run into them a few times, and so far as friends in this world go, Imin is the only one I've got right now.

Pulling up the chat, I see a screenshot of a hidden answer post on a topic I'd discussed the last time we were online. "Underground movements shift to broad daylight." The article is an anonymous post that discusses different trafficking options and how they have shifted out of back alleys.

The only problem is now that most shipments of illegal cargo are out in the open; they all look like regular deliveries.

Skimming through the article, one section catches my attention. The author mentions catering as a new shipping method, and it reminds me of footage I'd gone through days before.

Curious now, I switch to my primary system, which is tied directly to the warehouse quantum processor. HUNTER loads without delay, and I log in using my retina, fingerprint, vocal signature phrase: Blue Hawaii, and six-digit password: 568140.

Without perfect matches, access is denied for twelve hours. After a second incorrect input, it locks out for 48 hours. Three wrong attempts corrupt a portion of the code, inserting a trojan into the source.

A fourth attempt uses that trojan to infect the system, attempting access with an infinity worm, which not only locks the computer from any functionality but also copies all the files and sends them to my server.

Everything is destroyed if I don't log in once every seven days.

It should be foolproof.

If anything happens to me, there is no way to recover it.

Period.

This security was set up to prevent the technology from getting into the wrong hands. I've thought of adding additional users, Dante, Mason, and maybe even Cain because I know they would use this for its intended purpose.

Return people who are kidnapped, free innocents from monsters, and find the head of the snake.

Something has always stopped me, though.

With the system fully operational, I input the data identification for Deacon Marlo. One phone call with Dante gave me everything I needed to use his vocal signature to pinpoint his location anywhere in the world anytime as soon as he spoke.

The screens load to yesterday's feed, and I see him in his office. His webcam gave me a video along with the audio I could pull from any of the five devices in the room.

"La morte è parte della vita. Sarò lì entro un'ora, ciao," he says in Italian, causing me to run the recording back to translate. "Death is part of life. I'll be there within the hour, bye," it reads off, and I jump back to the feed in time for his secretary, a top-heavy brunette, to sashay her way in.

"I have a meeting with Orlando. Ensure the catering trucks unload in the east wing when they arrive in twenty minutes. Troy will oversee them," he says, grabbing his suit jacket off the back of his chair before leaving his office.

Bingo.

Using that information, I locate the business's east wing entrance cameras, move ahead just before delivery time, and wait.

Two delivery trucks with La Strada embossed on the sides roll through the gates. An older man steps out of the building as the driver exits the first truck. Losing them behind the vehicle, I scan for a better camera angle, finding one on the opposite wall. I pull from the phones the men are carrying to listen in.

"Twelve cases and ten pallets of ammo," the driver says to the man, who I assume is Troy.

"Do they have the accessories? Scope, extended mag, tripod stands?" he rattles off, giving me everything I need.

Fucking Jackpot.

"We were only able to get the extended magazines; scopes will be here in our next drop," he explains.

"And what exactly would you like me to tell our buyers? 'Here are the guns you ordered, but you will have to wait for the rest of the pieces.' This won't fly. You remember what happened last time?" Troy says, causing the other man to raise his arms in surrender.

"I know, but our shipment got caught up at the port. We can have them here first thing tomorrow. Tell him we will sweeten the deal when it does," the man says.

After saving the video and shots of the cases moving off the trucks, I devise a plan.

Blackmail him into backing off.

Get him to delay long enough for Dante to figure this out.

Fix what I broke.

Everyone keeps telling me this isn't my fault, but when you look at what happened, it all comes back to the one moment in the hall outside Cain's apartment.

The one moment I wish I could take back and do over.

I should have said something. Anything. Then she wouldn't have left. Hudson wouldn't have taken her. Deacon wouldn't have shown up for the exchange, and he would never have found out she was Unawakened.

If none of that happened, he wouldn't have filed a complaint with the LLC, they wouldn't have found out he was her father, and we wouldn't be fighting this war over her.

All because I didn't open my damn mouth.

Switching back to my laptop, I send a thank you to Imin for the article, leave a link to a CTF competition happening this weekend with the short message "Dynamic duo?" and log myself out of the Tor network.

Before I can talk myself out of it, I pull the throw-away phone from the stash we keep and download the evidence to it before shooting a text to the number I know Deacon Marlo has been using lately.

> How many years do you get for arms trafficking in the State of Nevada?

I send and include one photo of the cargo boxes being moved into his business.

> I'd imagine quite a few if you were caught, though those photos look like someone is having their event catered to me.

A smile forms, knowing he would say that, so I send along a second photo showing Troy opening the crate from the other picture and removing an automatic assault rifle.

> Delicious, it's no wonder they're so busy.

> Who is this?

> You can call me Cypher

> And what is it you want "Cypher"

> I want to make a deal.

Terms?

> You back off of the Vegas Pack, I don't send these to authorities.

Ah. One of baby Stone's loyal soldiers. No deal.

Wait what?

What the fuck does he mean no deal?

> Then I guess I will be sending these to the authorities. Homeland, ATF, NSA, FBI, LLC...

Send them to whomever you choose. I'm more interested in who you turned to get those images from my private surveillance. Tell me that information, and I'll consider delaying my takeover for a day.

A day?

> No deal. Your security problems are your own.

I have no security problems. My system is impenetrable; the only way those photos got out was through someone in my pack.

> Impenetrable? I do not think that means what you think that means.

I send, quoting one of my favorite movies.

> A Princess Bride reference? That's what you're going with? Couldn't go with 'What's your favorite scary movie, or I know what you did last summer?'

For a moment, I'm stunned. I wouldn't have guessed someone like Deacon Marlo had ever seen the movie, let alone enough to recognize the line. Then I'm pissed because he's mocking me.

Moving back to HUNTER, I pull up the live feed and find him in his office again. I grab a recording of him sending the response to me and forward it to the burner phone before sending it to him along with another message.

> I'm impressed you didn't even have to Google.

The message flashes on his phone, and I watch in real time as he realizes I can see him in his office right now. His head whips around, and I giggle at the wild look in his eyes.

> You want to make a deal? Tell me how you're doing this.

> What do I get in return?

> I'll call off today's advance.

Today?!

My heart sinks.

We aren't ready. We need more time.

> Your word.

> You have it.

He sends and nods to the camera I'm currently watching.

> I'm using one-of-a-kind software designed to track anyone anywhere in the world using image database recovery, vocal sound recognition, wireless, 5G, Bluetooth, and satellite. With a single image, video, or sound clip, I can find anyone anywhere in the world and use this software to penetrate all security so I can record, listen to, and identify them.

> That's impossible. Firewalls, passwords, and other security would prevent it.

> Try me. Give me a name.

He doesn't hesitate.

> Frank Marlo

Back on my primary computer, I use a Google search to find a photo of him. Once I have it, It's loaded into HUNTER, and the process begins.

In less than five minutes, I know his exact location and what he's wearing, and I have both a video clip and a still photo to send.

Pride fills me when Marlo's jaw drops at the information, and I wait while he video-calls his relative to confirm that what I sent is accurate.

> I'll take your silence and unhinged jaw as a compliment. Now, call off the attack.

I watch in real-time as he both makes a phone call and an email, delaying the push into Vegas.

Exhaling, I sink back in my chair, happy I bought us more time, even if it is only another day.

One more day means more lives are protected.

> Name your price.

> It's not for sale.

> Everything is for sale for the right price.

> Not this.

> Not even for a blood vow guaranteeing the safety of the entire Vegas Pack for the remainder of my reign as Alpha?

Holy Shit!

The phone falls out of my hand.

A Blood Vow?

I'd never known anyone to do one. They were fairy tales, legends, and bedtime stories told from generation to generation. If the Blood Vow were broken, he'd die.

> You'd give up the ability to ever take over Vegas?

> For exclusive access to this software, I would

Could I get him to leave his vendetta with us forever?

I could fix everything.

> Exclusive access for three months.

> You cannot use this technology to harm anyone in the Vegas Pack.

> You leave our Second alone and let him have his Mate

> It cannot be used in the mass murder of innocent people

This sounds an awful lot like you're giving me orders. I don't take orders. Your suggestions are noted.

If we are negotiating, I want six months, not three.

I'll agree not to use your software against the Vegas Pack so long as they keep the previously instituted peace treaty between us.

I will use it for whatever purposes I so choose outside of those restrictions, and I will vow to stay out of Vegas territory for one year.

Safety for everyone for a year.

A year to prepare.

> Deal.

Meet me tonight at 6 p.m. at the executive airport. To keep the exchange civil, you may bring a guard with you.

> I'll be there.

Holy shit, I'm doing this. I'm giving our biggest enemy software, which will make him unstoppable; not only that, but I have to go with him to make it work.

To protect our pack.

My wolf says, pacing beneath my skin with the adrenaline I have running through my body.

Looking at the clock, I see that I only have two hours. I need to pack, get everything here in order, and avoid my brother. Focusing for a minute, I make sure I'm blocking my emotions. The last thing I need is for him to feel my guilt for lying to him before I can save everyone.

***

Two hours later, I'm sitting with my back to the wall just inside the hangar where Marlo will be landing, feeling like a cat burglar. I've been prone to wearing more black lately, but it is the only color I have on tonight. Sweatpant joggers and a T-shirt hug my small frame while I anticipate his arrival.

The minute I hear the jet engine rolling my way, my nerves get the best of me, and I grab my mom's necklace for good luck, spinning the silver ring around to calm me.

I can do this,

I *can* do this.

When it comes to a stop, I stand, grab my suitcase, and roll it forward to where the staircase opens.

Straightening my shoulders, I watch as two men who are not Deacon Marlo step out of the plane, descending to the bottom and posting up on either side. The one on the right nearly blocks me from view, and I see him step through the door.

There's a powerful elegance to his stride as he descends, scanning the tarmac.

"It looks like he isn't here yet. Benny, check the parking lot. When this guy gets here, I don't want to take any chances that this is a setup," he says, overlooking me entirely as he pulls out his phone.

"Shocking, we have another narcissistic Alpha who thinks anything done well must have been done by a man," I say, slow clapping for effect.

Marlo's face snaps in my direction, and I swear he does a double-take.

A strong, sarcastic piece of me wants to shout, 'Yep, I'm a girl. Tada!' but his stillness unnerves me, as does the cold confusion on his face. My hand instinctively goes back to my necklace, and I swear I see his nostrils flare in response.

What is his problem?

Silence hangs in the air for several beats before he finally shakes his head and speaks.

"Presley Stone," he says, his voice unusually thick. He swallows and continues. "What are you doing here?" Irritation now fills the spaces he cleared out.

"Saving my brother's pack from you," I say, sticking out my jaw defiantly.

"Then I would venture to guess he doesn't know you're here," he says, his eyebrow lifting with the question.

"How about we keep this to business? You want the software. I have it. But I did forget to mention one thing," I say, pausing for dramatic effect. "It's completely useless without me."

"Useless without you? I'm sure we will manage," he says, head tilting to the side.

"The code will corrupt if I don't log in regularly, and my login cannot be duplicated or transferred. So if you want the software, you have to take me with you," I say, keeping every bit of the fear out of my voice.

"Take you with me?" he repeats, and I'm starting to wonder if the stories about how ruthless and intellectually sound he is are rumors.

He spends a moment contemplating, or at least that's what I think he's doing because his expression looks exactly like he's sorting out a complex math problem.

Standing here under his scrutiny is wearing on me, and I bite my lip absently.

"I can't have you in my territory against your will. We just dealt with this with the Unawakened girl."

"Brielle, your daughter…" I say and physically see his color pale.

"You will join the Reno Pack for the six months I have the software. This protects my pack from retribution from the LLC and keeps you from sending secret messages to your brother. These are my terms," he says, gesturing to the man on his right who produces what looks like a legal contract.

Marlo grabs it, signs it, bites his palm, and places it on the document before he hands it to me.

"Sign it, and we have a deal. Don't, and I'm prepared to attack at midnight," he says before pulling out his phone and excusing himself back into the private jet.

He stands just out of earshot, even with enhanced hearing, but where he can see my choice. His eyebrow lifts, and I can feel the challenge radiating off him.

You don't scare me, Deacon Marlo.

The pen glides over the contract, and I add my name before biting into the flesh of my palm, drawing blood, and stamping it to seal the Blood Vow.

Fates protect me.

The man standing guard takes the document and my bag and turns for the plane just as Marlo returns, places himself behind me, and bites into the skin on my shoulder— initiating me

Deacon: Welcome to the Reno Pack, Presley Stone, Pack Member 6,481.

With that, my connection to Dante is broken, and I belong to the Reno Pack.

Forgive me, brother.

Pack First.

Acknowledgements

Finally!

Thank you for being patient with me while I worked through this story. I know it was supposed to be a standalone fated mates story, and instead became a trilogy with a prequel in between. Thank you for taking this journey with me. You're the reason we authors throw our words onto pages in hopes our characters' stories come to life in the minds and hearts of others. The characters in this book certainly went off script and made this author want to quit more than I can express. The fate of the rest of the Reno Pack, and the Vegas Pack as well as Bri's inner circle will shake out over the next several books. I hope that you enjoyed the character back and forth, and felt every heartwarming, laughable, tension-building moment.

I want to thank my husband, I love you Rabbit. I will always be grateful for your patience as these books come to life. See I told you I could finish this book! And yes, there will be another one, and then another one, but if I don't write them, the readers will riot (back me up here guys).

And I have to thank my bestie, Juliet, my therapist, my sounding board, and most days the one who understood how hard it was to finish. You have been the greatest blessing I've gotten from being an author. None of these would have been possible without you cheering me on, picking me up, and pushing me across the finish line. I will never be able to express in words (and that's saying something since I'm an author) how lucky I am to have you in my life. You are a light, an inspiration, and a gift to this world. Someday we will move into our writing compound in the woods, but until then, know you are my absolute best friend and I love you.

Thank you to my Alphas, Betas, and ARCs for trudging through incomplete copies of this book to get to the finish line with me. I might only be one person, but I know I have an entire tribe behind me making this possible.

Thank you! Hugs!

About the author
Amanda Nichole

Amanda writes urban fantasy with a little spice. She believes her characters guide her stories and let them run amok busting outlines, timelines, and even causing series headaches. While writing was a passion she came to find later in life, her love for reading has always been a huge part of her. She spends her days teaching English Language Arts to 8th graders, and her nights and weekends chasing around her three wild children and husband, often on the slopes with a snowboard. In stolen moments in between, she sneaks in a chapter or two to satisfy the need to tell her characters' stories. Amanda lives her life trying to soak in every possible moment, and because of this, drinks an exorbitant amount of caffeine to fuel her busy schedule. Most of all, Amanda hates talking about herself in the third person and is also terrible at tooting her own horn.

Keep up with everything Vegas Wolf Pack at AuthorAmandaNichole.com and follow her on her socials:

TikTok: @authoramandanichole

Instagram: @author_amanda_nichole

Also by
Amanda Nichole

VEGAS WOLF PACK SERIES

- Unawakened Fate: Vegas Wolf Pack Series Book 1 – January 2023

- Fate Awakened: Vegas Wolf Pack Series Book 2 – September 2023

- Villainous Fate: Villain Origin Story Book 2.5 – May 2024

- Understanding Fate: Vegas Wolf Pack Series Book 3 – November 2024

- Fate Encoded: Vegas Wolf Pack Series Book 4 – Coming 2025

- Fate Abandoned: Vegas Wolf Pack Story Book 4.5 – Coming 2026

- Coded Fate: Vegas Wolf Pack Series Book 5 – TBD

- Fate's Prophecy: Vegas Wolf Pack Series Book 6 – TBD

- Fallon's Fate: Character Origin Story Book 6.5 – TBD

- Foreseen Fate: Vegas Wolf Pack Series Book 7 – TBD

- Fate's Adversary: Vegas Wolf Pack Series Book 8 – TBD

For the latest information about this series see the author's website AuthorAmandaNichole.com

All caught up on Amanda's books, Check out Juliet Thomas who writes Contemporary Romance with all the feelings.

- Uncaged
- Uncharted
- The Christmas Cracker Novella
- Uncertain

Milton Keynes UK
Ingram Content Group UK Ltd.
UKHW040230031224
451863UK00005B/340